ONE BULLET

Also by Mark Boss

Hired Guns
The Cultist
Dead Girl
Dead Girl 2: Fader Boy

ONE BULLET

Mark Boss

Copyright 2014 Mark Boss
Cover design by Jayson Kretzer
(http://wannabeheroes.com/)
1st Edition

All rights reserved.

The events and characters in this book are fictitious.
Any similarity to real people, living or dead, is
coincidental.

ISBN-13: 978-1497538931
ISBN-10: 1497538939

http://markboss.net

Dedication

Mom, thank you for your endless love and encouragement.

Acknowledgements

Thanks to the Cheshire Writing Group (Ruth C., Rich K., Carole L., Tony S., Marty S., and Milinda S.) for your camaraderie and advice.

Also, thanks to the Panama City Writers Association (especially Wayne G., Barbara W. and Ed P.), and the Panera Writers Group (Rob D., Mike L., Nick M., Chris and Eve W.). Much gratitude for the Coffee House Syndicate (Brady C., Lou C., Jayson K., Mike L. and Tony S.).

Special thanks to "Bill" for teaching me about money laundering.

Chapter 1
Joe

As I walk to the airport terminal, I check my pockets again. Make sure I have my cell phone, picture ID, ticket and boarding pass. And the password envelope.

I look back at my gal, Carly, but she's looking down at her phone. I left her with the keys to Vlad's Lexus, and told her not to smoke in the car. When I asked to borrow the Lexus from Vlad this morning because my Audi is in the shop, he was real reluctant. I guess he's particular about his cars.

Inside the terminal, a trickle of sweat runs under my shirt when I enter the TSA security line. My ticket to Philly is a there-and-back in business class, but I'm not going on any airplane ride. The ticket is just for show.

The TSA trolls send me through the cattle gate, then wand me, and I grab the plastic tub with my stuff. Except the envelope. That's still in my jacket pocket, damp with sweat. I've done a dozen exchanges like this, but there's always some nerves.

The trolls stop an old lady behind me and give her the choice of getting groped or x-rayed. She must be ninety.

It's almost lunchtime, and it's tough getting around all the families with baby strollers and the stressed-out business types just off the flight from Atlanta. I could use my size to push through, but I look at them and see the exhaustion on their faces and forget using my elbows and just walk.

8   Mark Boss

Find Gate A3 and take a seat outside the men's room. The setup is simple. We meet at an airport or a courthouse, anywhere with metal detectors, that way both parties have to go unarmed. Go in the bathroom, make the exchange, and walk out with a sack of cash. Security doesn't check people who are leaving.

The Cartel has used the same Mexican bagman twice now and I scan the crowd for him, but he's probably already in the men's room.

I pat the envelope for the tenth time, and go to the bathroom door. There's one of those wet floor signs in front, with a picture of a guy slipping and falling.

The bathroom is big and cold. There's a long row of sinks and dryers on my left, then a row of urinals. When I round the corner to the stalls, I see the kid. He looks half Samoan, half Sasquatch. He's even bigger than me, with cauliflower ears and some weird tattoo on his neck.

Definitely not the usual Mexican.

He smiles. "Whassup? You got something for me?"

"Where's the regular guy?" I take a step back. On my left, there's a boot.

A fancy stitched cowboy boot sticking toes up out from under the stall.

Ah hell.

Kid Sasquatch throws an overhand right.

Ten years ago, I'd have slipped it and punched him in the liver.

Instead, I take it on the forearm and stumble into the wall.

One Bullet

He comes in swinging and I pop him with a quick left that does nothing. Try to punch him in the throat, but his chin is tucked into his shoulder. He's a pro.

He grabs me in a clinch and shoves me against the wall. His mouth opens to take a breath and I try to fishhook him. He bites my thumb, and I yank it free while it's still attached. His knees shoot up like he's bouncing a soccer ball, one after another into my gut. I bend over to save my ribs, flex my knees to unload an upper cut and....

* * *

Chapter 2
Joe

Open my eyes. Blink. I'm in a bathroom stall. My cheek is on the cool, tile floor. The cool, sticky tile floor. My arm is across something--the dead Mexican bagman. I sit up. The stall door is closed and between the toilet and the little guy with the broken neck and me, there isn't much room.

There's blood on the floor. And more dripping off my chin. Check my pocket and the password envelope is gone.

The bag of Cartel cash I was supposed to trade the password for is gone, too. Mr. Cypress, and Vlad and the rest of the Syndicate will not understand this. Neither will the Cartel.

I slide up the wall, hook the Mexican under each arm and lift him onto the toilet. Dead people are always heavier than they look, so I'm careful about my back. The guys at the gym say, "Lift with your legs."

Open the stall door, peek out. Nobody. Spot a hole in the drywall shaped like the back of my head. Stagger around the corner and spit a mouthful of blood into the sink. Pull my head up to check my face in the mirror and the room does a lazy spin. I grip the sink, shut my eyes, and take a deep breath.

After a minute, I go back to my face. My lip is busted and leaking blood down my chin, but this bathroom doesn't have paper towels so I use the cuff of my jacket. Lost some buttons off my shirt and

One Bullet 11

my collar is torn. I look like a guy who just got mugged.

Damn, when's the last time I lost a fight? I don't lose fights. I knock them down or they run. Either way. I haven't lost a fight since I boxed. But Kid Sasquatch is big and fast.

The door swings open and a guy pokes his head in. "Is the bathroom closed?"

I blink. "Yeah. It's closed." Push past him. Walk through the airport with my head down, sucking on my busted lip and the copper penny taste of failure.

Feel a little fuzzy trying to walk fast, but gotta keep moving. Should have checked my pupils in the bathroom mirror. I probably have a concussion. Again.

Where would Kid Sasquatch go? He has a fifteen-pound bag of $700,000 in cash and the password to an overseas account with $700,000 more. Airports have Internet, but would he sit right here and log in to that overseas account? He has to do it fast, before I call the Syndicate and they change the password.

Pull out my cell phone to dial Vlad. I don't want to admit what happened, but he's gotta know so he can go online and change the password. That'll protect our half of the money.

A deep crack runs through the face of the phone and the screen is dark. I look around, but there's no pay phones anywhere these days.

Why am I alive? He killed the Mexican bagman, so why not kill me? Maybe he thinks he did?

If he thinks I'm dead, I have an edge. I need an edge. And a gun. Like something you hunt polar bears with. Hell. If Sasquatch logs in and steals the money, the Syndicate will kill me. Those guys don't like excuses.

And then fifty steps ahead of me there's Kid Sasquatch. Sitting in the waiting area, hunched over a laptop that looks tiny in his big mitts. An open sheet of typing paper is on the seat next to his, on top of the password envelope I carried. The one with my sweat and blood on it. A small, nylon duffel bag is slung crossways over his shoulder--it's got to be the cash.

I duck behind a pack of Canadian tourists, but no need to. His head is in the computer and he's typing slow with two fingers.

Gotta think, come up with a plan. But I'm not a thinker.

My hands shake. It's not adrenaline. I know what it is. Fear. He beat me senseless and I'm scared to take a rematch.

A couple of airport cops saunter by. One of the bastards is eating frozen yogurt. I eye the gun on his belt, but even I know that's a stupid play.

Walk past a couple trying to corral about ten squealing kids. They're too busy to notice me lift one of their carryon bags, the kind with the wheels and a pull-up handle. Carry the bag to the row of chairs behind Kid Sasquatch and set it down. Push it under the vinyl seats with my toe. Keep walking.

The Kid is still typing and I swear his lips are moving as he reads the password instruction sheet next to him.

One Bullet 13

I march across the wide hall to the nearest airline counter and flag down a lady in a navy blue outfit.

"Can I help you?" she asks.

"I know this sounds weird, but see that bag over there by itself?" I turn and point at the bag behind Sasquatch. "Yeah, this nervous-looking guy left it there and walked off. He looked Middle Eastern, you know?"

She bites her lip and puts a hand on the phone behind the counter.

"It's probably nothing, but..." I spread my hands.

She picks up the phone.

I walk to the window, get out my broken phone, and act like I'm sending a text message.

Thirty seconds later the cops are back. The fat one drops his yogurt in the trash and they start moving people away from the suspicious bag. Sasquatch looks up. The cop says something to him, and he looks over his shoulder at the bag and rolls his eyes. Gets up, the laptop open in one hand, the paper and the envelope in the other.

The cops herd everyone away.

The Kid shuts the laptop, sticks the envelope in his pocket and starts walking. He takes big steps. He's so big the duffle bag over his shoulder bounces like a little purse.

I stay just within sight of him through the crowded airport. As I walk past the little cafe, I slow down and lean over the railing by an empty table. Grab a napkin rolled around a fork and knife and unwrap it as I walk. I press the napkin to my busted lip, and check out the knife. It's one of those stupid, blunt-nosed knives you can't stab with, but I slip the silverware in my pocket anyway.

Maybe he'll just lay still while I saw his head off.

He tucks the laptop under one arm as he walks. Smiles at a pair of stewardesses.

The airport is packed. People are looking for their gate, or their ride home.

I think about Carly sitting there smoking and playing games on that damn iPad that never leaves her hands. But I wish I was with her right now and we were driving to lunch and my head didn't ache and my mouth wasn't bleeding and I hadn't got jacked and lost a combined 1.4 million dollars in ten seconds.

If Sasquatch has someone waiting in a car to roll in and pick him up, I'm screwed. But he hasn't been on the phone, and the cops won't let you sit in the fire lanes outside the doors. If he drove himself, he'll have to go find his car, and I have a chance.

The long-term parking is open to the sky, and you have to take a shuttle out there. But the short-term is in a huge garage.

The sliding doors open and he goes out. It's easy to follow a guy who's a head taller than everyone else. And he hasn't looked back once.

He crosses the street to the parking garage. The wind gusts and a blast of cold raindrops crash down. The rain washes away the dizzy feeling. I walk faster. Flex my fists and feel how tight my bruised thumb is.

One Bullet 15

There's a big white sign with blue letters above the parking garage. Something about security cameras, but I'm moving too fast to read it all.

What level is he on? Carly is on Level Two.

He skips the stairs. Goes straight up the ramp like a tank.

I run to the stairwell and dash up two at a time. Sweating. Panting loud. Hit Level Two and look out. He marches past. As soon as he turns the corner, I run to the Lexus and slap the roof with the palm of my hand. "Start the car."

Carly jerks. Leans to the open window with a cigarette between her fingers. "What? You scared the hell outta me."

"Start the damn car." I run to the trunk and use the blunt tip of the knife on the screws holding the license plate.

Sweat runs into my eyes.

Drop the screws and they roll under the car. Jump in and throw the license plate on the back seat. "Get out."

Carly looks at me. "Excuse me?"

I lean across her and open the passenger door. "Out. I'll be back to pick you up in a minute. Just wait here."

"It's forty degrees out, and you want me to stand here freezing my ass off?" She keeps talking as she climbs out. "My hair is gonna be a mess."

I hit Reverse and slide out of the parking space, punch it and head for the up ramp.

Level 3. Brake and look. No sign of Sasquatch unless he's sitting in a car, typing in the password.

Damn it.

16   Mark Boss

Spin the wheel and up the steep ramp to Level 4. Even in low gear, the Lexus is smooth. Powerful.

Sasquatch is walking along the row in front of me, one hand in his pocket, probably digging for his keys.

Pull my seatbelt down with my right hand and click it. Steer with my left. Hit the gas and the big sedan shoots forward.

He looks over his shoulder.

Bam.

The front bumper snaps both his legs and he's under the car as I hit the brakes and the airbag pops me in the face. I forgot the airbag.

When the car stops, I use the fork on the stupid airbag. It's like stabbing Jell-O. Look over my shoulder. He's on the ground. There's probably cameras recording all this, but at least they won't get Vlad's license plate. Pull my jacket collar up around my face, jump out and run to him.

Grab the moneybag and pull it free. Dig in his coat for the envelope. He moans and I flinch. Find the envelope and stick it in my pocket.

Take three steps toward the car, stop and go back for the Kid's laptop. I'll give it to the Syndicate hackers. Maybe something in the computer will tell them how Sasquatch knew about my meeting with the Cartel.

Run to the Lexus, throw the duffel and computer in the back seat and get the car turned around.

Sasquatch is sprawled in the middle of the row and I have to roll over his legs to get by.

One Bullet   17

The tires thump.

He screams higher than you'd think a man could.

Wish I'd put the windows up.

Almost hit the wall on my way down the ramp to Level Two because I'm speeding. I brake and see Carly standing there, cigarette in one hand, iPad in the other. Her hair is limp and hanging in her eyes, and she's wearing a cute yellow raincoat that can't hide her curves.

Damn she looks good.

Pull up, get out and open her door for her.

She looks up at me. "What happened to your face?" Then she looks at the hood of Vlad's Lexus. "What happened to the car?" she asks as she gets in.

"I hit a deer."

"In a parking garage?"

I shut her door for her and run around and jump in. "We're leaving. Gimme your phone, I gotta call Vlad."

* * *

Chapter 3
Joe

The Lexus weaves across the airport access road. My hands are shaking and my left foot stomps the floorboard over and over.

Carly slides across her seat until her back is touching the passenger door. Her eyes are huge. "What did you do?"

Gusts of cold air through the open window slap me awake. I lean and spit a glob of blood into the wind. "Big bastard jacked me. But I fixed him. Fixed him good."

Look over and Carly's nose is dripping and the cold, damp air slicks her hair down like she's running a fever. "Is he dead?" she asks.

I laugh. Thump. I felt the front bumper hit him. I didn't see much cause of the airbag, but I felt it. It felt good. Like slamming a left hook into the other guy and watching his eyes go blank.

"Joe, is he dead?"

"Shit. I don't know." The wave peaks, crashes onto the rocks. "He might be dead. I dunno." Slap the wheel. "He shouldn't have jumped me. You jump a bagman, what do you expect? Did he think I was gonna hand it over without a fight? Stupid." Kick at the airbag hanging over my knees, but now I'm as deflated as it is. "How did he know about the exchange? He got there first, killed that little Mexican, then waited for me. How'd he know?"

Carly shakes her head. Tries to light a cigarette but her hands are shaking worse than mine and the

One Bullet 19

wind is crazy in the car. "There were cameras watching. I saw a sign in the parking garage."

We're off the access road and onto State Road 388 heading west toward Panama City Beach. I can't remember if we passed any cops on the way out. Look down at the dash. I'm going 20 over the speed limit and it feels like we're crawling. Gotta slow down.

"Cameras, yeah, but I took the license plate off. If they can't identify the car, it'll slow them down. Still...." When the Cartel doesn't hear from their guy, they'll go looking. They don't know about Kid Sasquatch, so they'll figure I killed their bagman. Not good.

"Lemme have your phone, I gotta call Vlad."

Carly digs her phone out of her purse. "Pull over before you wreck us."

Slow down and bounce off the highway onto one of those dirt roads that ends after 50 feet. A sign saying, "Posted. No Hunting," hangs on a chain between two trees. There are buckshot holes in the sign. Rednecks down here are the same as in upstate New York or eastern California. Different accent, same behavior.

Dial Vlad's number and he picks up on the first ring and says what he always says. "Speak."

"It's Joe."

"Why are you calling on Carly's phone?" Vlad asks.

"Mine's busted. How do you know Carly's number?"

20 Mark Boss

"She didn't tell you about us?" Vlad laughs. Barks really. "She works at my restaurant. You think I don't have her number?"

"Right. Look, I need to talk to Mr. Cypress."

"He's at the urologist. Come on, Joe, anything you need to tell the boss you can tell me."

Sometimes I forget Vlad is the one who hired me when I had to get out of Phoenix. But Cypress is the boss. No one forgets that. "I got jacked."

Vlad says nothing.

I sit still and listen to the Lexus. It ran over a guy the size of a water buffalo and the engine is still purring. Good machine. Carly puts her window up and twists the dial for the defroster. The phone signal is weak out here but I can hear Vlad breathing.

"Did you lose the money?" he asks.

"Yeah, but I got it back. I ran the guy over in the parking garage, then I--"

"The Cartel bagman?"

"Dead. It wasn't the Cartel. Unless they killed their own guy. Which makes no--"

"The guys who jumped you?"

"Guy. One guy. Probably dead." It sounds weak when I say it, but I'm really not sure.

"One guy and you didn't finish him? Shit. Okay, yeah, you're a bagman, not a hitman."

I can hear ice jiggle in a glass. Vlad is reckless and deadly when he drinks. Cold and deadly when he doesn't. I say, "Kind of early in the day."

"Shut it, I'm thinking."

Hear glass break. Probably the glass. Maybe the bottle. Or a window.

One Bullet 21

"Is the car smashed?" he asks.

"Yeah, looks like I hit a deer. But it runs."

"A deer. Right," Carly mutters and lights a cigarette. I hit the button to roll down her window and she mashes her button to roll it up and the window freezes half way. The little window motor in the door whines.

Vlad's voice is calm. "Airports have surveillance cameras. We have to get that car off the road. They'll be looking for a gold Lexus."

"I took the license plate off."

"Smart. Okay, write these directions down. They're to an auto shop nearby. I know the guy and he won't ask a bunch of stupid questions. I'll call and tell him you're coming. Stay there and I'll come pick you up."

He goes over the directions while I scribble them on the back of the receipt from the Waffle House this morning. Seems like days ago.

Vlad hangs up.

I stare in the rearview mirror at my swollen face. My lip has stopped bleeding. Shift into reverse and get the car turned around.

"What will you do?" Carly says. Her voice is low. Almost like her pillow voice, but tighter.

"First, we have to get rid of this car before the cops find it. Don't worry. Vlad said he'll help us."

She shakes her head. "Vlad never helps anybody but himself."

* * *

Chapter 4
Vlad

Vlad dropped his cell phone on the couch, opened the sliding glass door and stepped outside into his back yard. One of his mastiffs--Amber--poked her head out of the doghouse, then the wind gusted and her face disappeared.

A large truck tire lay on a bare patch in the small yard. The house took up so much of the lot there was barely room for the dogs and the tire. Vlad peeled off his suit jacket and took up a twelve-pound sledgehammer. He adjusted his stance, swung the hammer high and brought it down right on the 'G' in Goodyear. Thump. The tire rocked.

By the tenth swing he found his rhythm. The tire began to hop off the ground as he whacked it with the sledgehammer. After forty hits he stepped back and took deep breaths of cold air until his lungs felt huge. His shoulders dropped as the tension bled out of his neck.

Vlad laughed.

Genghis and Amber poked their heads out of the doghouse, one on top of the other.

"I emptied the overseas account, you know," he told the sad-faced dogs. "The password in the envelope is real, but the account is empty. I was going to blame it on Joe, and say he stole it. But he got hijacked, so then I could blame it on someone else."

He chuckled and kicked his suit jacket into the air. The dogs watched the jacket go up and come

One Bullet   23

down. "But that Joe, he doesn't know how to quit. He got the money back and the password envelope, too. So I have to kill him before the Cartel calls Cypress and asks where their bag of cash is, and how come their bagman has a broken neck."

Vlad stood beneath the gray sky, imagining what it would be like to stand in battle against armored men and swing the big hammer. Shatter shields, crush helmets, smash skulls. Feel hot blood splash his hands. Hear their screams.

He smiled.

The dogs retreated.

Still carrying the hammer, he went through the open door to the living room, stepped over the broken bottle of vodka and picked up his phone. The Finn answered on the fourth ring.

"Is there a problem?" The Finn asked.

"Yes, we have to move it up. We need to kill Cypress today. Pick your location and text me this afternoon. I'll bring Cypress to you."

"I don't like to rush. It's risky to rush."

"The exchange at the airport went bad. Someone ambushed our bagman. The Cartel won't wait to act, and neither should we." Vlad paced, stepping over the broken glass. Outside, his jacket blew past the open door. Genghis chased it. "Do you have a twin?"

"Yes, but I killed it in the womb. Why?" The Finn said.

Vlad watched the big dog maul his jacket and laughed. "I have another job I need done today--our bagman, Joe Barrow."

"Why not use your Syndicate soldiers?" The Finn asked.

"I'm not their king. Not yet. Besides, Joe is new but they trust him. They won't believe he stole the delivery, and I don't need them asking questions. I'll have to get outside contractors."

"Who will you use?"

"I'll call some meth heads I know."

"You get what you pay for," The Finn said, then hung up and left Vlad staring at the phone.

The dogs looked in through the open door. One held a sleeve in its mouth.

"If you want to be the king, you have to kill the king," Vlad said. "When Cypress is dead, I'll run the Syndicate." He bent and scratched the dogs' heads. "It's too bad about Joe, though. I liked the guy."

* * *

Chapter 5
Joe

The auto shop is right off the highway, but the sign is small and I miss it and have to turn around. When we pull in, a fat guy with a couple of pit bulls trailing him comes out of the office. The place is L-shaped with the office on the left, and three bays facing the road. There's a dozen cars and trucks scattered across the lot and the grass on the side, and it's hard to guess which ones run and which don't.

As we get out of the car, I see two mechanics in the garage, standing under a big Dodge truck that's up on the rack.

"Can I help y'all?" the fat guy asks. The label on his shirt says, "Fred." His eyes crawl all over Carly.

She crosses her arms.

"Vlad sent me." That gets his attention. Point my thumb at the Lexus. "I hit a deer. I need that car cleaned up. It's Vlad's car. Don't worry about the dent, but get the blood off. Every bit. Hit it with bleach if you have to."

Fred leans and looks around me at the car. I sidestep and look, too.

The Lexus is worse than I thought. Huge dent in the front bumper, and half-dried blood blown across the hood.

Fred waddles to the car, passing close to Carly on the way. She glares at him. He looks in the window. "What about the air bag? Have to order a replacement."

"Just yank it out, clean the car and park it where no one can see it from the road."

"Got a tent out back we use to paint in. Could put it in there."

"That's fine."

One of the dogs grabs a radiator hose off the ground and the two play tug of war. Fred watches them. "If you're in the market for a yard dog, I figure to mate one of these."

"With you or another dog?" Carly asks.

"What?" Fred's small eyes scrunch up and disappear into his head. "Oh, you made a funny. I like my women sassy."

"I'll be in the office," Carly says and walks inside with her iPad in one hand, purse in the other.

Fred watches her walk. Even when she isn't trying, Carly jiggles. When she tries, grown men swoon. "Damn, girl, you want some fries with that shake?"

I grab Fred's fat head and shove the car key into his face just below his eye. "That's my woman. Clean Vlad's car. Now."

Up close, Fred smells like a port-a-potty on a hot day. I let go and he almost tips over.

"Okay, okay, I was just reading from the menu, didn't say I was trying to order." Fred, like Vlad's dogs, has a drool problem.

I push the key hard into his hand. Grab the duffel bag and Kid Sasquatch's laptop computer off the back seat and go in.

One Bullet

27

Inside, the office is a pit. Cluttered with parts catalogs and out-of-date nudie calendars and a coffee maker with no pot. Carly sits on a vinyl love seat, crosses her legs and lights a cigarette.

At least we're out of the wind and the noise from the highway. Maybe I can think, which for me always takes some doing.

She waves her phone while I pace. "You want I should call a cab?" she asks.

"No, Vlad is gonna pick us up."

I stand at the window and watch one of the mechanics thread the Lexus through the lot toward the back of the shop. The dogs are still playing with the radiator hose.

"So how much were you delivering this time?" Carly asks.

Rub my chin, look at the duffel bag on the floor by her feet. "Seven hundred thousand. I was picking it up, not delivering." Carly knows what I do. We started dating a few months after I moved down here, so I guess ten months ago. She's a hostess at Vlad's restaurant, and she knows he launders money through the place. But I don't usually talk details. I'm not sure how much she knows about the Syndicate.

"I've never seen that much cash." She pokes the duffel with her toe. "Can I look?"

Normally, the bag isn't opened. It goes from the Cartel bagman to me, and then I put it in Vlad's hands while Mr. Cypress watches. But Carly's had a tough morning, and I'll do anything to see her smile. "Sure, open it up. Just keep it on the floor so the grease monkeys don't see."

She stubs her cigarette out on Fred's desk. Her hands tremble when she touches the duffel bag. Unzips the bag and pulls outs a 10K brick with a blue rubber band around it. She riffles it like a deck of cards. "What the hell?"

"What?"

She throws the brick at me and I snatch it out of the air. The top of the brick is a dirty hundred dollar bill. Underneath, the rest is fake. Not even counterfeit money, just a stack of green and white paper cut the right size.

"Those bastards. They cheated," Carly yells.

"Keep it down, babe." I touch her shoulder and she flinches. I step back. She looks ready to punch someone, and I'm the only one here. I slump down on the vinyl seat and it creaks. "What the hell is happening? First Kid Sasquatch jacks me, now the money is fake. What the hell?"

Carly digs through the duffel. "Look, they're all like that. Fake. A rip off."

I run my hands down my forehead, over my eyes. Gotta think. Maybe the Cartel screwed us? Or Kid Sasquatch switched the money somehow? How long was I knocked out on the bathroom floor at the airport?

If I hand Vlad and Mr. Cypress a bag of fake money, it will look bad. A bagman is the only criminal other criminals trust with their money. But if you give them cause to doubt you, you're dead.

What happens when the Cartel asks for their money back? We can't tell them we don't have it.

This is bad.

One Bullet

She kicks the bag and marches to the window. "If this creep keeps looking at me, I'm gonna walk out there and kick him in the nutsack."

I zip the duffel shut and get up to look.

Fred waddles back and forth across the parking lot, a cell phone pressed to his ear. Every few steps he looks up at the office where we're standing.

Fred looks nervous.

"Something's wrong. Get your stuff, we're leaving."

A minivan shoots into the parking lot. Its brakes screech.

Fred holds his phone to his chest and looks up.

A shirtless guy in saggy jeans and big black boots jumps out of the minivan. With a machete.

Fred screams. Shirtless whacks Fred in the neck. Blood geysers straight up.

The yard dogs grab Shirtless by the ass, while three more guys burst out of the van. One levels a pump shotgun and starts firing.

I pull Carly down as the window explodes.

* * *

Chapter 6
Vlad

When Vlad got out of the shower, his cell phone rang. It was set to rattle, so it skittered across the vanity and tumbled into the sink. He grabbed it, read the caller's number and answered, "Sir?"

"The Mexicans called." Cypress had the hoarse voice of someone who screams at people. "They want to know where their bag of money is, why they didn't get the password envelope, and how come their bagman is dead."

"Yeah." Vlad ran a comb through his hair to slick it back from his face. Amber wandered in and lapped from the toilet. He looked at the dog and shrugged.

"You knew?" Cypress asked. "How did you know?"

He put the phone on speaker and set it on a hand towel. While he squeezed a fat ribbon of Colgate onto his toothbrush, Vlad said, "Joe called me. Said he got jumped at the airport."

Cypress cleared his throat. "Is he back yet? He should be back. Where is he?"

"Sir, we have to look at what we know. The Cartel bagman is dead, Joe is gone, and the money is gone." Vlad looked at himself in the mirror as he said the words that would seal Joe's death.

"Joe came with a half dozen good references. He's done bagman jobs all over the country and never lost a delivery. Shit. It was only $700,000, why did he pick now to get greedy?"

One Bullet 31

Vlad let Cypress rant. He knew the words meant little because Cypress would be thinking while he talked. Cypress might scream and throw things, but he rarely acted out of emotion. Besides, Joe had only been around for a year. How attached could the old man be?

While he dressed, Cypress went on. "Look, call the number two guy over at the Cartel. What's his name? Ernesto. Call Ernesto and set up a meeting. Don't let them pick the place. You pick the place and make sure it's somewhere private. Tell Ernesto I'll bring a bag of good-faith money they can hold onto until we find Joe and sort this out."

"Got it. You need me to pick up the money?"

"No. You work the phone. I'll visit a few banks, put together a pile, then meet you at the condo in Rosemary Beach."

"Yes, sir."

Cypress hung up. Vlad dropped the phone in his pocket and clipped a holstered Glock 19 to his belt. He slid a Gerber knife into the top of his boot, and took a five-shot Smith and Wesson revolver out of a drawer. He weighed the revolver in his hand, then put it in his pants pocket. The gun made a clear outline on his pants, so he switched it out for a tiny Taurus .380 semiautomatic in a wallet holster.

Vlad went out to the kitchen for his keys, and the mastiff followed, toilet water dripping from her muzzle.

Lacey sat on the couch in the living room with Genghis warming her bare legs. The TV had one of those shows where five people sit around and gossip about celebrities. Vlad wondered why he hadn't used the sledgehammer on the TV.

"You want some lunch? There's buffalo wings from last night in the fridge," Lacey said.

Her voice was thick, almost as bad as Cypress, but it wasn't from screaming. A pair of her jeans hung over the kitchen sink. The jeans stunk of marijuana, and there was a wet spot down one leg.

"How come movies cost so much to make? Isn't it all computers?" Lacey sipped from a big, plastic tumbler. Her words were slurred. "Genghis humped my leg again. You need to get him fixed."

"Which is Genghis?" Vlad pulled the jeans off the sink and dropped them into the trash. He wanted to check with The Finn and find out where they'd kill Cypress. The Finn didn't like to rush, but Vlad knew he had to move fast. If Joe used the password and found out the overseas account was empty, then told Cypress, the old man would suspect Vlad emptied the account because he was the one who set it up.

Still, if Cypress found out the account was empty, Vlad could blame Joe. He could blame everything on Joe. Then kill Cypress. And after the meth heads killed Joe, he could blame dead Joe and dead Cypress and run the Syndicate himself.

If.

If his meth heads found Joe and killed him. If The Finn could beat the Kwan brothers and kill Cypress. If.

Vlad drank straight from a bottle of orange juice on the counter. If they did this meeting like the others, he'd be in the back seat of the car next to

One Bullet 33

Cypress. Sitting next to the target of a hit was a dangerous place to be. He hoped The Finn was as good as advertised.

He set the bottle down too hard and spilled it. Held up his hand to the weak winter light. His hand wasn't shaking, but it trembled. Just a little.

"--and you should get him those fake nuts after he gets fixed. For his self esteem," Lacey said. "Genghis needs self esteem."

Vlad looked over the kitchen counter at her. "Who is Genghis?"

Lacey pointed one tattooed arm at the huge dog sprawled over her feet. "That one. Your dog. Don't you know your dogs' names?"

Vlad looked down at Amber, and winked. "I don't name them. It'd be like naming a shovel."

He went to the garage and climbed into a Porsche Cayenne sport utility vehicle. He decided to call The Finn on the drive over to Rosemary Beach to meet Cypress.

* * *

Chapter 7
Joe

I pull Carly down as the auto shop window explodes. Glass and shotgun pellets shred the back wall of the office. I hear the guy outside rack the pump on his shotgun up and down.

Reach up and tip the desk over. A phone and a bunch of other crap slides off, including a flat-head screwdriver.

Everything sounds distant, muffled. I see in black and white, the colors washed away. It's a narrow view--just what's directly in front of me. I grab the black and white screwdriver.

Instead of going through the door like a human, Shotgun Johnny steps through the shattered window. Jagged glass at the bottom catches his pants and he looks down.

I lunge up and put the screwdriver through the soft part under his chin and drive it all the way up into his brain.

He blinks, confused.

His mouth is pinned shut but it looks like he's trying to talk. I can hear Fred screaming outside, but he sounds very far away. Dogs barking. Guns firing. I look into Johnny's eyes and I can't break the stare.

Then he sags and falls backward out of the window. I grab the shotgun out of his hands on his way down.

"Let's go," Carly yells and tugs my arm.

One Bullet 35

I've never killed anybody before today. Beat people half to death, but never that last half.

I should feel something.

Look up. Shirtless is whacking a pit bull to death with his machete. The other dog is down. So is Fred, but fat Fred is still conscious and screaming.

Shirtless swings the machete and I shoulder the shotgun, take a second to aim and shoot him in the face. The birdshot mangles. One second Shirtless is a pale-faced kid with black teeth. A second later his face is a leaky blood orange and he's staggering around holding his skin on.

He trips over Fred and falls.

I rack the shotgun. The empty plastic shell pops out, but there's no more in the tube.

Turn toward the back of the office where Carly is heading for the door, the duffel bag in her hands. She opens it and I see a toilet. It's just a bathroom, not the way out.

There's a side door from the office into the garage bays. Run to it, ease it open an inch and look. One of the mechanics is down with a bunch of holes in his chest and a red pool underneath him. The other is rolling around on the concrete with one of the minivan freaks, gouging and biting each other.

Next to me on the wall is a square of pegboard with a bunch of keys on hooks. I grab three keys off the top row, just the ones that have keyless entry clickers attached.

"Carly, this way," I say it loud but I can barely hear my own voice.

Bullets poke holes in the office drywall.

Carly runs to me, head down, holding the duffel bag like a shield.

Yank open the side door and dash into the garage. The freak is straddling the mechanic now, choking him. I swing the empty shotgun like a golf club. It hits the freak so hard the wooden stock snaps. His head flops over, way past his shoulder. Way past what your neck is designed for.

The mechanic wriggles out from under the body.

I drop the broken shotgun and grab a long wrench off the floor. The mechanic runs past me, right into a bullet.

The mechanic spins around and the rest of the bullets hit him in the back and the head and legs and he jerks as he falls face down on the floor.

Out in the parking lot, a freak with a rifle reaches into the front seat of the minivan and pulls out a fresh magazine.

I turn in time to see Carly go out the back door and disappear into the yard. Follow her as fast as I can.

Outside and see her tugging on the door of a Honda Civic. She's screaming but I can't make sense of her words.

Yank a clicker from my pocket and hit the button. Across the lot, a horn sounds and I flinch. It's a jacked-up bubba truck with huge tires and a roll bar.

"Carly, come on," I yell and run for the truck. Bullets whine and it sounds like the freaks are shooting their way through the garage bay wall.

One Bullet

The truck has a little step to stick your toe in so you can climb up to the seat. I jump in and crank it. Country music blasts out of the speakers behind my head, and I bang my nose on the steering wheel. Carly scrambles into the passenger seat, the duffel bag still clutched to her chest.

Before she pulls her seatbelt down, she reaches over and cuts off the stereo. I could kiss her.

There's a beat-up, wooden privacy fence between us and getting the hell outta here. I have no idea what's on the other, but I hit the fence without hesitation.

The lot is empty except for an overgrown foundation for a trailer that never arrived. By the time we hit the highway we've picked up some speed and the truck leans over hard when I turn east. I expect a bullet through the back window, but there are no more shots. Just the loud hum of the big mud tires and the sound of my own breathing.

Next to me Carly hugs the bag of fake money and rocks back and forth. "It wasn't supposed to be like this. It wasn't."

It's her day off. After my exchange at the airport, I was supposed to take her out to lunch. We were gonna drive over to Seaside, eat some fish, get an ice cream cone and walk around and look at the fancy houses. Not run over a guy and fight a minivan full of rednecks.

But the job isn't over until you deliver the money. That's the deal.

* * *

Vlad

As Vlad drove west on Highway 98 toward Rosemary Beach, his phone rang. "Speak."

"Was he fat?"

"What? Who is this?" He sped up to pass a truck hauling a shaky pile of pine tree logs.

"It's Ladle. I'm at the auto repair shop." Ladle spoke slowly and his words were flat, each syllable given the exact same emphasis. "Would you say this fella, Joe, was an obese man?"

"No. He's my size, muscled. Why, what happened?" Despite the winter air outside, the back of his neck prickled and Vlad turned on the air conditioner.

"Well...the situation was confusing," Ladle said. "Lot of people running around. Yelling and such. The boys were pretty worked up."

Vlad switched hands and pressed the phone to his ear. "Is Joe Barrow dead or not?"

"I suspect not."

He heard Ladle clear his throat and spit.

"You know I've got some cousins in Texas I've been meaning to visit," Ladle said.

"Yes, do that. And throw that phone away." Vlad hung up and slapped the steering wheel. What had The Finn said? You get what you pay for.

* * *

Chapter 8
Joe

Unlike Vlad's Lexus, in the truck you feel the speed. Especially with the windows down and the cold air numbing my busted lip. I crank the handle and get the window up. Check the rearview mirror but there's no minivan full of zombie rejects on our tail. I guess after you shove a screwdriver through somebody's brain it sends a warning to his buddies not to follow you.

Unless they're his brothers.

I speed up.

I'm not sure how many scumbags I killed. People...people I killed. Carly is better at math than I am, but I can't ask her.

I don't know where adrenaline comes from or how much your body can make in one day, but I'm rocking back and forth in the seat of the truck. Smiling. But pissed. Those bastards tried to kill us. Fred was a creep, but the mechanics didn't deserve what they got.

"You think those freaks were after Fred or us?" I ask.

Carly says nothing. She's still holding the duffel bag to her chest and staring straight ahead.

I touch her arm and feel her flinch under the raincoat. "Baby? You think those meth heads were after Fred or us? Because Vlad sent us to that auto shop, so.... I'm not saying Vlad set us up, but we have to think here. He could have told Mr. Cypress. When I didn't show up with the money, they might have thought I ripped them off so they sent those freaks. But why wouldn't they use Syndicate soldiers? Unless it was the Cartel. Maybe the Cartel figured--"

"I have to pee. Now."

"Baby, those guys might be on the highway behind us. I'm not sure now is the best--"

"Now," she shrieks. It hurts my ears.

I look over. Her eyes are full of tears. Mascara is smeared down one cheek. There's sparkly bits of glass in her hair. Drops of blood on her cute yellow raincoat. Carly is a restaurant hostess. Sure, she was an exotic dancer once, but that was years ago. This whole situation is way beyond her experience. I think.

A quarter mile ahead there's a mini-mart with three gas pumps and weird sign with a frog on it. Not like a Circle K or a Seven Eleven, just some indie quickie mart out here in the middle of nowhere.

I glance at the gas gauge, but whatever bubba owned this truck left us a full tank. Slow down and work the wheel and the truck sways and leans over like sailboat. I pull past the pumps and park over on the side, out of view of the highway in case the minivan of freaks are still hunting us.

Carly pops out and bolts through the door before I can shut the engine off. When I step down from the truck my legs are shaky and I feel a hundred years old. Empty and weak. Everything looks grey. The sky is grey, the road is grey. But the pine trees are that same uniform shade of green, like an endless row of giant plastic army men.

One Bullet 41

The door jingles when I tug it open. At the counter on my right, a short, chubby girl looks up from her cell phone. She has vampire makeup on, and two bolts through her lower lip that wag like the barbs on a catfish.

"Do you have bandages?"

She nods. Points. "Back there by the condoms."

"Thanks." Walk down the row and look.

"Are you okay?" she asks.

I look up from the metal shelves. "What?"

She points again. "You're hurt--your lip is bleeding. Are you okay?"

In the parking garage at the airport, Carly said, 'What happened to your face?' and 'What happened to the car?' She didn't say, 'Are you okay?'

I make myself smile. "Yeah, I'm good. Thanks." Spot the bandages on the bottom shelf and kneel down to reach them. Hear a toilet flush in the back of the store. Carly must be almost done. Hear a car pull up outside.

Lean and look around the shelf.

The car is an old Chevy Caprice painted purple, with giant chrome wheels shaped like ninja throwing stars. Two guys step out, both wearing hoodies. The driver takes a sip from a beer bottle and drops it on the ground. Across the Caprice, the passenger hitches up his pants. He's got something tucked inside the hoody.

"Get down," I say in a loud whisper to Goth Girl behind the counter.

"What?" she asks.

The door swings open, the passenger levels a gun, a single-shot shotgun with the barrel cut short. The driver vaults the counter and shoves the girl into the wall so hard that cartons of cigarettes rain down on her head.

She screams, and he slaps her. "Open the register, bitch!"

The Gunner looks around and I duck lower. Carly, don't flush the toilet again. I picture her opening the bathroom door and this guy blasting her with the shotgun.

Slapper throws Goth Girl into the counter next to the register. "Open it. Open it."

He grabs her from behind, and his hands roam all over her. "You want something from me, bitch?"

She twists and gets an elbow into his gut. Good for her.

He punches her in the back of the head and she drops. He bends down behind the counter with her. I hear clothes rip.

Gunner says, "Come on, man, we don't have time for that." He leans to look over the counter.

I charge.

Guys my size aren't quiet.

Gunner's head comes up and he starts to turn.

Three steps. Four. If I can just reach him--

The shotgun comes around. A 2-liter soda bottle next to me explodes. Pops straight up in the air like a cork.

Gunner pulls the trigger again just before I slam into him. I guess he forgot he's holding a single-shot shotgun.

One Bullet 43

The barrel pokes me in the gut but I come around with an elbow and knock him stupid. His head hits the edge of the counter on his way down.

I start to climb the counter but Slapper jumps off the floor. Something in his hand. A knife. Shit. I didn't see the knife. Grab his wrist and lose my grip on the counter. Fall back and my weight yanks him over the counter and onto the floor with me.

He has a knife, but I have his wrist.

It's hard to throw punches from your back. He's howling. Trying to get the knife into me and punching with his free hand. I grab hold of his neck, get a good grip with my fingers and squeeze. His eyes bulge.

Slapper thrashes, but now he's not trying to get at me, he's trying to get away from me. When he tries to stand, I roll us both over. Still have his wrist, but now I'm on top. Let go of his neck and he tilts his chin back to gulp a precious breath of air and I drive my fist as hard as I can into his throat and feel it collapse under my knuckles, and snot and spit shoot out of him onto my face but he is dead. Or will be in a minute or two as he flops around on the cold tile, gagging for air through his crushed windpipe.

Turn around. Everything is so sharp. The colors of the candy wrappers. The neon beer sign in the window. The yellow plastic shell Gunner is trying to feed into his shotgun. What happened? Before it was black and white, now it's color so bright it hurts.

I grab the knife off the floor and rush him. Gunner looks up, drops the shell and raises the shotgun like a shield. I stab him. Underhanded. Nothing fancy. No waving the knife around like some moron in a movie. Just a straight on Folsom Prison Rush where you keep the knife low and drive it into them until your arm gives out.

I stab him twenty or thirty times before he stops screaming. Stops twitching.

Shit.

Rock back on my knees. I guess we're on the floor. My arm is tired.

Hear a door creak.

The bathroom door opens just wide enough for Carly to peek out.

"Carly, it's okay. Come out." My voice is raw. Thick. I push up from the floor, lean on the counter and look over it. Goth Girl is curled up in a ball. Her shirt is ripped and she has bright tattoos on her pale skin and tomorrow she'll have bright bruises. And nightmares for a lot longer.

"Are you okay?" I ask.

She doesn't respond. Her eyes are open, and I can see her breathing. One of the bolts from her lip is torn out, and blood drips on the floor.

I turn around and Slapper is still gagging. Croaking like a frog as he crawls toward the door. He collapses before his hand touches the glass. He shudders once and goes still.

Carly's high heels click on the floor. She steps carefully over one of Gunner's shoes that came off in the fight. Goes around Slapper, opens the door and walks slowly to the truck.

Yeah. The truck.

One Bullet 45

We better leave. I say to the Goth Girl, "I'm sorry about all this." My mouth is so dry it's hard to talk. She doesn't say anything. I grab three bottles of Gatorade from the shelf and go outside. The Caprice is still running, pumping exhaust into the cold air.

The engine sputters and quits. They were out of gas.

* * *

Chapter 9
Vlad

As Vlad cruised west over the bridge at Phillip's Inlet, his phone rang again. He glanced at the number and didn't recognize it, but answered in case it was The Finn.

The Finn said, "I've found a place."

"Already?"

"I scouted it last month when you asked me about the contract. This morning I revisited the site to confirm it is still abandoned."

Vlad cracked the driver's side window. Cold, wet air blew in, but it was a quicker wakeup than a cup of coffee and easier on his stomach. "I'm on the way to Rosemary Beach to pick him up. Can you be ready in time?"

"Yes. As soon as we hang up, I'll text you the directions. How many will be in the party?"

"Me, Cypress and the two Koreans--the Kwan brothers. Remember, these Koreans were ROKs, Republic of Korea army special forces or something. They're good."

"I'm better," The Finn said softly. "Do you know 'Kwan' means 'mountain'?"

"No, but these two are the size of mountains. All they do is lift weights and kick trees."

"Trees don't kick back. You'll be in the back seat of the car next to Cypress?"

"Yeah." Vlad unfastened the top buttons of his shirt to get some cold air on his neck.

One Bullet

"It's windy today, bad shooting weather. Don't sit too close." The Finn laughed and hung up.

Vlad opened the passenger window and pitched the phone out. He knew he should have pulled the SIM card, smashed the whole thing and dropped it in the ocean. But the roadside ditch would have to do.

He slowed down and followed a yellow pest-control truck and a few cars through the left turn onto State Road 30-A. He slowed down even more once he reached the pastel-colored gauntlet of condominiums, beach houses and restaurants. In the summer it would be jammed with sun-burned tourists, but it was the winter off season, and only brave Canadians wandered the streets, hunched beneath umbrellas.

The rain grew harder and he fiddled with the intermittent windshield wipers, never satisfied with the setting. Vlad turned left into the cramped, twisting streets of Rosemary Beach itself, where the tight-packed condos reminded him of the houses in Rome. There were only two parking spots beneath Cypress's condo, one with his Porsche Panamera sedan in it, and the other with the younger Kwan's sand-colored Jeep. The silver Panamera looked like a giant bullet.

"Shit." He thought about parking in someone else's spot, but with his luck, Vlad figured the owner would call a tow truck. Most of the places were empty during the winter, but he couldn't afford a single misstep today.

He circled back to the small park in front of Restaurant Paradis. Settled his suit jacket over the holster, and hopped out. Despite his fast march pace, he was half soaked when he reached the steps of the condo.

The door opened before he could knock. The older Kwan brother lowered his JS 9 submachine gun, and stepped back to let him in. The hall was narrow for two large men, and Vlad had to turn sideways to go past Greater Kwan. Looking down at the gun, he wondered why Kwan would use a Chinese-made submachine gun, but Vlad figured Kwan probably killed a Chinese soldier and took it from him.

He went through the living room, where Lesser Kwan sat in a rattan chair, loading a Heckler and Koch USP 9mm pistol. The TV was on the weather scan channel, with the sound off. As he went into the kitchen, Vlad heard a toilet flush down the hall. He ran a handful of paper towels over his wet face and hair, and studied Lesser Kwan's back. He could see the outline of body armor under the younger man's shirt.

"You go to the bank, yet?" Vlad asked. Cypress had said he'd bring a small bag of cash to keep the Cartel happy until they found Joe and retrieved the original $700,000. Of course, Cypress thought they were going to meet the Cartel. Vlad knew they were going to meet The Finn instead. But if the Cartel called while they were en route, Cypress would have questions. Vlad had seen the Kwans ask people questions before, and it always involved screaming.

"We went bank. Two banks." Lesser Kwan held up two fingers. One of them was crooked.

One Bullet   49

Vlad wiped his face again. "It's pissing down out there."

"In high wind, the pine tree bends. Not breaks," Greater Kwan said, and Lesser nodded. He slid the magazine into the H&K, chambered a cartridge and tucked the gun into his shoulder holster.

Down the hall the toilet flushed again, then the door opened. Cypress called, "Vlad, you here?"

"Yes, sir."

The bedroom door shut and Vlad stood with the two bodyguards, watching the weather scan channel. Rain beat on the windows, and on the TV green and yellow blobs drifted west to east across the map.

Vlad wondered if Cypress was sick. He'd been to the urologist, now he was taking forever in the bathroom. What if Cypress was too sick to go to the meeting? Could he do it here? No, taking on all three by himself was insane. He needed The Finn and they needed to set a trap. "He eat some bad fish or something?" Vlad asked.

Neither Korean answered. Greater Kwan held a hard, rubber ball in his hand. He squeezed it until the veins on his forearm looked ready to burst, then passed it to the other hand. Lesser Kwan loaded another H&K.

"Looks like you're going heavy today," Vlad said. "I know the Cartel is angry about their delivery, but they aren't crazy. A word with Mr. Cypress and a bag of money will make it right."

Lesser Kwan shrugged and loaded a magazine with 9mm cartridges, holding the stack down with his thumb and methodically pressing each cartridge in.

Vlad looked around the room, avoiding their eyes just as they avoided his. There was a huge coffee table with carved elephants as its legs. Pen-and-ink drawings of monkeys above the couch. A statue of a leopard, or maybe it was a cheetah, crouched in the corner. A blunt spear and a narrow shield hung on one wall. Like someone returned from a safari and brought everything from the hunting lodge with them.

Cypress came down the hall in a fast shuffle, his shoes in one hand, a cheap nylon bag in the other. "Chickens."

"What?" Vlad blinked.

"Fucking chickens. Filthy things. They raise them in these warehouses where they sit in piles of shit and peck each other to death." Cypress sat on the couch and bent to put on his shoes. "I ate Chicken Marsala last night and now I can't get off the toilet."

"Oh, yeah. You drink plenty of fluids?" Vlad asked.

"Fluids? What are you, my nurse?" Cypress struggled with his shoe laces. His face flushed.

Vlad watched Cypress's knobby, arthritic fingers. Noticed the glasses on a silver chain around the old man's neck. He wondered if the rumors about Cypress having syphilis were true. Manila Tommy said the cook at Cypress's house in Pensacola told him all about it. Vlad thought about a sore on Lacey's mouth. He'd noticed it last night during dinner. She said it was cold sore, but maybe it was time for Lacey to go...somewhere else.

"So where?" Cypress asked.

Vlad looked down. "Sir?"

"Where are we meeting Ernesto?" Cypress said slowly. "Damn, you deaf or hung over? I tell you, he's got that attention disorder crap." Cypress laughed and looked at the Kwans. They both shrugged. Cypress shook his head. "Like telling jokes to a pair of mimes. Pointless."

The old man stood and pointed at the nylon bag. "Vlad, you get the money. Kwan, get the car started and turn on the heater. Other Kwan, get my Thermos." While Greater Kwan went into the kitchen, Cypress stared at Vlad. "What's the problem? You're sweating."

Vlad ran the damp paper towels over his forehead. "I had to park at Paradis and walk through the rain. I'm soaked."

"I'm melting," Cypress said in a falsetto voice. "Don't be such a damn baby. Let's go."

They went out into the rain, and Vlad held the door for his boss, then went around and climbed in the other side. The back of the four-seat Panamera felt very small.

Lesser Kwan sat at the wheel. He put a thick arm on the center console and looked over his shoulder. "Where?"

"Out to Highway 98, then I'll give you directions from there. It's not far," Vlad said.

* * *

Chapter 10
Joe

My arms are so tired that just keeping the steering wheel straight is an effort. The bubba truck wobbles along the highway, big wheels humming. I drink one of the bottles of Gatorade, looking over the lip for cops or meth heads or whatever the hell else might be after us.

Hold a second bottle out to Carly but she shakes her head.

"They were going to rape that girl behind the counter," I say.

Carly nods. "I saw. Let's not talk about it." She reaches over and turns on the radio. Skips the preset buttons and scans manually. A reggae song strolls out of the speakers and suddenly the world isn't quite so cold and grey. I went to the Caribbean once and ninety percent of everybody was poor. I noticed because I was carrying $500,000 in a briefcase with a ballistic panel built into it in case someone shot the money.

The weird thing was almost all the people on the island were happy. Cooking fish on a charcoal fire, but happy. They must know something I don't.

We drive toward Panama City. The traffic picks up when I take Highway 77 south into Lynn Haven. My stomach rumbles. You'd think killing two guys in a mini-mart would spoil your appetite, but I'm starving. "You hungry, babe? It's past lunch time."

Carly stares at me. "You're kidding."

One Bullet 53

When the DJ on the radio starts the news, she turns it off. "Joe, we have to run. I don't know if Vlad set us up, or the Cartel, or Cypress. But we can't stay."

She's half right. She can't stay. I can't protect her and fix this mess at the same time. Although I could use her brains. Carly is definitely the smart one.

While we sit at a traffic light, I scrub my hand over my face and realize my fingers are covered in half-dried blood. Look down and see the splatter across my shirt from when I stabbed Gunner. Or maybe it was when I put the screwdriver through...what did I call him? It doesn't matter. Damn, it's hard to think.

The light turns green and Carly goes on. "We need clean clothes and money. New phones. Plane tickets somewhere."

"Guns."

"Not guns. I'm sick of men with guns." Carly looks out the window at the crowded lot of a grocery store. People putting bags of food through the side doors of minivans. Plopping kids down into the car seats and double checking the buckles. Hurrying because it's cold. "Maybe guns. Just until we get away."

"We'll go to my apartment," I say. "I've got some money stashed there. Not a lot, but any's better than none."

"Will there be cops when we get there?" she asks.

"Maybe they've got video from the airport parking garage, but we switched cars. Nothing from the auto shop connects to us, except Vlad's car. The mini-mart was random, and the poor counter girl can't tell them much."

"The Cartel?"

"It's possible, but they'd have to move pretty quick to put someone on my place before we get there."

"The Syndicate?"

I take a long, slow breath. "I dunno. Vlad sent us to the auto shop, then those meth heads showed up. But were they there to kill Fred, or us? Did the Cartel send them? Or did someone follow us from the airport? I dunno. We have to be careful."

Carly shakes the second Gatorade and opens it, so I drink the third bottle. It's a lot to consider. More thinking than I usually manage in a week.

My stomach growls. I've got half a Porterhouse steak in the fridge in my apartment. If there's time I can heat it in the microwave, stick it between a couple pieces of toast and eat it on the way to wherever we're going next.

My apartment complex has one of those security gates where you have to stick a plastic card in to make the flimsy wooden arm go up. It also has a little forest behind it. I slow the bubba truck down and cruise by the gate. The security card is in my wallet, but I'm not going in through the front.

Take a side street and cut through to the next road, and park across the street at a veterinarian's office that looks busy. Button my suit jacket and pull the lapels up, not only because it's cold but because I have blood all down the front of my shirt.

One Bullet   55

"I'll take a quick look at the apartment. If it's clear, I'll come back and get you."

Carly nods. She's chewing her bottom lip hard enough to draw blood. Her eyes look big again, like this morning.

"It'll be fine." I lean across the seat to kiss her but she turns her head and I get a mouthful of hair and a pebble of window glass. Pick the glass off my tongue and drop it on the ground as I step down from the jacked-up truck.

Across the street, the woods are scrappy little pines that somebody planted twenty years ago. But the growth beneath them is thick. I look around, but the only people in the vet's parking lot are a couple trying to coax a big Labrador down out of their Chevy.

Jog across the road and into the woods, then stop. Listen. I hear car noises. A siren somewhere south of here, probably on 23rd Street by Gulf Coast hospital. A squirrel in the tree above me works, raining bits of pine cone down to the ground. He seems calm, so I guess everything is cool.

It's hard to walk a straight line because I have to keep going around trees and blackberry bushes and stepping over ant mounds. Up ahead it clears out and I see the edge of a deep ditch. When it rains around here, the runoff can be huge. Streets and parking lots flood all the time.

Something screeches and a blue jay dive bombs my head and I squat low. It takes another pass and the damn thing is so loud and aggressive I lay down.

From this angle, I can see below the smaller trees down into the ditch. There's a tall, concrete drainage pipe on my left, then the ditch, and farther along a thicket with bottles and garbage caught in it.

But there's a shape that doesn't fit. At the end of the drain pipe, something sticks out. Something metal.

My heart kicks up a notch, but I don't feel the rush. Maybe I'm too tired and hungry, but it's almost like I'm watching it on TV. Distant.

The gun barrel sticking out of the drain pipe moves. Rises, then lowers as the gunman adjusts his position to peek out at the blue jay.

I bury my face in the dirt for a minute, then look.

The gunman is turned in profile, looking down the length of the ditch. He's dark haired, and tan or naturally brown. The collar of his denim jacket is turned up and he looks like a ranch hand. He's wearing work gloves and holding an old Mac 10 submachine gun like most men hold a newspaper. He squats in the pipe and watches the blue jay, and I sink lower.

He leans and spits a stream of tobacco juice into the weeds along the bank of the ditch.

Looks up again at the blue jay as it zips back and forth in the air, and waits.

I wait, too. Until the bird wears itself out and shuts up.

Unless it's a woman across a bar, I won't stare at a person because sometimes they sense it and look right at me. But I can't help it, and I take another look at him.

One Bullet 57

His face is weather beaten. Or maybe life beaten.

He looks a few years older than me, and his eyes probably aren't as sharp as they once were. He looks calm, even content, squatting in that drainage pipe with the rainwater drifting past his boots.

He's probably Cartel, but I'm not sure. There are very few old gunmen in the drug cartels. They're all either dead or in prison, so it's usually young guys. But here's this middle-aged ranch hand waiting in a ditch for me.

There's probably more men inside my apartment. Digging through my cabinets for my rolls of cash, checking the pistol under my bed, eating my delicious Porterhouse.

Meanwhile, this poor bastard is stuck out in the rain, thinking about Old Mexico, I guess. Thinking about his gal, or maybe his wife and kids and his dog.

It's a terrible thing to kill a man.

I did it an hour ago. I can't do it now.

I put my chest to the ground, hug the earth and slither away. Leave the blue jay and the gunman together in the woods.

Carly and I need a new plan.

* * *

Chapter 11
The Finn

The Finn left her car in the woods and lugged her frame backpack and a duffel bag down a dirt road to the back end of the job site. The slow patter of rain hit her wool watch cap and soaked down into her hair, but to her the Florida cold was a weak, unremarkable thing.

She used a pair of long-handled bolt cutters to cut a flap in the chain-link fence. Shoving the bags ahead of her, she crawled through, and left her gear in the bushes while she scouted the area inside the fence.

South of her position in the overgrown bushes was a low section of buckled black asphalt with a pond in the middle. She walked around the pond and realized it was simply a large puddle of rainwater, big enough to swallow a car. The Finn took a stick, poked it into the water and found it was half a meter deep.

Next was a large building shaped like a 'C,' with the open end facing away from her. She checked the back door of the building and it was unlocked. After the buildings, there was a blue, single-width trailer on the west side of the property. Two rusty shipping containers at the southern end near the road. The main gate was to the east, but she'd noticed a narrow gate on the western side as well.

The Finn wasn't sure what business had run here, but it had moved away or failed. The main

One Bullet 59

gate was wide enough for large trucks, and there were still piles of sand and gravel heaped here and there. Some type of gantry system ran on old tracks next to the 'C' building, close to a metal chute painted green.

She stood under the roof edge of the building and stared at the gate as the rain fell. The target's car would come through the main gate, and she reminded herself to retrieve the bolt cutters and cut the chain off the gate. If they were smart, one of the bodyguards would get out and walk around to check the perimeter.

On the south side by the shipping containers, the bodyguard would be in view of the car. But on the north side, he'd pass behind the 'C' building and out of sight. Since the enemy outnumbered her, separating them was important.

If she could kill the bodyguard on foot behind the building, and without making much noise, how would she kill the second bodyguard and the target in the car? A sniper shot from the roof? The report of a high-powered rifle could carry for kilometers, and even in a deserted area like this, there might be hunters or country people.

No, she had to get them inside the building.

She checked her watch. Vlad and the target were already on their way. If Vlad wasn't in the car, she could simply bury an anti-vehicle mine at the gateway and activate it when the car came through. But Vlad was paying her, so killing him would be a problem. Also, the one time they'd met in person she'd found him attractive.

It was a tricky problem.

The Finn smiled. If killing people was easy, she wouldn't get paid so much to do it. She went to get the bolt cutters.

* * *

Chapter 12
Vlad

Vlad shifted in the back seat of Cypress's Porsche Panamera. The four men rode in silence, except for the continuous squeak of the windshield wipers. Cypress took a satellite phone out, raised the stubby antenna and leaned against the window. He dialed, then waited and listened, but said nothing.

The Kwans stared at the pine trees swaying in the wind.

Vlad tried to get comfortable, but the car was too hot and trickles of sweat ran down his neck. He took out his phone, looked at the directions again, and put it away. "Look for Wild Hog Road, and turn left."

Lesser Kwan nodded.

Cypress ended his call and dropped the satellite phone on the floorboard. "You know what the temperature is in Montreal today?"

"No." Vlad took a small calendar from his pocket and scanned the pages without really reading what he'd written on them.

"Kwan, gimme my Thermos," Cypress said. Greater Kwan passed the plaid Thermos back and Cypress unzipped his pants. While he urinated into the Thermos, Cypress blew out a long breath. He reached over and poked Vlad's calendar. "What's that sticker? It looks like a beaker. Why is yesterday marked with a beaker? You getting into the drug trade?"

62   Mark Boss

Vlad looked at the small, green sticker shaped like a beaker on his calendar. "It's a reminder. The dogs are due for their flea medicine. They put stickers in the box so you don't forget." He touched his throat. "If I don't apply the medicine, they get ticks under their chins where they can't bite them off."

Cypress stopped, squirted once more into the Thermos and winced. "I bet your girl Lacey gets jealous of those dogs. You fucking coddle them things."

The car dropped two inches and Vlad flinched. Looked up.

Lesser Kwan said, "Wild Hog Road. Now where?"

"North until you get to the first cross street, then right and we should see the job site." Vlad put the calendar in his back pocket and his hand brushed the holstered Glock. "We should have built the ATMs."

Cypress screwed the top on the Thermos and dropped it on the floorboard. "What?"

"Last year when those bankers approached us about ATM machines? We should have built our own network of ATMs. Scatter ten or twelve ATMs from Pensacola to Port St. Joe. We could mix the dirty money in with the clean. Launder all the money we wanted." Vlad stared down the road at the fence up ahead.

He thought about standing in his backyard with his sledgehammer crashing down on the truck tire. Only in his mind, it wasn't the tire, it was Greater Kwan's head. Then Lesser, then Cypress. His

One Bullet   63

shoulders relaxed. He looked out at the rain and smiled. "You should have listened to me."

Cypress grunted. "We got check cashing joints, strip clubs, pawn shops. Plenty of places to launder money. Why get into all that banking crap?"

Greater Kwan tapped Lesser on the arm. Lesser slowed the car, turned left onto an access road and stopped at the gate. Greater Kwan opened his door, got out and pushed the door slowly shut until it clicked.

Greater swung the gate open and held it while Lesser drove through. Then Greater trotted away, holding his Chinese submachine gun ready.

As they eased through the parking lot, the Porsche hit a pothole and the Thermos rolled next to Vlad's shoe. He nudged it away.

Cypress ran his sleeve down the side window, wiping away the moisture. He stared at the job site. "I don't like sitting here in the open. Kwan, pull up by that building over there." He pointed at a 'C'-shaped structure.

Lesser Kwan shook his head. "Brother is checking. Fence first, then building. We must wait."

"Wait for a sniper to shoot me in the head?" Cypress asked. He reached forward between the front seats and slapped Lesser's arm. "Pull up to that building."

Lesser Kwan shrugged and the car bounced forward, splashed through a puddle and stopped in front of the big building shaped like a 'C.' The building had three wide, rollup doors standing open.

64 Mark Boss

Old wooden pallets and 55-gallon drums were stacked along the back wall, but otherwise the building looked empty. Cypress pointed again. "Pull into the middle bay, then get out and look around. What time did you tell Ernesto?" he asked Vlad.

Vlad checked the clock on his phone. "We're a few minutes early. It gives us chance to secure the area before the Cartel arrives."

"Sure." Cypress grunted. "Hand me my Thermos."

* * *

Chapter 13
The Finn

The Finn lay beneath the water in the cold pond, trying to breathe slowly and minimize the bubbles that rose to the surface. She lay stretched out on her stomach, a scuba regulator clenched between her teeth and a speargun in her hands. Her air tank was next to her and the hose stretched to her mouth--she didn't wear the tank because she would need to move fast. In the rush to get to the site, she hadn't packed a wetsuit, so she wore her clothes and shivered.

The water was filthy, and it was difficult to see through her mask unless she raised her head to just below the surface. She wasn't wearing a snorkel because she thought a sharp-eyed bodyguard might spot it.

With the rain tapping the top of the water, the pond was almost peaceful. Except for the cold. Her leather gloves were soaked through and she felt her grip on the speargun weakening as her hands grew numb.

Something brushed her shoulder and she flinched, but it was only a plastic soda bottle.

To her south, she heard a rumble, a car engine. She checked her watch, but in the dark water the luminous dial was insufficient.

She heard a metallic screech, something scraping across concrete that she could half hear and half feel. It had to be the main gate opening.

She counted to sixty in her head and kept her breathing slow to preserve the air tank.

The Finn pushed up until her mask was centimeters below the surface. A shadow rippled across the water, moving from her left to her right on the back side of the 'C' building.

The first bodyguard.

She pushed herself higher, tracking her target. If she could ease up from the water without splashing and take careful aim, she might be able to kill him with one shot. If not, she had a second speargun next to her leg.

The bodyguard moved to the back door of the building, then paused to speak into his mobile phone.

Something brushed her hand.

She looked, saw a black snake swimming next to her. She held her breath and kept still.

The bodyguard opened the door, peeked in, and then shut it.

The snake bit her wrist just above her leather glove. A quick, piercing bite that her cold-numbed arm barely felt.

She shook it off. Splashed. The snake shot away, slithering fast across the water.

The guard turned. The Finn fired. The spear hit him sideways through the throat.

He dropped his gun and fell to his knees. They looked at each other while she dug in the water for the second speargun. Then he toppled over and curled up in a ball, facing away from her, his boots touching the back wall of the building. He tried to yell, but it was a thick, wet gurgle.

One Bullet   67

She stood, water streaming from her clothes. Hesitated. Cypress was on the other side of the building, or maybe inside. But the snake was getting away. She wasn't familiar with American snakes, and to receive the right anti-venin from a doctor she needed to know what type of snake bit her.

The Finn turned back to the pond. The snake was almost to the far edge, heading toward the bushes. Her right hand was numb with cold, but her left wrist was already beginning to burn. She spit the regulator out and took a breath of rainy air. Sighted the second speargun. Fired.

The spear pierced the snake. She dashed around the edge of the pond, knees high trying not to splash. Grabbed the snake by the tail and slapped its head against the asphalt until it stopped thrashing. She pulled her duffel bag from the bushes, took an AK-74 with a folding stock out, and dropped the dead snake in the bag.

She heard muffled thumps from inside the building, and sprinted around the pond. As she passed the bodyguard, she saw a mobile phone lying next to him. Dying and unable to speak, the big Korean might have texted his brother a warning.

The Finn ran to the door.

* * *

Chapter 14
Vlad

Vlad watched Lesser Kwan search inside the building. The tall Korean held his 9mm pistol in both hands, close to his chest in a tactical posture. As he stepped around a stack of pallets, he pushed the pistol out, then relaxed and brought it back.

Vlad breathed out.

He wondered where The Finn was, but then again, if he spotted her she wouldn't be as good as his contacts said she was.

Cypress dug in his pocket and brought out a bag of pistachios. He cracked them open and dropped the shells on the floor mat. "Ernesto probably can't find this place. Why are we in the ass-end of nowhere?"

"You told me you wanted privacy, so you can talk to them." Vlad shrugged. His hand drifted back to his holster. He waited for Lesser Kwan to return and sit in the driver's seat. He would shoot him in the back of the head, and then Cypress.

Through the front windshield, he saw Lesser Kwan stop and take out his phone with his left hand. Lesser stared at the screen, then dropped the phone and ran toward the car.

Cypress spit a mouthful of pistachios out. "What now?"

Vlad pulled his Glock 19, shoved it into the side of Cypress's head, and yanked the trigger. One, two, three. The blasts drove Cypress into the door, the side window shattered, and blood erupted over the leather seats.

With the doors closed, the noise inside the car was shocking. Physically painful. Vlad reached across with his left hand, opened his door, and tumbled out backward. His brain shook inside his skull.

He got to his knees behind the car.

His ears were useless and he couldn't see Lesser Kwan. The gunshots would bring Greater Kwan, too, unless The Finn got him. Maybe The Finn had failed?

In the side mirror, he saw Kwan creeping around the back of the car.

Vlad fired the Glock, pulling the trigger as fast as his finger could.

Kwan disappeared.

The Glock's slide locked in the rear position, breech empty. Vlad stared at it.

The Porsche rocked on its tires as Kwan scrambled onto the roof. Vlad dug in his pocket for the tiny .380, looked up and saw the Korean take aim.

An unseen, massive force knocked Lesser Kwan off the car. He fell on top of Vlad with three smoking holes in the back of his coat.

But no blood.

Vlad remembered Kwan wore body armor, the heavy kind designed to stop a rifle bullet.

Kwan pushed up with one hand and tried to swing his 9mm around. Vlad drove the tiny .380 under his chin and pulled the trigger until the gun was empty.

For a long minute, he sat on the cold, concrete floor with the dead man across his legs. Looked in the open door of the car and saw Cypress slumped in the back seat, his ugly head a red mess.

He looked up. The Finn stood above him, holding a Kalashnikov AK-74 at the ready. Her face was pale, and one eyelid twitched. "A snake bit me. I must go to hospital."

Vlad saw her lips moving, but the sound was muffled. Indistinct.

"I'll help you clean up before I leave. We'll put them in the car and roll down the bay doors. It will be weeks before anyone finds them." She walked to the back door, opened it and looked out.

Vlad watched her raise the rifle and retreat into the building. "What?" he called. He wasn't sure how loud he said it, so he tried again. "What?"

The Finn came back, her stony face pinched with cold or pain. "Greater Kwan is gone."

This time he read her lips. Vlad took Lesser Kwan's pistol and kicked the dead man aside.

* * *

Chapter 15
Greater Kwan

Something punched Greater Kwan hard in the side of his neck. He stumbled. His next breath felt wrong, and he fell to his knees. Choked.

He collapsed against the side of the building near the back door. Heard splashes from the pond behind him, and wondered if the Cartel had decided to take revenge for their dead bagman.

Kwan reached for his JS 9 submachine gun, but it wasn't there and he knew he should have used a sling to keep the weapon attached. Sloppy. Not like his army days. However, he noticed his phone was on the ground between him and the building wall--it must have spilled from his pocket.

He gasped for air but something obstructed his breathing. Kwan looked down. At the edge of his peripheral vision, he saw the bloody head of a spear near his right shoulder. Without actually turning his head, he shifted his eyes left and saw the other end of the spear over his left shoulder.

More splashing behind him.

There was no time to find the JS 9, but the phone was there.

Kwan didn't pick up his phone because he was afraid he'd drop it. He simply rotated it on the rough concrete until he could read the screen. He sent his brother a simple text message: "Trap."

Footsteps came toward him.

Gunfire sounded inside the building. Three quick shots, probably a pistol. Then a flurry of shooting.

The door of the building opened, and Kwan caught a glimpse of a dark-haired woman dart inside. She held a Kalashnikov rifle, which meant his brother was outgunned.

Kwan rolled over onto his stomach. The spear brushed the wall and he tried to scream, but only a growl came out.

The big Korean spit a mouthful of blood onto the ground and took two slow breaths, then got to his knees. He swayed, swayed like the pine trees in a storm.

The gunfire inside the building stopped.

Kwan put his forehead against the wall and reached down to his phone. Tapped the screen. "?"

While he waited for his younger brother to respond, his mouth filled with blood. It hurt to spit so he simply opened his lips and let the thick mix of blood and saliva stream down onto the asphalt.

The target had to be Mr. Cypress, and the secondary target would be his lieutenant, Vlad. Kwan knew he and his brother were only collateral damage. Still, careful assassins would come back to make certain he was dead.

He knew that if his brother was alive, Lesser Kwan would still be shooting or racing outside to help him. No, his brother was surely dead. And he would be next.

Kwan put his hands on the wall for balance, and then pushed up to his feet.

One Bullet 73

The rain gusted and he blinked away the drops as they ran down his shaved head. He turned, careful not to bump the spear in his neck, and walked north on stiff legs. Around the pond, into the bushes.

He spotted a frame-style backpack and a duffel bag hidden a few paces inside the woods. Hoping the bags contained weapons, Kwan unzipped the duffel. He reached into the dark bag and felt something cold and slick. Pulled.

Snake.

He rocked back and flung the snake away, bumping the spear as he did so. Fresh blood ran down both sides of his neck into the collar of his jacket. Kwan kicked the duffel aside, wondering what kind of evil bitch kept a snake in her pack.

The spear must have missed his carotid arteries, or Kwan knew he'd already be dead. But the blood loss made him dizzy and he would continue to weaken if he didn't do something. He unzipped the frame pack, and peered inside before he put his hands in.

He found a compact first-aid kit, four packets of QuikClot powdered wound treatment, several spare magazines of 5.45mm ammunition and two bottles of water. But no weapons.

Back across the parking lot, he heard the rear door of the building scrape open.

Kwan tossed the ammunition aside to lighten the pack, then grabbed it by one strap and staggered into the woods until he hit the fence. Reasoning the woman must have cut a hole in the fence, he looked for a gap, but the brush was heavy and he couldn't spot the opening.

He took three steps back, then surged forward and slammed into the fence. It bent. The two nearest support posts uprooted from the rain-softened earth. The world tilted and Kwan was on his hands and knees again, the metal loops of the fence digging into his palms. He pushed up and stumbled across the fence and into the woods.

There was a thicket of trees and he walked with one hand extended to keep the low-hanging limbs from snagging the spear in his neck. He pulled the frame pack along with his left hand, but every vine and root seemed to snare the pack.

The woods opened onto a one-lane road of loose sand and Kwan paused in the tree line. By reflex, he turned to check for cars before crossing the road, and pain rippled through his neck and up his jaw. He growled.

Kwan took a step, saw the car and stopped. A car sat parked close to the trees just fifty paces down the road. It was a plain, silver four-door Toyota. New or close to it.

Voices sounded behind him, back at the fence. He swallowed hard and trotted down the road. His sneakers sank into the wet sand, and he struggled to move faster. Yanked the door of the Toyota open and saw the keys in the ignition. Kwan threw the frame pack in, then bent his knees and slid sideways into the car, careful of the spear.

The Toyota cranked instantly. He forced himself not to accelerate hard, worried the car might sink in the soft sand. Kwan let the car roll forward, applied gradual pressure to the gas, and turned the car around.

If the assassins came out of the trees from the same path he'd taken, he didn't want to drive right by them and get shot, so he steered west until he hit a crossroad. Took a slow left turn, and drove south until he hit Highway 98. As he picked up speed, he adjusted his side mirrors so he wouldn't have to turn his head.

Kwan reached into the pack for the QuikClot. He had to stop the bleeding before he passed out at 55 miles per hour.

* * *

Chapter 16
Vlad

Vlad slid the magazine out of Lesser Kwan's H&K pistol and counted the remaining cartridges. Seven. Had Lesser Kwan fired so many times?

When he looked up, The Finn was trotting to the back door of the building. Her wet clothes clung to her and Vlad admired her ass for a moment, then followed.

She stood to one side of the door, rifle up. "Ready?"

His hearing was still recovering, so Vlad watched her lips move, then nodded. "Ready."

She pushed the door open, ducked low and to the left. Vlad went right. Swept the pistol left to right across his field of vision. Woods, a pond, more woods, then the fence on the far right. There was no cover and The Finn was already circling the left side of the pond, so he went right until he reached the tree line.

Rain drops hit his thick hair and soaked down to his skull. His head pounded from shooting inside the closed car. Without sound, nothing felt real. Much like the one time he'd tried LSD and felt his mind take a long step back from...everything. Vlad thought about Cypress slumped over in the seat, his brains leaking onto the leather. From boss of an innovative crime organization to a hunk of old meat in three bullets. Three seconds. Three pulls of the trigger.

One Bullet 77

The forest air scrubbed the gun smoke from his lungs. The iron sky dropped rain on his face and Vlad felt the strength of his grip on the gun. He was alive. Alive, armed and ready for battle. Life as a man should live it. He smiled and stood tall. Let Greater Kwan come.

He felt eyes on him and turned to see The Finn watching him. A slight smile crossed her lips and she met his gaze. "It's good to be the one that lives, yes?"

Vlad heard her. It was distant, like a voice in a tunnel, but he heard her and read her lips and pieced it together. "Yes. It's good."

They entered the woods together.

The Finn stopped and pointed down at a duffel bag. A dead snake lay a few steps from the bag. Vlad knew the locals called it a water moccasin or cottonmouth. The Finn poked the barrel of her rifle under the dead snake and tried to lift it into the duffel bag, but the wet snake slid off. She tried a second time.

Vlad grabbed the snake just behind its mashed head and threw it in the bag. "We're wasting time."

She nodded and took the lead. They reached the crushed fence and Vlad looked at it and chuckled.

"He ran over it," The Finn said.

"That is Kwan's way."

"Schist. My car." She dashed off.

He followed at a measured pace, always looking for a tree thick enough to stop a bullet that he could shelter behind. In a few minutes, he reached a dirt road that ran east and west behind the job site. The Finn stood at the side of the road, examining fresh tire tracks. "He took my car."

"What? Damn. You left your keys in it?" Vlad wasn't sure how loud he was speaking.

"Yes, I left my keys in it. Why would I think anyone would steal it? No one has ever survived my ambush." She glared at him.

Vlad looked away. This is a hard woman, he thought. Tougher than even the strippers at the club. "This is all Joe's fault."

The Finn set the lever-style safety on her Kalashnikov. "Who is Joe?"

"Our bag man," Vlad said. "The one who screwed everything up. I told Cypress we needed to spread the deliveries out and use a different bag man each time, but no, he said Joe Barrow was the best. The bag man who never lost a delivery. So we used Joe again, and he screwed it all up."

"You're talking too loud. Lower your voice." The Finn turned into the woods, back toward the job site.

Vlad marched beside her, waving his free hand as he spoke. "Joe lost the delivery and blew the exchange with the Cartel. I'd already emptied the overseas account, but the password in the envelope he carried was correct. When the Cartel used the password and found the account empty, I was going to blame Joe. But no, he got himself ambushed. Then chased the attacker down, took everything back and disappeared."

The Finn rolled her eyes. "He is a bag man. Isn't recovering the money his job?"

One Bullet

79

"His job is to make the delivery without getting ambushed in the first instance." Vlad took long steps, stomping the undergrowth. "The Cartel will wonder why Cypress and I haven't met with them to explain the loss of delivery and their dead bag man." He laughed. "I'm going to tell them Joe did it. 'All bag men are thieves waiting to be born.'" He smiled down at her. "My father said that."

The Finn shrugged. "This Joe is probably on a plane, or in a speeding car three states away."

"No, Joe won't run. Joe will try to fix this. And Greater Kwan will try to kill us."

She stopped to pick up her duffel bag, then they circled the pond. The Finn stayed several steps from the water. She held her left arm bent, close to her body.

Vlad watched her. "Let me see the snake bite."

The Finn held out her arm. Her wrist was swollen so badly the skin had curled around the band of her dive watch.

"We have to get that watch off," Vlad said. She stepped close to him and rested the back of her hand on his chest while he struggled with the watch buckle. He finally pried it lose and she hissed in pain as the blood returned to her fingers.

The Finn looked up at him. "What will you do next?"

Vlad marveled at her eyes. They were dark, dark gray. Almost black. "First, we take you to a hospital. I'll tell the Syndicate employees that Joe and the Kwans killed Cypress and tried to kill me. And then I'll take command of the Syndicate."

They walked to the building and he opened the door for her. "I know how to get to Joe. He has a weakness and her name is Carly," Vlad said.

They crossed the concrete floor to the Porsche. Lesser Kwan lay dead by the open car door. Cypress was slumped across the back seat. Blood covered the car's interior, and there were bullet holes in the trunk and rear bumper, but somehow all four tires were untouched.

"I don't think we should take this car on the road," The Finn said. "Bullet holes and blood will attract police attention."

Vlad kicked Lesser Kwan in the head. "This is all Joe's fault."

* * *

Chapter 17
Joe

I trot back through the woods behind my apartment complex and climb up into the truck. Carly is slumped in the seat, smoking a cigarette and staring at the rain clouds. When I slam my door shut she looks over and asks, "What happened?"

Blow on my hands for a minute and rub the blood flow back into my bruised knuckles. At least the cold numbed my face and my lip doesn't hurt as much. "We can't get into my apartment. There's Cartel soldiers in the woods and probably inside, too."

She reaches over and touches my arm. "Joe, we should run. The Cartel wants their money back, the Syndicate thinks you stole the delivery, everything is bad." Carly gives me a long look, like she's searching for something in my busted-up face. With her leaning forward I can see the top edge of her bra peeking up from her shirt--the bra is black and lacey. She wears nice stuff under her clothes, and it's always a treat to unwrap her like the world's best birthday present.

"Without going in your apartment, how much money can you put your hands on today?" she asks.

I blink. Pull my eyes away from her breasts and try to think. "I've got three bank accounts in different names. One here in Panama City, one at the beach, and one in Destin." Look down at my watch, but the crystal is shattered and the hands are gone. "It's late in the day, but there's plenty of time to get to the one here in town."

"How much?"

"About fifty five hundred."

"That's it?" Carly sits back. "All the money the Syndicate pays you, and you've saved five thousand? You ever buy airline tickets on short notice?"

"No. Mr. Cypress has a guy that makes all our travel arrangements." Across the parking lot, a big guy comes out of the vet's office with a German Shepherd. He looks like a cop. "Speaking of travel, we need to move."

I crank the Dodge, turn the defroster on max and roll out into traffic. Drive up to 23rd Street and pull into the Sonic drive through. Find a spot in the back, as far from the road as I can get. Get my wallet out and realize I have 80 dollars total--a twenty, a ten, and a fifty. Not much for going on the run, but plenty for a feast at Sonic. "Babe, you want something?"

"I'm not hungry."

I roll down the window and reach for the red button to place an order. "You sure? How about a Cherry Limeade? You love those."

A little smile flits across her lips. "Okay. A Cherry Limeade. A big one."

"You want a snack with that? We missed lunch."

"No, I'll eat your tater tots."

I order two Chicago dogs, a double cheeseburger, and two orders of potato tots, her Limeade and a Coke. While we wait for the food, I

One Bullet 83

think about who set me up at the airport. There's a limited number of people on the Syndicate end who knew about the exchange, and who-knows-how-many people on the Cartel side who knew. Then I think about how I can't protect Carly and fix this mess at the same time. Carly has a temper, so I bring it up carefully. "You need to leave."

"What?" She puts her iPad in her lap and stares at me.

"I've got to figure out who set me up at the airport. Then find the money and give it back to the Cartel. And the Syndicate will want their password envelope back, too. I can't do all that and protect you."

"You protected me at the auto shop."

Open my mouth, stop. Yeah, I did.

"And at the airport," she says.

True.

"Joe, we can't run without money. Even if we get that $5,500 from the bank today, it's not enough. We've got to find the bag of cash, the real $700,000, before we can go." She kicks the duffel of mostly counterfeit money sitting on the floorboard.

Three slots down from us, a little Hyundai with a fat muffler pulls up and a kid gets out. He sits on one of the picnic tables with his feet on the bench, and takes out a phone.

"I got an idea. I'm gonna call Mr. Cypress, skip Vlad and go straight to the top. Cypress is mean and he's been extra crazy lately, but he has the power to fix this." I pop my door open.

"Wait." Carly waves one hand. I see the rings on her fingers and wonder if we could pawn them. "There's no pay phone here."

"I'll buy that kid's phone off him." I point at the kid, who's holding the phone almost to his nose while he's texting. Damn, how did this half-blind kid just drive here?

Carly grabs my wrist before I can get out. "Joe, you're covered in blood. Wait a second." She digs in her purse and tears open a tiny, lemon-scented hand wipe. Leans over and cleans up my face. She doesn't scrub, just wipes the dried blood off and manages it without getting the alcohol on my busted lip. Her face is inches from mine, and I don't care that her hair is a wreck, or that the rain washed her makeup away, or that she's ten years past being some hot young thing. I push her hair back from her eyes and I know why I have to fix this.

I have to do this for us.

"Dude, a little help?" a voice says.

My head whips around and there's a middle-aged guy in a visor standing there with our food and an embarrassed look. I grab Carly's Limeade before it slides off the tray and pass it to her.

Pay the guy, tip him, and set the food on the seat between us. I'm starving, but I gotta get to the kid with the phone before he leaves.

Make sure my suit jacket is buttoned up as I drop down from the truck into a puddle. Step up onto the concrete and approach the kid. "Hey, is that phone new?"

One Bullet   85

He's wearing one of those beanie hats pulled down to his eyeballs, and there's a ring of long hair spilling out all sides of it. "No, this is last year's model. New one came out six months ago."

"You interested in selling it?" I hold out the fifty dollar bill.

"For fifty bucks? No way. This phone costs me $200 and I'm locked into a contract for two years. Two years." He holds up two fingers in case I don't get the concept of two.

I'm tempted to snap his fingers off.

Instead, I walk back to the truck and get in.

"What happened?" Carly is working her way through the box of tots, and half my burger is gone.

"Kid wouldn't sell his phone for $50. Guess it's some kind of pricey model." I plunk down in the seat and start on the nearest hot dog. The relish spills between my fingers onto my lap. It's the best thing I've eaten since yesterday.

Carly reaches down to the duffel bag at her feet and opens it. Holds up a $10,000 brick made up of cheap, green paper and a single, real, hundred-dollar bill on top. "There's 70 bricks, each with a $100 on it, so that's $7000. Go offer the kid $200 for his phone and he'll jump at it."

"We can't. Put that away." I push the brick away.

"Why not?"

"That's not our money. It was supposed to go to the Syndicate. $700,000 in Cartel cash in exchange for a Syndicate overseas account loaded with $700,000. I'm a bag man. It's my job to deliver it. If I steal even one dollar, I'm breaking my contract." I take the brick from her and drop it in the duffel bag. "We're not touching this money."

Carly kicks the dash so hard the glove box pops open. "Are you insane? They're going to kill us. We can use this $7,000 and whatever else you can put together to get out of Florida. But oh no, you won't touch it because you gave some other scumbag your word."

People in neighboring cars look over at Carly yelling, so I roll up the window. "I have a code. There are things I'll do, like today when I went to the airport to exchange money with a drug cartel. But there are things I won't do, like watch two thugs rape a girl in a mini-mart. Or touch money I said I'd deliver. That's my code."

"You act like you're some samurai, but you know what you are, Joe? You're a chump. You're the guy other guys snitch on when the cops catch them. We're going to die because you won't take a few thousand in drug money."

We sit and don't talk. I eat all of my food, drink my Coke and wish the rain would start again. When the last tater tot is gone, I start the truck. "We better get to the bank before it closes."

* * *

Chapter 18
Vlad

Vlad stood just inside the rollup metal door at the job site, and held up his phone. The rain stopped, but clouds still hid the sun and the temperature was dropping. He looked over his shoulder and saw The Finn sitting on a stack of wooden pallets with her snake-bitten arm held close.

He checked to see if the phone was getting a signal and saw one tiny bar in the upper left of the screen. "Good enough."

He scrolled through the phone's contacts list, and thought about which Syndicate soldier he should call to come pick him up. Manila Tommy talked too much, and he'd never keep quiet once he saw the bloody job site. Simon was too smart, and might figure out that he killed Cypress, not the Kwans. If Simon knew, he'd use that against him. Fergus, Arturo and Lars were good soldiers, but they'd been with Cypress before they'd formed the Syndicate together, and their loyalty was to the old man. Vlad scrolled back up. Jorg. The ex-kickboxer was nervous and slow witted, but when he was sober he followed orders and he knew how to keep his mouth shut.

He dialed Jorg and waited.

Music blasted from the phone, loud enough to make him wince even with his temporary hearing loss. "Jorg?"

The music was some bass-heavy club mix and he caught people talking in the background. A woman with a squeaky voice said, "My nose burns. Is it supposed to burn?"

Then Jorg said, "Slow down, girl." He slurred the 's' and the 'r.'

"Jorg, listen to me. I have a situation," Vlad said.

"How come I can't be happy?" Jorg asked. "I just want to be happy for one whole day."

The woman said, "How come we can't ride zebras? They're just horses with stripes."

The phone went silent. Vlad stared at the screen. "He hung up on me."

Vlad thought about who else he could call, but the Syndicate had more hackers than soldiers.

"Problem?" The Finn asked.

"Four problems." Vlad stuck Kwan's 9mm in his belt and walked across the bare concrete floor to where she sat.

The Finn held a small folding knife like a pencil and cut an 'X' over the snake bite. She turned her arm over to let the wound drain, but held her hand inside her duffel bag. "Don't want to leave my DNA here for the police to find."

Vlad sat beside her. "You need a doctor, we need to leave here, we need to do something with the bodies, and we need to get rid of the car." He nodded at the shot-up Panamera. "We have four problems."

"Who did you call?"

"A Syndicate soldier named Jorg. He was not coherent." Vlad felt like sighing, but it would appear weak. "I'll call Fred and...damn it. Joe."

"What?"

One Bullet 89

"I could have called Fred to come tow the car, but he runs the auto shop where I sent Joe. So he's dead." He squeezed the scrap wood pallet beneath him until a chunk broke off in his hand. "Joe ruins everything."

The Finn turned her wrist over to check the wound. "You should kill this Joe."

"Yes. I should." Vlad got up and took off his suit jacket. Went to the row of big 55-gallon drums along the wall and pried the rusty lid off one. The empty drum was about three feet tall and maybe two feet wide.

"Do you have any dry clothes in your bag?" he asked.

"Would I be sitting here shivering if I did?" she asked.

"Good point." He peeled off his collared shirt and his T-shirt. The air was cold on his back and he rolled his shoulders a few times. Vlad crawled into the back seat of the Panamera and took Cypress by the lapels of his jacket. Pulled him out through the door and paused to get his hands under the old man's armpits. Cypress stank of blood and urine and arthritis ointment. He was heavier than he looked.

Vlad half carried, half pulled Cypress over to the drum, tipped him in head first, then folded his legs on top. He put the flat lid on, then secured it with the steel loop and bolt ring. Without a wrench he had to hand tighten the bolt ring, but he made it tight enough to keep animals out.

He bent his knees and grasped Lesser Kwan, but it was like trying to grab a boulder. The bullets that killed him went into his skull but didn't exit, so he hadn't bled all that much. Vlad grunted with effort. After two tries, he dropped the dead man and stood up to catch his breath.

"Take the barrel to him," The Finn said.

"Then how will I get it back to the wall so it blends in with the other drums?"

The Finn raised a round steel dolly with four metal casters. "I think they roll them with this."

"A drum dolly. Very good." He took the dolly, put the empty drum on it and rolled it over to Kwan. Lifting him into the drum was impossible, so he turned the drum on its side and tried to stuff the corpse in. "He's too big. All those steaks and steroids." Vlad kicked the body again, but it wasn't as much fun this time. "I'll have to cut him in half, and use two drums."

The Finn sat back with her head against the wall, eyes shut. "Maybe you could call a friend with a car, first. They could be on the way here while you work."

Vlad stared at her for a moment while her eyes were closed. He wondered if he would need another drum for her, and the thought gave him a sudden, weird ache in the center of his chest. He reached up with one bloody hand and touched his sternum. Felt his heart flutter in his chest. Too much caffeine, Vlad told himself.

He wiped his hands on the back of Lesser Kwan's shirt and then took out his phone and ran through his contact list again. Dialed one of the accountants. Nothing. Not even voicemail. A recording said, "This line has been disconnected."

He thought about calling Pudge Loomis, but Loomis was an errand boy and a drunk, and this was too important to screw up.

Vlad blew out a long, slow breath and stared up at the ceiling. He thought of the team of hackers the Syndicate kept in a pair of houses in Fort Walton Beach. The chief hacker, Sir Hax A Lot, might be able to handle this. He called Hax.

Hax answered, "Whassup?"

"It's Vlad. Listen--"

"I know it's Vlad, dude. Cause my phone says, 'Vlad.' They do that now."

"Shut it. Where are you?" Vlad asked.

"The Sleep House. Why?" Hax asked. The tremble in his voice came straight through the phone, even with the weak signal.

"I'm texting you directions. Come here immediately. Tell no one. Come alone and bring two padlocks. Do you have a saw?"

"Ah, maaaaaan. This is bad, isn't it?" Hax asked. "Oh God, I don't do well with bad. Damn it, I need my inhaler. Where the hell is my inhaler?"

Vlad heard the hacker banging around, slamming drawers. He hung up and sent a text with directions to the job site. When he went back to The Finn, she opened her eyes and blinked at him. "Let me see your wrist," he said.

She turned her palm over. Even with her dive watch removed, the swelling around the bite mark was significant, and spreading up her arm to the elbow. Blood collected beneath the skin at the wound site, and the skin was turning dark.

The Finn held up her phone and then tipped the duffel bag with her boot. The dead snake spilled out. In the light from the rollup doors, the snake was still dark, but not pure black. Vlad saw dark brown bands along the snake's body.

"I looked up my friend with the fangs," The Finn said. "It appears to be a water moccasin, a pit viper common to Florida."

"Is it..."

"Deadly?" The Finn smiled, then coughed. "Wikipedia states, 'Adults are large and capable of delivering a painful and potentially fatal bite.' The key word is 'potentially.' If I receive antivenom within six hours I should keep my hand, and my life. Besides, I'm too resilient to die of snake bite." She sat up and fainted.

Vlad caught her and eased her to the floor, then looked around. He had a shot-up Porsche, a dead crime boss, a giant Korean half way inside a drum, an unconscious assassin with a snake bite, and an asthmatic hacker who'd never seen a dead body in his life on the way to help.

"Damn you, Joe."

* * *

Chapter 19
Hax

After Vlad hung up on him, Hax sat on the edge of his bed in the Syndicate-owned Sleep House in Fort Walton and stared at his phone. "Do I have a saw? And two padlocks?" The young hacker shut his eyes, took deep breaths and wondered if there was a saw among the computers and servers at the Hack House next door.

They kept a few screwdrivers at the Hack House to open the cases of the servers, but not much else. Probably not worth the time to check, especially since Vlad had told him to hurry.

Hax touched the window with his fingertips, winced at the cold, and put on a long-sleeve T-shirt and his heaviest hoodie. He opened his bedroom door quietly so he wouldn't wake the others, and went down the stairs to the kitchen. The Sleep House was warm, with the comforting aroma of marijuana and leftover pizza. And feet. The Sleep House always smelled a little like feet.

In the kitchen, Root sat at the bar, smoking a fat marijuana cigarette and buttering a batch of bran muffins. When Root turned on the barstool, Hax flinched, then tried to keep from laughing. Obviously, Root had passed out without locking his bedroom door and someone had drawn all over his face with a green Sharpie.

Root pointed at the smiling whale drawn on his forehead. "Know anything about this?"

"Definitely not." Hax shook his head. Root smoked meth for two and three days straight while he hacked for the Syndicate, but there was the inevitable crash. In crash mode, Root slept like he was in a coma, which made him perfect for pranking.

"Do we have a saw?" Hax pantomimed the sawing action, like a magician cutting his assistant in half. "And some padlocks?"

"There's some old tools in the garage. Why?" Root closed his eyes and took a long inhale.

"Vlad called. He has a situation. One that calls for a saw." Hax tried to say it low and cool, but his voice cracked. "Dude, I think he killed somebody."

"Did he ask you to bring a shovel?"

"No."

"Then he didn't kill anybody." Root took a bite of muffin. Butter ran through his beard and dripped onto the counter.

"Could I take one of those muffins with me? I don't have time for breakfast," Hax asked.

"Make your own damn food. I'm not sharing." Root turned away. The TV on the counter played an episode of 'Big Bang Theory.'

Hax glared at Root's back. "Have you seen my inhaler? I left it on the counter."

Root pointed at the microwave oven. "Last night Lulz put it in the microwave and blew it up. Didn't you hear that?"

"No. I was next door, working. Something you guys are supposed to do now and then." Hax knew he had a spare inhaler in his car, so there was no point in arguing about it, but Lulz had crossed a

One Bullet 95

line and he would respond later. He checked his cargo pockets for his phone and keys and went into the garage. A rusty toolbox sat in the corner, left behind by the previous owners of the house.

He found one combination lock with the number written on tape on the back, and figured he could take a second lock off the gate outside. A narrow keyhole saw lay in the bottom drawer of the toolbox. Hax examined it for a moment, and tried to imagine sawing someone's head off with the flimsy blade.

He dropped the saw in the box and stomped the lid shut.

"I can't believe those clowns blew up my inhaler." He went out into the cold morning air and cranked his new Ford Mustang. He revved the engine, hoping to wake the idiots inside, then backed out of the driveway.

It's true Vlad didn't ask me to bring a shovel, Hax reasoned. Maybe it won't be that bad.

* * *

Chapter 20
Joe

We're almost at the bank on 23rd Street when Carly finally decides to talk. "Joe, you can't go into a bank with blood all over your clothes. They'll call the cops."

"The kid at Sonic didn't notice," I say.

"He had his nose in his phone. He's probably blind without his glasses." She rattles her straw around the bottom of her Cherry Limeade, but doesn't slurp. "Turn around and head up to Dillards. I'll go in and buy you some decent clothes. If you think we can spare the money."

"I don't have much left. Maybe we better go to Target." By late afternoon, traffic on 23rd Street is thick, not like Boston or LA thick, but slow for Panama City. It takes us fifteen minutes to get to Target. I give Carly my fifty dollar bill and she slides down out of the bubba truck.

The rain has stopped. She peels off her yellow rain coat and tosses it onto the seat, then checks her face and hair in the side mirror. She's so short and the truck is so tall that she has to stand on her tiptoes to look in the mirror.

Watching her primp, I can't help but smile. She's fussy about her looks, but I like girly girls.

She winks at me, then takes off across the lot in that swaying walk that leaves men dizzy and grinning. Including me.

Once she's inside, I sit up in the seat and turn on the radio. All the channel presets in the Dodge are set to country music stations, so I scan manually for the news. I figure the police will have found the rapist wannabes at the mini-mart, and probably the dead meth heads at the auto shop, too. There's no reason for them to connect the two crime scenes, but I have enough problems already without looking over my shoulder for the cops.

When I hear a voice instead of a song I stop scanning, but it's just some political junkie griping about the opposition like they're not two sides of the same filthy coin. Turn the radio off and pick up Carly's iPad. Poking the touchscreen makes me feel like a kid in a finger painting class. It's hard to believe these things are made for adults.

I slump down in the seat so people in the parking lot won't see me.

Find my way to the Internet and search for local news sites. Swipe my finger along the screen like I've seen Carly do. Considering how many people died today, there's not a lot of crime news. But one story catches my attention, a hit and run out at the airport. There's a link to a video. I swallow hard. Will it be a security camera in the parking garage showing me jumping out of Vlad's Lexus to take the bag of fake cash from Kid Sasquatch's body?

Turns out the video is a 30-second loop of two EMTs, two sheriff's deputies and an airport cop trying to lift a huge guy into an ambulance. Kid Sasquatch is on the gurney in a neck brace, his big hands folded across his chest. It's weird they didn't pull the sheet over his face. They usually do that for dead people.

There's no sound with the video, but one of the EMTs leans over him, and Sasquatch moves his hand.

What?

I try to pause the video and replay, but my big finger mashes the screen and the window closes. I get it open again, and read the text below the story, which says, "Unidentified airport victim taken to Bay Medical Center in Panama City for treatment."

Son of a bitch, he's alive. Kid Sasquatch is alive.

I'm not a murderer.

But I put a screwdriver through a meth head's brain an hour after I ran Kid Sasquatch over. Beat that guy in the mini-mart to death. Okay, I'm a killer. But not a murderer.

That doesn't make me feel better.

I ran Kid Sasquatch over because I was afraid to fight him again.

That makes me garbage.

But I had to get the money back any way I could. That's what a bag man does--protect the money. It was dirty, but I did my job. So why do I feel like shit?

Drop the iPad on the passenger seat, sit and rub my hands over my face. My busted lip still stings.

Will Kid Sasquatch describe me to the cops? Does he know my name? I look around the parking lot. No tactical team closing in, no helicopters. Just a bunch of late afternoon shoppers trying to get home.

Kid Sasquatch won't tell them the truth, because that means telling them he killed the Cartel

One Bullet   99

bagman and stole $700,000 in cash plus the password information for $700,000 more. No, he won't talk, but he will try to contact his secret partner as soon as he can.

The Kid had to have a partner. Someone told him about the exchange so he could ambush me.

Kid Sasquatch is my link. The link to finding who set me up.

That's what I have to do. Figure out who set me up, and find the money.

The Kid's partner won't like leaving a loose end, especially not a badly injured giant Hawaiian that the hospital will shoot full of painkillers and then let the cops in to question. His partner will want to silence Kid Sasquatch, which means I have to talk to the Kid before that happens.

I look up and see Carly walking toward the car with bags in each hand. A guy putting his shopping cart in the cart corral stares as she sways past.

I crank the truck. We're not going to the bank, we're going to the hospital.

* * *

Chapter 21
Hax

Hax left Fort Walton Beach and followed the directions Vlad texted him. Highway 98 east toward Rosemary Beach, and then side roads north into the vast pine forest. Within minutes of leaving the highway, he was on a dirt road with no other cars or buildings.

He turned the radio off and sat forward in the seat.

When he reached the job site and saw the open gate, Hax stopped the Mustang and sat wondering if he'd done anything particularly stupid that week to piss Vlad off. Mr. Cypress might be mad about something--he was unpredictable. But Vlad supported the hackers because they generated money from their scams at little risk to the Syndicate. The hackers stole without breaking windows or busting heads, and that meant less police attention.

"I'm the future, not these Neanderthals. Me. Sir Hax a Lot." Hax gripped the steering wheel and rolled through the gate. For a second he wondered if it was an ambush and someone would jump out and shoot him.

But the job site felt abandoned, quiet, almost peaceful.

Ahead on his right, Vlad stepped out from under a tall, rollup door and waved. The Syndicate lieutenant was shirtless, and blood coated his thick chest.

One Bullet 101

"Oh, shit." Hax fished in his pocket for his inhaler, then remembered Lulz blew it up in the microwave.

Vlad knocked on the car window, then snatched the door open before Hax could find the button to roll it down. "Park inside by the Porsche. Hurry up." Vlad slammed the door and Hax flinched.

"Okay. Gosh." Hax lined the Mustang up carefully with the door so he wouldn't scratch the side mirrors. He drove into the gloom of the building, and stopped well short of Mr. Cypress's Porsche Panamera.

A woman sat slumped on a stack of wooden pallets by the back wall. Hax looked again and realized she held a rifle. The barrel of the gun tracked him as he pulled up. Behind him, Vlad pulled the rolling door down to waist level and the interior of the building grew darker.

"Oh, maaan. This is bad, this is very bad," Hax whispered.

He opened the center console and dug through a pile of napkins and fast food receipts for his backup inhaler. All he found was a USB cable and a single peppermint. He took the peppermint, and opened the glove box to continue searching for the inhaler.

Vlad yanked the door open again. "Did you bring a saw?"

Hax shook his head. "The Sleep House didn't have one." He swung his legs to get out but his seat belt was still buckled. He fumbled with the belt and scrambled out.

102   Mark Boss

Up close, Vlad smelled of sweat, and blood coated his arms to the elbows. He held up a small knife. "This cleanup is taking forever. Did you bring the padlocks?"

"Yeah, yeah. We have those. Locks." Hax wanted to get the locks off the passenger seat but didn't want to turn his back on Vlad.

Vlad looked...focused. Calm, even. Despite the blood dripping from his fingers onto the smooth concrete floor. "What's wrong?"

Hax leaned and looked around the big mobster. A rusting, blue 55-gallon drum lay on its side.

With a pair of legs sticking out.

"What's wrong?" Hax asked. "There's a dead dude in that barrel. You called me to a murder scene. I'm not...this isn't my thing. I do computers, I program them, I--" His lungs seized up and Hax went stiff in the knees. Reached out and grabbed the open car door to steady himself. He took a slow inhale and a slower exhale, then another breath. "Is that Lesser Kwan?" he asked. He looked around for the other Korean.

Vlad took him by the arm and walked him to the barrel. Pointed at a second barrel and waved the knife. "Look, it's not that bad. I got his torso in there, but the legs and head wouldn't fit. That's why I needed the saw. But you took so long getting here that I'm nearly finished without it."

"S-sorry." Hax took out the peppermint, fumbled with the clear wrapper and dropped the candy on the floor. He looked down. The mint sat in a pool of blood. The blood had a thin skin on

One Bullet 103

top, like gravy left out too long on the kitchen counter.

Hax bent over and gagged. He hadn't eaten, but something burned its way up his esophagus. He tried to spit it out but it was too thick. Hax hung his mouth open and let the bile drain down into the blood pool.

Vlad waited a moment, then dragged him over to the wall. He opened another drum. "Here's Cypress. Look."

Hax hugged himself. Looked. Cypress was mashed into the barrel, staring up at the ceiling with a surprised look on his face. "Oh. Shit."

Vlad slapped him. A quick, stinging pop. "Listen. Joe Barrow and the Kwans attacked us. They killed Cypress and they almost killed me. I shot Lesser Kwan, but Joe and Greater Kwan escaped. Do you understand what I'm telling you?"

"No." Hax shook his head.

The woman with the rifle watched him. Her face seemed drained of blood and expression. He looked at her and it was like staring through the glass wall of a terrarium at a snake.

"Joe the bag man?" Hax asked.

"Yes, Joe the bag man," Vlad said as he closed the drum on Cypress.

"He's the big guy with the hot girlfriend, right? Carly. She works at your restaurant." Hax looked away from the woman with the gun.

Vlad patted him on the shoulder. "That's right, Hax. Good. Now I want you to email everyone that Cypress is dead and that Joe and Greater Kwan killed him. Notify everyone in the Syndicate."

104 Mark Boss

Vlad tapped the lid of the drum tight. "And tell them I'm running things now. I am the new boss."

Hax swallowed. His mouth tasted like stomach acid. "Okay." He got his phone out and checked for a signal, then walked a wide arc around the bullet-riddled Porsche until he reached the rollup door. Ducked under and out into the cold. The wind pushed fresh air into his lungs and he stood still and counted prime numbers. "Two, three, five, seven, eleven, I don't want to die, thirteen, seventeen, I don't want to die."

He looked back at the building, then at the trees outside the fence. Should he run? Could he make it through the gate and into the woods before they shot him? Then what? No, the safest move was to do what Vlad said. That's how you stay alive, Hax told himself. Do what Vlad says. He pulled up his contacts list and sent a Syndicate-wide message: "joe bag man & grtr kwan killed mr cypress & escaped. vlad is new boss. lssr kwan dead."

He took a deep breath of cold air and went back inside. Vlad rolled the third drum against the wall. A pistol was tucked into his waistband just below a large, bone-white scar. Hax squinted in the gloom at the scar. Years ago, someone had literally stabbed Vlad in the back.

"That explains a lot," Hax muttered.

The big man turned. "You sent the message? Good. Now we take my friend to the hospital. She has a snake bite." He dried his hands on a bright, white T-shirt, smearing the cotton with blood. Vlad held out his hand. "Give me your keys. I'll drive."

* * *

Chapter 22
Greater Kwan

After he escaped the battle at the job site, Greater Kwan followed Highway 98 east toward Panama City Beach. He kept his hands locked on the steering wheel and simply focused on driving the stolen Toyota without crashing. The pain was tolerable and a packet of QuikClot had stopped the flow of blood, but he felt dizzy and disconnected.

Traffic increased in the late afternoon, but since it was January the cars actually moved. Kwan forced himself not to look at the drivers on either side of them, hoping they wouldn't notice a giant Korean with a spear through his neck. But the drivers that passed him were busy talking on their phones or texting.

For the first few miles he was so geared up his hands shook, but now he felt tired, almost drowsy. His fury at his brother's death gave way to a guilty sense of relief at surviving the ambush. Kwan blamed the feeling on blood loss. Now he had to think. Plan.

Going to any house or apartment associated with the Syndicate would be foolish. He had no way of knowing how much the assassins knew, and if they had inside help from rogue elements of the Syndicate. He needed a safe place to treat his wounds and regroup.

The past few years in northwest Florida had taught him that two thirds of the rental houses on the beach were empty in the winter. There would be some Canadians, what the locals called 'Snow Birds,' but they tended to rent at the big condominiums rather than the individually owned beach houses.

Kwan turned left, away from the beach, and entered an old neighborhood of small, wooden houses probably built in the 1960s. The houses were single story, with sagging roofs and narrow yards. The ground they sat on was more valuable than the structures themselves.

He cut down a side street and cruised with his foot off the accelerator. Counted empty driveways and looked for overgrown yards. Kwan braked in front of a squat, white house with faded blue shutters. The mailbox hung open, with catalogs and flyers spilling out. The only neighboring house that had a car in front was two doors down across the street.

Kwan eased the car along the circular driveway and snugged it between the front door and an overgrown azalea bush. Took the rest of the QuikClot and the bottled water and walked slowly to the front door, one hand trailing on the peeling paint of the wall.

He rang the doorbell once, then knocked. Waited. Set the supplies down, braced himself on the wall and drove a powerful side kick into the door, just above the knob where the dead bolt was installed.

The door shook.

Kwan said, "Damn it," but it only came out a weak growl.

One Bullet   107

He took a deep breath and kicked again. His foot barely cleared the knob, but the door rocked in a few inches. His third kick hit the knob and the door swung open. Kwan carefully turned his entire body around without moving his head, and looked down the street. Saw no one. Listened. Heard nothing but the sound of traffic a quarter mile south on the highway.

Stepped inside, dropped his supplies on a chair, and twisted the deadbolt so he could shut the door. With the frame warped the door wouldn't stay closed, so he shoved the chair against the door.

The little house was quiet and musty. The furniture looked like garage-sale purchases the owner figured were good enough for a rental. It was impersonal. No photographs on the walls, no family heirlooms, no pet bowls on the kitchen floor. Just a functional place to sleep that sat within walking distance of the powder-white beach. But a place no one had rented or maybe even entered in weeks.

It was perfect.

Kwan checked the narrow kitchen, then the bathroom and both bedrooms. As long as renters or a yard service didn't show up, he was safe. He took the QuikClot and went back to the bathroom. Pushed his shoes off with his toes and stood on the cold, tile floor.

In the mirror, the spear through his neck looked unreal. If it was a bullet hole, or even a bayonet wound, it would make sense. But a spear through his neck? It was hard to comprehend. He stared at the mirror for a few minutes and tried to make sense of it.

The assassin had to be in the pond at the job site, hiding beneath the water. Or she'd hidden in the woods and used a crossbow. He looked at the spear, and it seemed too large to fire from a crossbow, so it had to be a spear gun. Kwan wondered how many people had purposely been shot with a spear gun, and how many survived.

Perhaps he'd do a Google search. After he killed everyone responsible.

He searched beneath the sink and found a half bottle of rubbing alcohol, two bottles of suntan lotion, a box of Band-Aids, and a bottle of Tylenol that had expired two years ago. Went out to the kitchen and slid open the drawers until he found the silverware.

He needed something to cut the point off the spear so he could slide it out of his neck. Kwan examined a few dull steak knives, and one rounded bread knife and growled. He heard a hiss and a low, drumming sound. Grabbed the bread knife and peeked through the plastic blinds above the sink.

Next door, sprinkler heads popped up from the ground like land mines.

He let go of the blinds and turned on the tap on the sink. The water was still on, and after a few seconds, the flow turned from rusty brown to clear. Kwan took a roll of paper towels off the holder, plus a handful of kitchen rags from the drawer, and put them and the bread knife on the back of the toilet in the bathroom.

One Bullet 109

After he spread a beach towel on the tile under his feet, he took a deep breath and sawed the bread knife across the spear.

The shaft of the spear quivered deep in his throat and he stifled a cough. Sawed more slowly. A trickle of fresh blood pushed through the caked QuikClot and ran down his shoulder. He stopped, took off his shirt and looked at the spear.

The knife had barely scored the metal shaft.

Kwan turned his shoulders and examined the spear's head in the mirror. The point was like the pyramid-shaped tip of a nail, except for two wings beneath the point. The wings were designed to pop out and secure the fish, and each wing stuck out about two inches.

He wondered if there was a hack saw or maybe some garden shears anywhere in the house or back yard. His stomach rumbled. Kwan realized he either had to cut the point off and draw the spear out to his left, which meant moving it about eight inches. Or leave the point on and draw the entire spear to the right and through his neck. About 24 inches.

His stomach churned, like the one time Mr. Cypress had taken him deep sea fishing. Kwan shoved his pants down. His bowels cut loose before he'd even settled on the toilet seat.

After a few minutes, he sat with his elbows on his knees and wiped the sweat from his forehead. What would his brother say if he saw him like this?

He wondered if his brother had died fast. A quick, decisive bullet to the head, or a gut shot, something painful and slow?

"I will destroy your killers," Kwan said, but again only a growl came out. A sound like a dog. He flushed the toilet, stood at the mirror and locked eyes with himself.

Kwan wrapped his thick fingers around the spear point and slid the long end of the spear through his neck, watching his own eyes the entire time.

Blood dumped down his shoulder, over his tattoos and down to the waist of his pants. He threw the blood-slick spear into the bath tub. The spear bounced and slung bright spots of blood across the yellowed tiles.

He used the second bag of QuikClot and a thick wad of folded paper towels, and secured them with a kitchen rag tied around his neck like a cowboy's bandanna.

Kwan staggered out to the living room and sat facing the door. The couch sagged beneath his weight and he propped one foot up on the wooden coffee table.

His work phone rattled in his pocket. Not the personal phone he'd dropped at the job site, but a smartphone the Syndicate supplied him.

Kwan smiled. Maybe they would ask him to come in and talk.

He couldn't talk. He had nothing to say, anyway.

The giant Korean slid the phone out of his pocket and poked the screen. Read the message: "joe bag man & grtr kwan killed mr cypress & escaped. vlad is new boss. lssr kwan dead."

One Bullet   111

Vlad was alive and he'd framed Kwan for the murder of Mr. Cypress. Framed Joe Barrow, too.

Kwan turned the phone off, opened the back and pried out the battery. Dropped it all on the couch next to him. Vlad's hackers could use an active phone signal to track someone down, but this didn't feel like a ploy, especially since the message was sent to the entire Syndicate. Now Vlad's Syndicate.

With control of the Syndicate, Vlad could use the hackers to search for him, and then send his soldiers to kill him. Plus he had the services of a very clever assassin, a woman who used spear guns and kept a dead snake in her backpack.

Kwan realized he was in enemy territory, and unable to even speak the English language he'd struggled to learn or his native Korean. He knew few people outside of the Syndicate, and couldn't trust anyone within the organization. He was injured, unarmed and alone.

The smart move was to run. Run until he reached South Korea, where he could blend in, and where anyone coming for him would stand out.

Or he could fight. Fighting meant not waiting for Vlad to move. It meant finding those who betrayed him and striking first. And when he found the woman with the spear gun, Kwan guessed she'd be standing next to Vlad.

He recalled his army training and what they'd taught him about attacking the enemy's weak points. Going after their logistics and supplies, wrecking their communications and intelligence, spreading chaos and destruction behind the front lines. Yes, he would kill the assassin and he would kill Vlad, but first he would burn down everything Vlad hoped to rule.

Kwan dipped his index finger in the sticky blood above his collarbone. Leaned forward and wrote "VLAD" on the wooden coffee table.

Sat back on the couch and stared at the name.

Tonight, he would start with the hackers.

* * *

Chapter 23
Vlad

At the job site, Vlad watched Hax take deep breaths and then straighten up. The skinny hacker's eyelids fluttered. Vlad put the car keys in his pocket, and opened the passenger door of the low-slung Mustang. "Get in back. I'll drive."

Hax crawled into the back seat, sat with his hands on his boney knees and stared straight down at the floor mat. Vlad shrugged and walked to the back wall where The Finn sat dazed next to the three drums containing Mr. Cypress and both halves of Lesser Kwan.

He threw his bloody T-shirt into the barrel with Lesser Kwan's head and legs, then fixed the lid and tapped it down. The Finn stirred and her rifle moved toward the sound.

"It's me," Vlad said quickly. He stepped around the barrel of the gun and checked the snake bite on her wrist. The swelling was considerable, and her face was so pale he thought he could see her skull underneath the skin. For a moment, Vlad did see her skull and he flinched.

"What?" she asked.

"You look unwell." He scooped her up in his arms and her head lulled against his chest. Even with the rifle, she weighed far less than one of his mastiffs. He thought of his dogs and wondered if Lacey had remembered to feed them. Vlad imagined introducing Lacey to The Finn and smiled.

114   Mark Boss

He carried the assassin to the Mustang and gently set her in the passenger seat. Reached up to pull her seatbelt across her chest. Her eyes opened and he pushed her bangs aside. Her forehead felt clammy. "Keep watch for the other Korean. He'll know that when we leave, we have to go through the front gate," she said.

Vlad nodded. He had assumed Greater Kwan would escape to fight another day, but there was the possibility he would circle back and ambush them as they left the job site. Vlad shut the car door and went back to the stack of wooden pallets. He slung the pack with the dead water moccasin in it over one shoulder, stopped to check the cartridges remaining in his pistol and found just eight rounds.

As he walked past Mr. Cypress's shot-up Porsche, he picked up the all the loose weapons. Started to shut the doors of the car and noticed a small bag on the floor of the back seat. And a plaid Thermos full of Cypress's urine. Vlad laughed out loud as he grabbed the small bag of money Cypress had planned to give to the Cartel to placate them.

He shoved the rolling garage door up and the rusty rollers screeched. Vlad stood in the shadows and searched the job site--the trailer stood on his right, the Conex shipping containers straight ahead, and the gate on his left. But Greater Kwan didn't leap out with a rocket launcher.

Vlad dropped into the Mustang, cranked the big eight cylinder and slammed the accelerator down. The pony car leaped forward, back wheels spinning. The rear end kicked out and he used the car's

One Bullet 115

momentum to sling through the open gate like a drift racer.

Stomped the brakes, jumped out and ran back. Pulled the rolling door down, took a padlock from his pocket and snapped it shut. Still no Greater Kwan. Vlad sprinted to the gate and dragged it closed, then secured it with the second lock. Breathing hard, he scrambled into the Mustang and took off down the dirt road.

They splashed through puddles, and he grabbed at the stalk on the wheel. "Where are the wipers?" He hit the turn signal, clicked it off.

Hax sat forward between the seats and pointed a shaky hand. "Twist it toward you. No, I mean, away from you. Yeah, like that."

The wipers slung mud off the windshield and Vlad hit the lip of the highway at 40 miles an hour, barked the tires as he yanked the car around and shot toward Panama City. "I like this car," Vlad said. "American muscle."

"Yeah, uh, it's new. Just made my second payment, so...." Hax stared over Vlad's shoulder at the speedometer.

Vlad adjusted the seat. The leather seat stuck to his bare back. The Finn reached over and turned on the air conditioner. Vlad glanced at her. Sweat ran down her pale cheeks.

He sped up.

They passed the intersection with Highway 79 and continued east until they reached Panama City Beach. Vlad slowed and turned left.

116   Mark Boss

"Dude, the hospitals are that way," Hax said and pointed. "Gulf Coast or Bay Med, but either way you gotta go into town."

Vlad nodded. Passed a slow-moving mail truck and turned onto his street. He didn't see Greater Kwan sitting in a parked car, but then again, Kwan wouldn't be that obvious. Still, his driveway was empty and there were no odd cars on the street.

They bounced up into the driveway and stopped outside the garage. Vlad set the parking brake but left the engine running. "Drive her to the hospital. Straight there, no stops. I have business to handle with the Cartel." Vlad got out.

"Whoa, whoa, what?" Rather than push the seat forward, Hax slithered across the center console and out onto the wet driveway. "You wanted me to come pick you up and I did and--"

"You'd leave a woman to die of snake bite?" Vlad asked.

"No, of course not, but I thought you'd take her. Does she even have health insurance?"

Vlad unzipped Cypress's small duffel bag and pulled out a brick of cash. Shoved it into the hacker's hands. "Here's $10,000. Tell them your insurance company is very understanding. And don't forget the snake is in her bag. The doctors will want to know what type it is." He clapped Hax on the shoulder. "Get moving."

Hax rubbed his shoulder. "Yeah, okay." He looked down at The Finn. Leaned toward Vlad and whispered, "She's not gonna kill me, is she?"

Vlad smiled with just his mouth. "No, but if she dies before you reach the hospital, I'll put you in a drum next to Cypress and Lesser Kwan."

Hax jumped into the Mustang. Revved the engine, then whipped out of the driveway. Vlad waved to The Finn but she just stared at him.

He shrugged. "Women." Turned and went up the driveway. Saw the day's copy of the News Herald sitting neatly bagged in clear plastic on his front step. Tucked the newspaper under his arm and pulled out his house key.

The front door wasn't locked. Most of the time, he couldn't rely on Lacey to even close the refrigerator, and she regularly left the doors unlocked, but.... Vlad reached back and pulled the Heckler & Koch 9mm. His hand brushed the line of scar tissue along his back and he thought of his mother and wondered if she still held the grudge.

It was awkward to walk with the pistol held beneath the money bag, but Vlad figured the sight of a large, shirtless man holding a gun might send his neighbors to their phones. He went around the side of the house to the fence and whistled for the dogs.

Waited. Usually when the mastiffs heard him whistle they would rumble and chuff like lions until he spoke to them. But the yard was quiet. If Lacey was home, they might be in the warm house, probably sprawled on the furniture asleep. Vlad went through the gate, saw their empty dog house and followed the wall until he reached the back door.

The glass door was shut, but when he tugged the handle it was not latched. He set the money bag on the dead grass and stepped inside. Got out of the doorway and behind a chair as fast as he could without making a noise.

No sign of the dogs, or Lacey. He opened his mouth to call out, but hesitated. He could smell the dogs, but not Lacey or the cloud of marijuana smoke that usually hovered above her head. Ice rattled in a glass in the kitchen.

Vlad raised the 9mm as Ernesto came around the bar into the living room.

The slender Cartel lieutenant held a highball glass full of orange juice. He smoothed his silk tie with his free hand, unbuttoned his suit coat and sat in Vlad's favorite recliner. "Hola, my Syndicate friend." Ernesto smiled and sang, "'Meet the new boss, the same as the old boss'.... I like those old hippie songs."

"Where are my dogs?"

Ernesto sipped his juice and nodded. "Mmm. You know in the winter time when there is no sun, I get a little depressed. They call it Seasonal Affective Disorder. S.A.D. My doctor advised me to drink more orange juice, and he sold me a special lamp. I like the Florida orange juice, but a lamp is not the sun."

"Where are my dogs?"

Ernesto blinked. "Our bag man is dead, murdered in an airport washroom. Our $700,000 in cash is missing. And you're worried about a few dogs?"

Vlad pointed the pistol at Ernesto's face.

One Bullet   119

The Mexican gestured. "In the laundry room. Resting."

Vlad marched down the hall. The rest of the house was quiet and appeared empty. One of Lacey's sandals lay by the front door, but there was nothing broken or out of place. He opened the door to the laundry room, but the door hit something heavy and stopped. He pushed it open far enough to poke his head in.

The two mastiffs lay on the hard tile. Their eyes were shut and streamers of drool ran down their muzzles to pool on the floor. Plastic zip ties bound their legs. Vlad reached down and held his fingers beneath Genghis's nose. Felt the dog's hot breath. Saw their ribs expand as they breathed.

Vlad squeezed the grip of the gun for a moment, then forced his hand to relax. Went back down the hall to the living room.

Ernesto sat watching the clouds. He rattled the ice around the bottom of his empty glass.

"You drugged my dogs," Vlad said.

The Mexican nodded. "We tried to make friends, but they were very aggressive. Like their master. So, indeed, we drugged them."

"With what?" Vlad found himself squeezing the gun again.

Ernesto shrugged. "Something they use on horses, perhaps? I'm not sure. The darts took some time to work." He set his empty glass on the floor. "You missed our meeting today. This upset Calm Ruben. It's not like Mr. Cypress to miss a meeting. But I suppose with his being dead, we must excuse him." Ernesto smiled.

120   Mark Boss

Vlad imagined putting his heel into the man's goatee and driving his head through the wall. He also wondered who on the Syndicate's email distribution list had told the Cartel about Cypress getting killed. "Cypress is dead. I am the boss." He glanced around, but there was no sign of Ernesto's men. Yet the slim Cartel lieutenant couldn't have dragged the mastiffs inside the house by himself.

"Did Cypress die well?" Ernesto asked.

Vlad tilted his head, and thought about it. "Da. Well enough. Joe Barrow and the Kwan brothers betrayed him, but the old man died with a gun in his hand." It was a lie, but one he thought would appeal to Calm Ruben.

"So Joe the bag man, the same Joe who killed our bag man and took our money, killed his boss? With help from the overlarge Koreans?"

"Yes."

"Interesting. How about the airport this morning? We're told there was a third man at the exchange. A Hawaiian." Ernesto raised one eyebrow.

Vlad looked him in the eyes and shrugged. "Maybe Joe has a partner we don't know about. But we will find him and--"

"Calm Ruben instructed me to give you this." Ernesto reached into his suit coat.

Vlad put his finger inside the trigger guard of the pistol and relaxed his right arm. Focused. Ready to whip the gun up and fire.

Ernesto took out a single sheet of thick, cream-colored paper. Unfolded the page, held it at arm's

One Bullet 121

length and squinted. "Item one. You owe us $700,000 to replace the money we lost at the airport. Item two. You owe us $100,000 for the loss of our bag man, Raymond. In lieu of the second amount, Calm Ruben will accept the head and hands of Joe Barrow. We take the hands to indicate he was a thief. The head is to console Raymond's uncle." He carefully folded the paper and set it on the arm of the chair.

"Fair enough."

"Vladimir, our arrangement is simple and convenient. We sell drugs to stupid Americans for cash money. Your Syndicate launders that money through the banking system so we can more easily manage it. That marvelous arrangement is now in jeopardy."

Vlad tapped the gun against the side of his leg. He thought of his dogs lying helpless. He thought of Joe and Carly sitting in an airport lounge somewhere, drinking champagne and laughing about their escape. And he imagined Ernesto looking up at him from the bottom of a 55-gallon drum. "Tell Calm Ruben I will fix this. I will find Joe and the money, and deliver both to him."

"I believe you, but Calm Ruben is...impatient." Ernesto spread his hands. "We, too, will look for Joe and our money." He raised his arm and consulted the Grand Seiko on his wrist. "It's nearly dinner time. If you return what is ours by dinner time tomorrow, we will consider the matter resolved."

"And if not?"

"Calm Ruben will torture and kill you."
Ernesto stood and buttoned his coat. The slim
Mexican walked down the hall, speaking over his
shoulder. "Oh, I almost forgot. The police called
and left a message on your answering machine.
They found your Lexus at an auto shop, along with
seven corpses. They said to call them back."
Ernesto chuckled as he shut the front door.

* * *

Chapter 24
Joe

I steer the bubba truck south on Highway 77 until we see Bay Medical Center on our left. Turn in by the main lobby and cruise the parking lot for a spot, but it's packed and no one seems to be leaving.

Carly points at a sign. "That says they have valet parking. Let them find us a spot."

"We're in a stolen vehicle."

"They don't know that."

Shake my head. "I'll find a spot. With my luck, if I use the valet he'll recognize this truck--it's probably his cousin's." We drive back around the hospital complex until we reach a sign that says, "Emergency, Surgery and Heart Institute Entrance." A guy in a Mazda pulls out, so I race up the aisle and grab his parking spot. Sit for a minute with the windows down and try to think ahead for once. The air outside smells wet and iron flavored.

"You want to come in?" I ask. "People don't notice couples as--"

"As much as they do big, Irish-American thugs by themselves," Carly says. "I wish you'd stop saying people don't notice me. How do you think that makes me feel?"

"I didn't mean it like that."

"You know, I work hard to look good for you."

I reach out and smooth her hair. "I know, baby. You look amazing."

"I look like a drowned cat." She reaches down on the floorboard for her purse, sets it on her lap and crosses her arms. "I don't want this giant creep to see me. Maybe I can just stay in the hall while you talk to him. You are just gonna talk to him, right?"

Spread my hands. My knuckles are still sore. "I just want to ask Kid Sasquatch two questions. How did he know I was meeting the Cartel bag man at the airport this morning? And what did he do with the $700,000?"

"Okay." She tilts the visor down and checks her face in the vanity mirror while I get out and come around to open her door.

The jacked-up truck is so tall that her heels don't reach the ground, and she slides off the seat before I can catch her. When she slips down, her skirt catches and hikes up around her thighs. I grin.

Carly gives me a little chest bump. "See something you like, sailor?"

I lean in for a squeeze and a kiss, but then lightning cracks a mile or two away. We both jump. Laugh. The rain clouds are back, and the thunder with it. I take her hand and we hurry to the crosswalk. There's a circular drive for ambulances to pull up, and we reach the covered area just as the first drops of rain smack the road.

There's no point in searching the Emergency Room, since I'm sure Sasquatch has already been admitted. Probably best to start in the main lobby. Bay Medical isn't huge, but it still takes us five minutes to cut through the hospital to the main lobby.

It looks like hospital lobbies always do. Rows of vinyl chairs with sad people sitting in knots.

One Bullet 125

Most of them look surprised to be here. A few look resigned, like they've been here before. There's a kid in cleats holding a bloody towel to her nose. Her teammates sit close but they're all busy texting. An old guy sitting forward in his seat, leaning on a cane, wearing one of those black, mesh caps with the name of a Navy ship he served on forty years ago. A skinny kid messing with his phone, perched next to a petite but athletic looking woman who's holding her wrist. Maybe it's the fluorescent lights or her sickness, but she's paler than a snow drift. They make a weird couple, but I don't see any cops or even a hospital security guard.

We get to the elevators, but when the door chimes I hesitate. "I don't know Kid Sasquatch's real name. I'm not sure how we'll find him, other than walking the halls and looking in rooms."

Carly winks at me. "Hang on, I'll ask the desk."

I watch her walk off, perfectly balanced on her high heels. Dealing with people is something Carly is good at. If I asked the desk about a giant Hawaiian with two broken sticks, they'd call the cops. But Carly? She can sweet talk anybody. Well, any man.

She's back in a minute, smiling. "His name is Dwayne Kimura. Fourth floor. Room 419. One bed."

I pull her into the elevator. "Good job, baby. This won't take long. Then we'll pick up some dinner, find us a hotel, and take a long shower."

The elevator stops on the second floor. A nurse in scrubs and a sweater rolls an old lady in a wheel chair into the car and turns her around to face the doors. The old woman's hair is white and so thin I can see her scalp when I look down. She has an IV in her arm, and a metal pole on casters to hold the drip bag. When she raises her hand to massage the back of her neck, the skin above her knuckles is almost clear, with wormy blue veins underneath.

I stare until Carly elbows me.

They get out on the third floor and we go on up to the fourth.

When we step out of the elevator, I see a couple of nurses at a desk, nod my head and smile. Hold Carly's hand. Try to look nonthreatening as we walk by. Go down the hall like we know where we're going, reading the room numbers on the wall outside each door.

"This is it." It's a wide door, wide enough to wheel a gurney through, and cold to the touch. I look down at Carly. "You sure you want to stay out here?"

She stands by a wall-mounted container of hand sanitizer. "Yeah, just hurry."

I ease the door open. The room is dim. There's a dark bathroom on my left, a TV mounted high on the wall straight ahead. The picture is on, but the sound is off. I hear somebody sniffle.

Fill my lungs with cold air and wonder how many germs are mixed in with it. People catch weird stuff in hospitals, like flesh-eating stuff. I've never spent a single night in a hospital. Always just got my stitches and left.

Take a step. Heart is thudding. Hands tighten into fists.

One Bullet 127

Kid Sasquatch knocked me out this morning. Beat me in a straight-up fist fight. But then I hit him with a car, like a damn punk. He's got broken legs, so why am I worried? Because looking him in the eye won't be easy.

I hope he doesn't start screaming.

Take two steps into the room and stop. Sasquatch is on the bed, casts on both legs. His eyes are shut, and there's monitor machines all around him. There's a young woman on a chair next to him, holding a rosary and a wad of tissues.

Oh shit, is he married?

She stands up, and damn, she's built like he is. Not as tall, but almost as wide. She has brown skin and big, round eyes turned red from crying. Hair pulled back in a ponytail and wearing a blue hoody that's tight through the shoulders. They look like twins. She must be his sister.

"Hi?" she says.

"Hey, uh, sorry to interrupt. I think visiting hours are until eight, so I..." I don't know what to say. I wish Carly would get in here. "Hang on." I retreat to the door and lean out. "Carly, come in."

She follows me, eyes wide.

"Are you friends with Dwayne?" the sister asks.

Carly smiles, puts out her hand. "Yeah, we know Dwayne. I'm Carly, this is Joe." She looks down at Sasquatch. He hasn't budged. "We heard he got hit by a car. How's he doing?"

Sister bites her lip. "Not good. He's in a coma." Fresh tears roll down her chubby cheeks. I feel like a turd.

128   Mark Boss

"I'm Pono, Dwayne's little sister. Maybe he mentioned me?" Her face is open and hopeful. When she smiles it's genuine. Some people can't fake it because it's not in their nature.

"Oh, yeah, he talked about you lots of times," Carly says. She pats Pono's shoulder and moves around the bed. "I wonder if he can hear us?"

Pono shrugs. "They say some coma patients respond to voices, or songs they like, but I've been talking to him for hours and he hasn't moved."

"How did you get here so fast?" Carly asks.

"Oh, I flew over to the mainland a few days ago. I came to visit Dwayne to ask him to come home. He's been in some trouble here and the family is worried about him. This morning he got up early and said he had something to take care of, and he never came home." She starts to cry again. Pono is maybe college age, even younger than I thought when I first saw her.

I want to go in the bathroom and shove my own head in the toilet.

It's not normal, seeing this. You do a job, maybe you have to beat somebody stupid, but then you get the hell out of there. You don't come visit them and see them with tubes down their throat and their family crying. I feel sick.

Carly reaches back and squeezes my hand. "Dwayne was supposed to deliver a bag to us today. That's probably what he was talking about when he left this morning. Did you notice a bag at home?" Carly holds up her arms to indicate the width of a duffel bag.

One Bullet 129

"No. He left with a big bag this morning, but he didn't come home and I don't know anything about it." Pono's face sets. When she looks up at me, I get a hint of what I saw in her brother's eyes at the airport. "Are you involved with Dwayne's drug business? I know he was dealing, and probably using, too."

I look away. Anywhere but her eyes. There's a rolling table by the bed, but no food tray on it. A landline phone on the nightstand, and an empty bottle of Mountain Dew. Next to the bottle are two cell phones, a man's wallet, a fat, gold pimp watch, and two sets of keys. One set has a white plastic tag with the license number on it, obviously for a rental car. The other is a regular ring with a big car key, several smaller ones like house keys, and a stubby key with a blue tag clipped on.

"We don't know anything about drugs." Carly touches her chest above her heart. "But Dwayne did invest with us on some foreclosed homes we're buying. He was supposed to bring us the money today so the deal can go through."

Pono looks at Dwayne as if she's trying to read his face, not Carly's.

"Joe, why don't you get us some sodas? Pono, you want another Mountain Dew? I'll take a Diet Coke." Carly turns me around. "Let us girls talk for a few minutes, okay?"

I go out the door and turn toward the elevators. Not sure where the drink machines are, but I can ask the nurses at the desk. Except there's already a guy at the desk, and he's holding a wet, green windbreaker. I can't read all the letters on the jacket, but I know the type. Cops call them raid jackets.

Down here all the investigators wear a long-sleeve dress shirt and a tie, but rarely a jacket because most of the year it's too hot. He leans against the counter to talk to the nurses, and I can see the badge on his belt. The gun must be on the other side, on his right hip. He's smiling at the nurses and brushing his mustache with one finger.

He looks up and I turn away. Stand at the sanitizer and pump germ killer onto my hands. It stings like hell on my knuckles. I'm facing away but I try to listen. At the far end of the hallway, the metal door to the stairs opens.

A short, dark Mexican pokes his head out. Looks down the hallway right at me. Yanks his head back fast.

Oh hell.

I snatch open the door to Sasquatch's room and bolt inside. "Carly, we gotta go. The Cartel is here. The cops, too."

* * *

Chapter 25
Vlad

Vlad sat on the floor of the laundry room and watched his dogs sleep. Genghis rolled over onto his back, legs sprawled since Vlad had cut the plastic zip ties. Amber was curled into a ball, snoring next to his foot.

Lesser Kwan's H&K pistol was on the top of the washer next to him, and Vlad held the wire cutters he'd used to cut the zip ties. He wondered if he should cut the dogs' nails while they were still drugged, but he figured they'd been through enough in one day.

He considered Ernesto's visit, and Calm Ruben's threats. When he'd helped Cypress form the Syndicate, Vlad remembered his school boy lessons on ancient city states. The city states learned that standing armies were expensive because they ate a lot but produced nothing. The Syndicate didn't need soldiers to collect protection money from businesses or guard drug dealers, because they didn't do those types of crimes. They'd embraced the future, where cybercrime and money laundering could reap millions with minimal risk.

Since Vlad and the Kwans could handle most situations themselves, the Syndicate had few soldiers. In contrast, the Cartel had many soldiers to protect their farms, labs, shipments and dealers.

Vlad stroked the soft, loose skin around Amber's neck. He'd already stolen the money from the overseas account that was supposed to go to the Cartel. If he could find and kill Joe before the Cartel did, he could take the $700,000 in cash and say it went missing. Let dead Joe take all the blame.

He sat back against the cold, metal side of the clothes dryer and the whole unit slid a few inches. Genghis twitched in his sleep, paws moving like he was swimming.

Ernesto, you should not have touched my dogs, Vlad thought. Maybe I'll cut your ears off and pour orange juice down the holes. See if that cheers you up.

His phone rattled, and he straightened his leg so he could pull the phone out of his pocket. It was a text from Hax that read: "@ bay med lobby. joe & girlf just walked past me."

Vlad read it a second time. What is Joe doing at the hospital? Perhaps he or Carly was hurt in the fight at the auto shop?

He dialed Hax and the hacker answered immediately. "Hang on, I gotta go outside."

After a minute, the hacker spoke again. Vlad heard rain in the background. "Joe and his hottie walked right past me, dude. Right past me."

"Did he see you?" Vlad asked.

"I don't think so."

"Where's The Finn?"

"They admitted her for treatment. I'm waiting to hear from the doctor," Hax said. "Oh, and a guy in Sheriff's Office jacket went in a minute ago."

Vlad shrugged. "That cop could be there for anything. How would he know Joe was in the

One Bullet 133

hospital? Listen, we have to get to Joe before the Cartel does. Watch in the lobby and text me if you see him. I'll call some guys and--"

"Oh crap." Hax dropped his voice. "I think you're too late."

"What?" Vlad said it loud and Genghis stirred but didn't open his eyes.

"Three Mexican dudes just got out of a truck and they're walking this way. Two of them have tool bags. One's got a, holy crap, he's got a guitar case."

"Don't stare at them," Vlad said. "Where are they going?" He waited for Hax to respond but only heard a thud. And then the patter of rain on a sidewalk, and the sound of distant thunder.

* * *

Chapter 26
Greater Kwan

The wind off the Gulf of Mexico rattled the busted front door of the beach house. Greater Kwan's eyes snapped open and he sat up.

It was full dark, and the unlit wooden house creaked as the wind strummed the shutters. He checked his watch and realized he'd only slept a short while. When he stood, the disassembled Syndicate phone slid off the couch onto the floor.

Kwan planned to discard it, but changed his mind and put the phone and battery in his pocket. If he had to, he could re-assemble it later and check for messages from the Syndicate. Apparently, they'd forgotten to delete him from the distribution list. In the meantime, he didn't want Vlad's hackers tracking him.

Moving carefully between the furniture in the unfamiliar house, Kwan went to the window and peeked out. A few houses down the street were lit, but the house directly across was dark. He was unable to see to the sides because of the overgrown azalea bushes.

He stared at the Toyota he'd stolen from the job site. It didn't look like a rental, and he doubted Vlad's assassin would report the theft, so it was probably safe to use for a few days. This thought led him to a mental checklist.

Transportation? Check.

Weapons? None, but a visit to the cache at his storage unit would fix that.

One Bullet 135

Communication? He lost his personal mobile phone, but still had the Syndicate model. Money? He opened his wallet. The Syndicate hackers could track credit card purchases, so the cards were useless, but he had just over a thousand in cash. Enough to begin operations. As for Intelligence, well, thanks to driving Mr. Cypress he was familiar with nearly all of the Syndicate's properties in northwest Florida. And if you knew where people lived and worked, you could find them.

His stomach rumbled, reminding him he hadn't included Logistics in his check list.

Kwan fished the car keys out of his pocket and went to the door. Pulled the chair away, and the door swung open by itself. A cold blast of air drove him back a step. He shoved the door closed and kicked the chair back into place.

Walking around in a bloody shirt was foolish, but walking around without a shirt in January was asking for attention. He went back down the hall to the first bedroom and searched the closet. Beach towels were abundant, but the clothing choices were limited. Kwan figured he could risk a light for a minute, so he flipped on the overhead.

There was a small stack of T-shirts on a shelf in the closet. The top one was a blue shirt with the sleeves cut off and a picture of some sort of carnival ride and the words "Vomit Comet." Kwan put it back. The second T-shirt was white, with long sleeves, and a cartoon picture of sea turtles.

He rolled it up and tugged it down over his shaved head, careful not to disturb the bandage around his neck. The shirt was too tight through the shoulders, but better than nothing. He pulled the blue Vomit Comet shirt on over it. Layers would help with the cold, and wearing a bright, white T-shirt wasn't ideal for sneaking up on people.

Kwan turned off the light and went back up the hall. He stopped to clean up the bloody towels and clothes in the bathroom. Carrying the wad of wet cloth and empty bags of QuikClot, he went outside and dumped them in the trash can.

There were no cars coming down the street, and no one out in the miserable weather walking their dog. Kwan unlocked the Toyota, started to get in and stopped.

He went back inside and down the hall to the bathroom. Under the weak, yellow light above the sink, he stared down at the two-foot spear in the tub. The spear was still wet with his blood. Kwan opened the tap, but there was no hot water so he rinsed the spear with cold until it gleamed bright and clean.

Spear in hand, he got in the Toyota and drove slowly back to Highway 98. The side-by-side Hack House and Sleep House the Syndicate owned were only an hour away in Fort Walton, but he knew he wouldn't make it without stopping for food. His stomach already felt like it was eating his other organs.

The beach traffic thinned out after the initial rush to get home, and he drove west fast enough to keep up but not so fast as to draw attention. Kwan turned off at Smoothie Queen and got out. The restaurant door jingled as he marched inside, and a stocky girl at the counter looked up and smiled.

One Bullet   137

He held up three thick fingers. "Three strawberry-banana Muscle Pumpers with whey protein."

It came out a long growl, like a dog's final warning before it bites.

The girl's eyes went wide. She stared at the bandage around his neck. "Omigod. Do you have throat cancer? My granddaddy has throat cancer, I mean, he's not really my real granddaddy but he raised me and my brother and he always dipped, you know, and now he has throat cancer and mouth cancer and they removed part of his jaw and...." She took a deep breath and covered her mouth. Tears flooded her eyes.

Kwan stared. Then he reached into his pocket for his phone. Opened a blank text message and typed in his order. Put the phone and his money on the counter.

She scooped up the phone, read the order, then typed her own message beneath his.

He took the phone and read it while she prepared his smoothies.

Her message read, "I will pray for you."

She put the three cups in a cardboard holder and handed him his change.

He thought about typing another message to explain that he didn't have throat cancer, and that he got shot with a spear gun, and was now on the path of revenge and would probably be dead long before her grandfather, but he had work to do. So Kwan nodded, took a straw and a handful of napkins, and went out.

Greater Kwan drove to the storage unit in nearby Laguna Beach where he and his brother stashed their arsenal. He coasted down the long aisle between the low buildings and parked the Toyota with the trunk facing the rollup, metal door of the storage unit.

He popped the trunk, and stepped out. There were floodlights on the roof of each row, but they were spaced just far enough apart to leave his unit in shadow. Kwan leaned in the car and found an expensive Surefire tactical flashlight in the glove box. He wondered how much Vlad was paying the assassin if she could afford such quality equipment.

No other cars were parked on his row, but he could hear a band warming up a few rows over. One night when he and his brother had come to pick up some ammo, they learned that local bands often practiced in the storage units.

While the drummer took a few, tentative whacks at his set, Kwan used the flashlight to open the lock. The Surefire had two settings, one for normal light and one bright enough to blind someone, which might prove useful. Having restored himself by drinking all three smoothies during the drive, he pushed the rolling door up without effort.

The storage unit was trashed.

He grabbed the spear off the car seat and dashed inside.

The metal shelving he and his brother had installed was tipped over. Boxes torn open. All of the tall, plastic long-gun cases were gone. He stepped over an empty ammo can and opened the ice chest where they hid the pistols. The handguns were gone, too.

Breathing hard, Kwan worked his way through the long, narrow storage space until he found what was left of his brother's scuba diving equipment. They'd taken almost everything but Lesser Kwan's flippers and a few pieces of miscellaneous gear.

The lock on the door didn't look tampered with, and Kwan wondered how the thieves had entered until he brought the flashlight around and saw the hole in the wall. Someone had entered the unit next door, and then bashed a hole in the wall and climbed through. The jagged hole was just big enough to fit a rectangular gun case, or a skinny thief.

Kwan stood in the dark room, hands trembling. A growl burbled up from his throat and he kicked an empty milk crate into the wall. He went out and stood in the cold, wet air in his too small T-shirts and took deep breaths. The cold air made his throat ache.

The rock band transitioned from a hard jam to a weepy, arena-pleasing ballad and Kwan listened until the tension bled out of his shoulders. He clicked the flashlight on and went back into the unit to see what he could salvage.

Without guns, the remaining ammunition was useless. But he found a plastic bag of .44 Magnum pistol ammo Lesser Kwan had prepared for use with a bangstick. Greater Kwan didn't dive, but he knew his brother carried a bangstick for protection from sharks. Loaded with a single cartridge at its tip, the two-foot long bangstick could be jabbed into an aggressive shark. Since a bangstick worked with the barrel pressed against the target, the escaping gas from the gun powder did an enormous amount of tissue damage, even more than the bullet itself.

Kwan stepped over the fallen shelves and dug through the boxes. He found two bangsticks wrapped in a towel at the bottom of a box. He carried the bangsticks and the bag of ammo outside and sat in the Toyota. Lesser Kwan had sealed the cartridges with red nail polish to protect them from the salt water. At the time, he'd kidded his younger brother and asked if he was going to paint his toenails.

He smiled as he loaded the bangsticks. They were simple devices, but reliable. However, he wondered how loud they would be when fired.

He went back into the storage unit and found a small, blue cooler where he'd stowed three homemade sound suppressors and a crude pipe bomb made with black powder and roofing nails. Two of the suppressors were too narrow to fit the head of the bangstick, but the third was wide enough. It was a little loose, but he figured it might stay on for a few shots.

A thorough search of the remaining boxes netted him a cheap pair of binoculars, two empty gas cans, and a badly rusted hatchet.

Kwan hefted the hatchet. It was time for war.

* * *

Chapter 27
Joe

I snatch open the door to Sasquatch's hospital room and bolt inside. "Carly, we gotta go. The Cartel is here. The cops, too."

Carly jumps up from the chair next to Kid Sasquatch's bed. The big thug is still unconscious, his brown toes sticking out of the casts on both legs. His sister, Pono, lets go of his hand and glances around the corner at the door. "What? What cartel?"

"The drug cartel he stole $700,000 from." I point at Sasquatch and wonder if he can hear us. Who knows what's happening inside his head?

Carly stands over him for a moment, biting her lip. She does that when she's thinking. One time I saw her bite her lip so hard it bled, and she was trying to decide between two pairs of shoes.

I grab her hand. "We gotta go." Turn to Pono. "The Cartel guy who saw me will come back with his friends. You should leave. Come with us."

Pono's eyes bulge. She raises her fists. "I'm not leaving Dwayne helpless so a bunch of scumbag drug dealers can kill him. I'll die first."

I should clock her. Knock her out, pick her up and carry her out of her so they don't shoot her full of holes. But I can't hit a woman. Only punks do that.

Wait, the Cartel thinks I stole the money. That's what Vlad must have told them. If I run, those guys will chase me and leave Carly and Pono alone.

I look at Carly and she looks scared and ripe and beautiful and I just want to protect her and give her nice things and sit on the beach somewhere and watch the waves with her. "Baby, I'll meet you at the truck in two hours."

"What? Where are you going?" Carly reaches for me, but I pull my arm back.

"I have to lead them away from you. They think I took the money, so they'll chase me. I'll get away and meet you back at the truck."

Carly looks hard at me, then nods.

The door is well oiled and opens without a squeak. I do a quick head out/head in move to check the hallway. On my left there's a Mexican in the door to the stairs with his phone pressed to his ear, and another guy trying to look over the top of his head.

"Just walk normal," I tell myself as I set off down the hall toward the nurses' station, walking fast but not running.

A voice calls from the stairwell. "Senor Barrow? You have something of ours."

Ahead at the nurses' station, the sheriff's investigator is making time with a cute redhead. I fill my lungs and yell, "Help, those guys have guns!"

Cops are suspicious types, but from his view he sees a big guy run toward him, yelling for help. And down the hallway, two guys with guns spilling out of the stairwell.

One Bullet 143

For the investigator it's a rush decision, but an easy one. "Sir, get down," he yells as he goes for his gun.

I look back just as the first gunman levels his pistol.

There's a room on my right, so I jump inside the doorway for cover. I see the investigator draw his pistol and step into a two-handed stance that looks straight from a cop training film.

The first shots are loud.

And right away, people start screaming. Nurses yell, patients scream, and visitors hit the floor so fast I can feel the thuds.

I drop to one knee and peek out. The two Cartel gunmen fall back to the safety of the stairwell, firing without aiming. I've got a few seconds to move.

Grabbing the metal doorframe with my right hand, I sling myself into the hallway and the hard turn nearly blows my knee out. I make three full steps before the first bullet cracks the air. No time to zig or zag . I just pump my arms, mouth open, legs driving me past the investigator.

He's busy shooting at the Cartel, and whatever high-capacity pistol he has is cranking out a lot of bullets.

Something burns my right calf, but there's no thump so the bullet didn't hit me square. I veer right behind a wall and into the alcove for the elevators.

The elevator chimes and the doors open.

A skinny gunman in a blue windbreaker runs right into me.

I weigh twice what he does.

He staggers back. Reaches under his jacket. There's a second guy behind him in the elevator, eyes wide.

I've still got momentum going, so I bring my foot up and boot the guy into the elevator. The back of his head cracks his buddy right on the nose, but somehow the guy squeezes off a random shot.

Shit. I've got to get a damn gun.

But not now. You can't wrestle two guys at once.

While they're trying to get to their feet, I push off the wall and dash down the corridor, and I can feel it in my hamstring. Why did I kick that guy? I'm not flexible enough for that kung fu stuff. I'm not built for a track meet, either, and I'm panting when I hit the door to the other set of stairs.

The first two flights go fast but I'm fading, almost falling down the last two sets. My knees feel like they might collapse. I have to slow down before I hit the lobby because there might be more gunmen. Damn, did they bring the entire Cartel?

What does the Syndicate have for soldiers? Like five guys. The Cartel has dozens.

But the Syndicate could be here, too, so I can't just look for Mexican pistoleros. I crack open the door and look out into the lobby.

Except it's not the lobby, it's a hallway. What? Where am I?

While I'm trying to figure it out, a private security guard runs down the hallway past me. He's talking into a radio, but he's running and I can't figure out what he's saying except, "Shots fired."

One Bullet 145

He blows by without noticing me and I wait a few heartbeats, then walk down the hall in the opposite direction. It's quiet in this corridor and I can hear the hum of the lights above me, and the distant sound of gunshots. The floor is freshly waxed. My shoes squeak with each step.

Take a left and see a beautiful red 'Exit' sign and a steel door with a push bar. I ease the bar in and step partway out. It's black outside and I can't see a damn thing. Standing in the doorway with the light behind me makes for a perfect target, so I step to my right and let the door swing shut.

For a long minute, my eyes strain to catch up with the change from bright light to cloudy night. My ears are still ringing from the gunfire, and I have that weird, metallic taste in my nose and mouth that you always get with guns. My clothes probably stink, too.

The smart move is to find the bubba truck and drive away. Hide out for a few hours and then come back for Carly, and hope that maybe Kid Sasquatch has woken up and is ready to answer my questions. Still just two questions. Who set me up? Where is the money?

How can something so simple get so complicated?

And how come I have no idea where the damn truck is parked? I must be on the wrong side of the complex because none of this looks familiar. Once I can see well enough not to trip, I start down the sidewalk and see a sign. "Women's and Children's Pavilion." Okay, I don't know where that is in

146   Mark Boss

relation to where we parked, but if I keep circling around eventually I have to find the truck.

Traffic and sirens are way off to my left, so that's probably Highway 77, which is on the west side of the hospital complex. I don't see anyone else around, so I walk up the sidewalk, the car keys ready in my right hand.

I take a left around something labeled the "Tommy Cooley Building" and think I'm going the right way. Up ahead a set of doors opens and two guys do what I did. Dash out, realize it's too dark to see much, and stop. They're both short. And speaking Spanish.

And looking my way. Damn it.

I turn and run back the way I came.

One shouts at me. The other saves his lungs and just opens fire. Three quick shots that poke holes in the cold air, but not in me.

As soon as I round the corner of the Cooley Building and have some brick between me and them, I cut left into "Patient/Visitor Parking." I don't want to run back inside the hospital, so hiding behind the cars is my only option.

For short-legged guys, the Cartel boys are quick. Hell, they're probably still in their twenties. As I duck behind a minivan, I risk a glance back. They're closing in, and now that the chase is on, they're saving their ammo.

I lean on the van for a few seconds and suck up some oxygen, then it's back to the foot race. There are trees on the far side of the parking lot, so I head for those. Hear voices on my right now and when I

One Bullet 147

turn my head to look something slams my left shoulder and spins me around.

Slumped against a car I try to get my fists up, but my left arm isn't working. Look up and see the big side mirror on a pickup truck hanging loose. I ran into a mirror, and broke it. That figures.

Now my fingertips tingle like I slept on my arm and just woke up. It's hard to run with one arm dangling, but I get my speed up and plunge into the tree line. Cold air or not, I've sweated through my clothes and my tongue tastes like paste and gun smoke.

I have to slow down. I can't keep this pace and if I step in a hole in the dark and break my ankle, they'll walk up and shoot me while I'm crawling. I'm no Tarzan, but I know in the woods you can either go fast or go quiet, but not both. So I scoot across the wet leaves without making much noise, and although I can hear the gunmen, no one is shooting.

Just ahead, a narrow road curves away to my right. I wait a second, then dash across. That's when the bullets start again. I'm into the trees on the far side and cutting right when my shoes hit a smooth, flat surface--a driveway to a house or a business.

There are no lights on and a bullet hits a window two steps to my left. Running away sucks, but I keep thinking of Carly and Pono trapped in that hospital room with that useless thug Sasquatch and no way out. I hope the sheriff's investigator took out those shooters, although it's weird to be pulling for the cops.

148   Mark Boss

I dash across the back yard, and the hamstring is really tightening up. Zig around a big, old tree and then I just flat run out of land. There's a slope, and my feet go out from under me and my ass hits the water.

It's a bayou or a bay or whatever they call it around here. A finger of water that cuts inland just deep enough for rich people to build a house with a dock. Footsteps thump the grass behind me and I can feel them through the earth. Before I can move, a guy lands on top of me, and he's more surprised than I am.

We're half in the water, half in the mud and the tree roots, and he's thrashing like he fell in hot lava. I grab for the gun and get my mitt around the slide, and my finger lands between the hammer and the firing pin. In the dark, this is sheer luck.

I roll him so I'm on top with my weight pressing him down. When he tries to scream for his buddies, I feel his chest swell. I grab a handful of mud and cram it into his open mouth. Shove his jaw shut so hard it snaps his head back.

He punches me in the eye with his free hand, and the thumb gets it there and it hurts and I see weird flashes. I bite his fingers to trap his hand, and yank him back toward the roots of the tree. If I put him in the water he'll splash and his friends will hear us.

Drop my shoulder into his nose once, twice, and by the third time he's still thrashing but not as much. Grab him by his wet hair and slam the back of his head into a root. Drive my elbow into his throat. He's either out or dead, cause he isn't moving. The gun comes right out of his limp fingers.

The barrel is hot.

There are more voices up by the house, descending into the yard. I wonder how many bullets are left in this gun, and how many guys are by the house, and when will the cops get here?

Screw it. I learned to swim when I was seven, and I float pretty good for a big guy.

Besides, I can see lights on the opposite side of the bayou. How far can it be? I slip into the water, trying not to splash. Just hunch over and wade out until my next step doesn't hit the bottom and I'm swimming. Nice and easy, no noise. Yeah, the water is cold but I'm so jacked up I barely feel it.

The water isn't salty enough to really sting, but it doesn't exactly feel good on my eye. Navigating mostly with one eye, I aim for a light across the bayou and take my time. But fifty strokes into my relaxing crawl I don't feel so good. Lungs are burning, my left shoulder aches like hell, and my legs feel heavy.

I don't want to kick off my shoes because I'll need them later on the streets to get back, but damn they feel heavy. Where is that light? Off to my left now. I can't feel a current but somehow I'm off course.

There's no boats, and few lights and no moon. As I get closer to the light I see that it's a house, and there's a dock with a boat house. But my arms are so tired that it's hard to reach out and grab the water and pull. My legs save me. Something in my brain says, 'Swim.' So I slither through the water until my forehead hits a wooden post on the dock.

Reach up with my right hand and grab a plank, and a barnacle cuts right into my ring finger. Son of a bitch it hurts, too.

But I hang there and pant and blink my right eye until I can see well enough to do something. The boat house above me has a white boat sitting nose out. I work my way along the boat, pull myself up onto the walkway beside it and roll onto my back.

Raise my left hand and realize the gun is still there. I didn't drop it. I forgot about it but I didn't let go and that makes me very happy. In the dark I run my fingers over it until I hit the magazine release. The magazine drops into my hand and it's light.

I sit up to count the bullets. I feel for the top of the stack in the magazine, but it's just the metal tab with the spring underneath. The mag is empty. So I draw back the slide and a bullet drops out of the chamber into my lap.

I have one damn bullet.

Typical.

* * *

Chapter 28
Carly

Carly watched Joe--strong, stupid, can't-break-my-code Joe--rush out of Dwayne's hospital room. She heard boots thump down the hallway and caught a glimpse of men with guns running by as the door swung shut.

The first gunshot she heard made her flinch.

She imagined Joe taking a bullet in the back and shut her eyes for a second. Pono pushed past her and Carly watched as the big girl snatched up a heavy chair.

"Joe said the Cartel is here. I have to protect Dwayne," Pono yelled over the gunfire.

Carly nodded. She was trapped. Joe was gone, and the cops, the Cartel, and maybe the Syndicate were having an all-out gun battle in the hall. It was too much. She stood beside Dwayne's bed and held her purse to her stomach and tried to think.

The huge Hawaiian shifted on the bed, and his eyes opened. "Turn the TV down," Dwayne rasped. He cleared his throat.

More gunshots sounded from the hallway. Across the room, Pono dropped the chair to the floor and pushed it against the door.

Dwayne looked at Carly and his glassy eyes slowly focused. "Carly?"

Carly's head snapped up. She yanked a compact 9mm pistol from her purse and ran around the corner of the bed toward the door.

Pono's back was to her, but as she got closer Carly realized how big the young woman was--a head taller than her, and twice her weight. As gunshots cracked in the hallway, Pono tilted the chair to prop it under the door handle.

Carly swung her pistol with both hands. The steel barrel hit Pono behind the right ear and the big girl fell over the chair and slid off.

The bed creaked, and Dwayne crashed onto the floor. His IV bag and one of the monitors tipped over as the giant crawled forward, dragging his broken legs. "Pono?"

He swiped at Carly's ankle but she jumped back and raised the gun. "You ripped me off, you bastard. We had a deal. I gave you the time and place of the exchange. All you had to do was steal the money and the password envelope. Then you were supposed to take the envelope and I was supposed to get the bag of cash, a 50/50 split."

Dwayne rolled onto his side. And laughed. A high, almost hysterical laugh, that kind that comes from morphine and fear. "You dumb bitch. You betrayed your boyfriend and sent him into that bathroom to get killed, and you're crying about me ripping you off?" He laughed harder, and tears rolled down his fat cheeks.

Carly tucked the gun under her arm, lit a cigarette and then aimed the pistol at his face. "Tell me where the bag of cash is. The real money, not that bag of counterfeit crap you were carrying when Joe found you."

"Hey, you can't smoke in here, it's a hospital," Dwayne said, and hiccupped once. "I'm not telling

One Bullet 153

you a damn thing. Go ahead and shoot me. I got so much morphine in my veins I won't even feel it."

Carly took a step to her left, leaned down and put the pistol to Pono's head. The Hawaiian girl lay face down on the floor, breathing but unconscious. "How about now? You feel like talking now?" Carly asked.

Dwayne stopped laughing. His eyes went wide. "Pono isn't part of this. She isn't in the business. You can't--"

"Yes, I can," Carly screamed. "Don't you get it? I'm desperate. The Cartel wants their money back, the Syndicate wants their money back, and stupid Joe wants to find it and prove he's not a thief. They. Will. Not. Stop."

Dwayne stretched out his hand. "Okay, okay. When I went to the airport, I brought a bag of counterfeit money with me and stashed it in a rental locker. After I ambushed the Cartel bagman and your boyfriend, I took the bag of real money to the locker and switched it with the fake. I was walking out to the car to give you the bag of fake money when a car hit me."

"Where's the locker key?" Carly asked.

The big man looked at the table beside the bed. "On my keychain. Take it. Just don't hurt Pono."

Carly walked around the broken man. She scooped his keys and the keys to Pono's rental car off the table, along with both cell phones. Then she grabbed a pillow from the bed.

When Dwayne rolled over onto his back to see what she was doing, Carly shoved the pillow into his face, pressed the gun to it and shot him four times. Even with the pillow, in the enclosed room the shots were painfully loud. Smoke drifted up from holes in the pillow, and Dwayne went limp.

She stepped over Pono and dragged the chair away from the door. The gunfire had stopped. Carly peeked out and saw no one with a gun, so she went for the stairs. In the corridor, a nurse in royal blue scrubs sat against the wall, trying to stop the flow of blood from a bullet wound in her stomach. The young nurse moaned and reached up to her, but Carly slapped her hand away and kept walking.

When she reached the door to the lobby downstairs, she watched as two cops ran by, guns drawn. Otherwise the lobby was empty. She pushed through the door and went out into the parking lot. Carly held the key to Pono's rental car high and hit the button until the horn sounded on a subcompact car a few rows over.

She dropped into the car, cranked the engine and watched for cops as she pulled out onto Highway 77. Carly figured she could make it to the airport in an hour, get the money from the locker, buy a plane ticket, and be in the air by midnight.

* * *

Chapter 29
Hax

Hax stood in the cold drizzle outside the lobby of Bay Medical Center, and whispered to Vlad on his phone. "Joe and his hottie walked right past me, dude. Right past me."

"Did he see you?" Vlad asked.

Hax shrugged, even though his new boss couldn't see him. "I don't think so." Across the sidewalk, a pickup truck wedged itself into a narrow parking space and three guys climbed out.

"Where's The Finn?" Vlad asked.

"They took her in for treatment. I'm waiting to hear from the doctor," Hax said. "Oh, and a guy in a Sheriff's Office jacket went in a minute ago."

"The cop could be there for anything," Vlad said. "How would the cops know Joe was at the hospital? Listen, we have to get to Joe before the Cartel does. Wait in the lobby and text me if you see him. I'll call some guys and--"

"Oh crap," Hax said.

The three short men from the pickup surveyed the parking lot for a moment, and then marched across the street to the sidewalk.

Hax hunched his head down between his shoulders and shuffled off the sidewalk until he was deep in the bushes next to the wall. "I think you're too late," he whispered into the phone.

"What?"

"Three Mexican dudes just got out of a truck and they're walking this way. Two of them have

156   Mark Boss

tool bags. One's got, holy crap, he's got a guitar case."

"Which way are they going?" Vlad asked, but Hax dropped the phone and stomped it into the wet dirt so the Cartel men wouldn't hear. Thunder rumbled to the south, out over the bay. Hax stood very still. The Cartel lieutenant, Ernesto, had visited the Hack House a few times with Mr. Cypress, and he always had bodyguards with him. It was possible one of the gunmen might recognize him.

The three men walked abreast down the wet sidewalk, the one with the guitar case in the middle. They were almost past his hiding place when the man on the left stopped. His head rotated slowly, searching the shadows.

Hax knew he should stay still, but when the man looked right at his spot, Hax bolted. He burst out the bushes and ran toward the lobby.

One of the men yelled something in Spanish, and all three surged forward. After five steps, Hax knew he was screwed. The hospital wall was on his left, the sidewalk on his right, and the gunmen cut off his angle to the lobby door. Simple geometry. A dog could figure it out.

Hax stopped running and raised his hands. "Hola, dudes, whassup? My wife called and the baby just dropped so I gotta get inside and--"

One gunman punched him in the stomach, and the second pinned his arms. The third gunman straggled a few steps behind with the guitar case. The guy who punched him pulled out a phone and held the lit screen to his face. Then he flipped

One Bullet 157

through a dozen photographs on the screen until he found a picture of Hax.

The gunman turned the phone around and Hax saw his old, high-school yearbook picture onscreen. His mortar board was as crooked as his grin.

"We know you," the gunman said. "The Syndicate computer boy. They gave us pictures, and told us to watch for you and your friends. What are you doing here? Where's our money?" the gunman asked.

"I'm not a boy, douche ba--"

The man hit him again, and his fist sank half way to Hax's spine.

When he slumped over to gulp for air, he heard a sharp crack and something wet hit the back of his neck. The guy pinning his arms collapsed on top of him. Hax's chin hit the dirt but he rolled over and looked up. The second gunman reached under his jacket and turned toward the sound.

Two quick shots from the darkness and the gunman staggered back, hands to his face.

The Finn stood up from the bushes, holding a short, blunt pistol with one hand.

The third gunman fumbled with the clasps on the guitar case, but The Finn put two bullets into the center of his chest and he fell over.

While Hax crawled out from under the dead gunman, the man in front of him fell to his knees, still holding his face and groaning. The Finn walked up, put her gun to his head and executed him. She tucked the gun into the sling holding her left arm, and grabbed the guitar case with her right hand. "Hax, get your keys, we need to leave," she said.

Two deep bangs sounded from inside the building. And then a flurry of shooting.

Hax sprang up. She pushed the guitar case into his arms and they ran to the parking lot. When Hax opened the Mustang, she helped him shove the guitar case into the back seat. In the dark, he felt the wet case and wondered if it was rain or blood.

* * *

Chapter 30
Greater Kwan

As he headed west toward Fort Walton Beach, Greater Kwan stopped at a well-lit gas station and filled the stolen Toyota and the two gas cans from the storage unit. Having drunk all three of the smoothies, he went inside the quickie mart to use the men's room. While inside, he checked the bandage around his neck. Thanks to the QuikClot the bleeding had stopped, and since the bandage hadn't soaked through he decided to leave it alone.

He bought a 20-ounce bottle of green tea and simply dropped his money on the counter and walked out without having to growl or type text messages. Kwan figured he could pretend like it was years ago when he'd first arrived in America and couldn't speak English. Now he couldn't speak at all, but it wasn't much different. He could do a lot without talking. Like take down the entire Syndicate.

It was past the dinner hour and traffic on Highway 98 was intermittent--clogged up at the major turnoffs or at bridges, but fast on the open stretches. In Destin he slowed down. Even in the winter there were tourists--cars from Canada and Michigan and Illinois full of snowbirds looking for seafood restaurants and outlet stores.

After he crossed the bridge into Fort Walton, he drove north on Ferry Road and then turned east toward Choctawhatchee Bay. Finally, he cut north again into a nice, almost rich, neighborhood where

160   Mark Boss

the houses looked like they should be next to the water but weren't.

When the housing market collapsed, the Syndicate bought two homes that sat next to each other. One was a Sleep House where the hackers lived, and the other was the Hack House where they ran their phishing and spamming operations. Kwan knew the hackers were responsible for a lot more than just spam. Using their computer skills, they laundered Cartel money into the US bank system in a three-stage process of placement, layering and integration. The money that came out on the other end was clean and ready to spend.

Hitting the Hack House would cost the Syndicate its main source of income, plus cripple its surveillance and intelligence operations.

Kwan lowered his window and rolled slowly down the street past the Syndicate houses. The Sleep House was three stories tall--a narrow building on a narrow lot, with a single car garage at the end of a straight driveway. There was one car in the driveway, and he saw another inside the open garage. Two lights were on in the upper floors, but the lower level was dark.

Before his death, Mr. Cypress had told him the hackers slept all day and worked all night, swilling energy drinks and snorting lines of powdered methamphetamine. But on previous visits, Kwan had always waited for Mr. Cypress and Vlad in the car, so he'd never actually been inside either home.

After the Sleep House came the Hack House, and there were lights on in almost every window. The Hack House looked vaguely Spanish, with a

One Bullet 161

ripple of curved tiles running across the steep roof. There were many windows, but Mr. Cypress had heavy blinds installed so neighbors couldn't see the hackers sitting at their computers all night.

Kwan estimated he faced four to six opponents, but he doubted they were armed, or at least not well armed. Mr. Cypress wouldn't trust them with guns. Sitting at a desk all day meant they'd be soft and fat, unprepared for the mayhem he was about to unleash. Kwan gave a happy growl.

He went to the end of their street, turned and came back up a parallel street. As he drove up the parallel street, he counted houses until he was directly behind the Sleep House. However, the house there was occupied, so he drove until he found an empty house with a 'For Sale' sign in the front yard.

The houses here had garages instead of carports, so he couldn't just pull in. Kwan turned off his headlights and left the Toyota running by the mailbox. He walked up the driveway, and looked in the windows. The house was empty, and a realtor's key box hung from the front door knob.

He went around the side of the house and saw there was no fence. The next door neighbors had a fence, but no 'Beware of Dog' sign. Kwan listened but nothing barked, so he went back to the car and pulled it up the driveway and through the grass until it was hidden behind the house. If cops came down the street, they wouldn't spot it.

Kwan gathered his tools, including the two bangsticks and the bag of ammo, hatchet, spear, two gas cans, a lighter, one pipe bomb and the Surefire flashlight. It was a lot of carry, and he didn't have a pack. He left the Toyota unlocked, but put the keys in his pocket.

He trotted across the wet grass and into a thicket of bushes and scrub pines that hid a deep drainage ditch. The ditch smelled like stale urine and rotting logs. On the way down he slipped and his shoes went into the cold water at the bottom. He yanked his feet back.

Switching on the flashlight was too risky, so he sat on the slope and waited for his eyes to adjust. Kwan caught glimpses of the stars above as rain clouds moved through. When he could see the stars clearly, he looked down in the ditch and spotted what he needed. Further along the ditch was a crude bridge, probably made by neighborhood kids so they could cut across to their friends' houses.

Holding his tools close, Kwan eased across the rickety bridge and crept along the far side of the ditch until he was behind the Sleep House. If the sound suppressor on the one bangstick worked, he could kill whoever was in the Sleep House without alerting the hackers working in the Hack House.

Kwan lay in the bushes at the top of the ditch and surveyed the rear of the Sleep House. There were four points of entry, including a set of French doors, a regular door, a big window, and a small balcony on the second floor if he felt like climbing.

For a moment, he rested his chin on his forearms and thought about Lesser Kwan. He recalled how the two of them ran the streets together as kids, taking on other gangs, always sure he had his brother there to protect his back. Now

One Bullet 163

the two-Kwan army was gone, and he was one man against an entire organization.

He looked away from the house. He could run, flee to South Korea, and--what? There was nothing there. No relatives, no gang, no purpose.

The only thing left was revenge.

He pushed up and ran across the yard to the French doors. A security light above the doors snapped on, flooding the back yard with light, but Kwan was already at the door. He tried the handle, then wedged the blade of the hatchet between the doors and pushed. The doors popped open.

No alarm sounded, and forcing the lock hadn't made much noise, so Kwan went into the unlit room as quietly as possible. It was a bedroom with two narrow beds, two chests of drawers, and the stink of unwashed clothes. And feet. The room actually smelled like feet.

A half open door led to a hallway, but as Kwan crept over the carpet, he heard another door down the hall shut. He raised the bangstick.

* * *

Chapter 31
Hax

"Reduce your speed," The Finn said. "You don't want the police to stop us."

Hax eased off the accelerator and the Mustang coasted down the Hathaway Bridge toward Panama City Beach. He sniffled and rubbed one hand over his ribs. "I think that guy ruptured my spleen when he punched me."

"He's dead now." The Finn leaned back in her seat and closed her eyes. "I'm sure you'll be fine. Wiry fellows like you are always more resilient than they look."

As he drove, Hax cleared his throat. "What did the doctors say about your snake bite?"

"They administered vials of something called CroFab antivenom. This occurred within the recommended six-hour window for treatment, so I should recover without complication." She wiggled the fingers of her left hand. "The physician's assistant told me to 'take it easy for a few days.'" The Finn chuckled.

The young hacker sneaked a glance at the assassin. With her eyes shut and her hair dangling loose and the streetlights playing over her face, she was remote and beautiful and unforgettable. He knew everything would get worse if he chased her, but Hax thought getting killed over this woman might just be worth it.

Then she shifted in the seat and he saw the butt of the pistol she'd stashed in her sling. And he recalled she'd just killed three men without hesitation or apparent remorse. The leather seat of the Mustang felt cold against his neck.

Every ten seconds he checked his rearview mirror to see if the Cartel was following them. But when he veered right onto Back Beach Road, he didn't see any cars filled with gunmen or police.

The Finn opened her eyes and tugged at her seat belt where it crossed her shoulder. "Don't worry. No one is following us or they would have attacked by now."

"I'm not so sure. Maybe they're waiting for us to hit a lonely stretch between here and Fort Walton. Although everything is so built up, there aren't many stretches like that anymore." Hax gripped the wheel and accelerated to five miles per hour over the speed limit.

"Fort Walton? I thought we were returning to Vlad's house?" The Finn asked.

"Are you crazy? No, I mean, I know you're not crazy. I take that back." Hax took a breath. "That Cartel guy at the hospital recognized me from my picture. It looks like it's open season on Syndicate employees. First Mr. Cypress, now Joe, Vlad, me, maybe you. Maybe not you, if you're like, an independent contractor or whatever."

The Finn slipped her arm out of its sling and extended it. Flexed her fingers. "And this is a problem?"

"Yeah, it's a problem. We can't go near Vlad's house. The Cartel may be waiting to ambush us."

166 Mark Boss

She checked the magazine in her pistol and nodded. "I do need ammunition and equipment. Body armor and an assault rifle, at minimum."

Hax put on the defroster and passed a camper with Minnesota plates. "The Cartel knows about the Hack House because they've visited it, but they may not know about the Sleep House next door. If we can get there first, I can grab my laptops, my data backups, and maybe my action figures, then get the hell out of there."

"Where will you go?"

"I don't know. You gotta understand, I'm not like Lulz and Root and the rest of those guys. They're all from eastern Europe. They'll be on the next flight back to Ukraine or St. Petersburg or Wherever-stan. I'm local. I grew up around here and went to school in Pensacola. My cousins live in Cantonment and Shalimar and Port St. Joe. I can't just leave."

When he referred to the other hackers, Hax realized he didn't even know their real names. He only knew them by their online handles.

"Perhaps your cousins will hide you. But you will bring them trouble," The Finn said softly. She shut her eyes again and Hax concentrated on the simple task of steering the car.

* * *

Chapter 32
Root

In the Sleep House, Root shuffled barefoot down the hallway and into the bathroom. He shut the door, turned on the exhaust fan, and sat on the toilet. As he waited for his slow, stubborn bowels to work, Root lit a joint and sat back against the toilet lid. Sucked in a lungful, held it, and blew it out his nose like a fat dragon sitting on a bed of treasure.

The pudgy hacker liked that idea: sitting on a bed of treasure. What he didn't like was Vlad calling him every hour asking if Joe Barrow had used a credit card or made a call on his Syndicate phone or visited an ATM machine for cash.

"Who does he think we are, the freaking NSA?" Root muttered while he rubbed his belly and considered eating more fiber. Lulz ate fruit like a monkey. "I bet he craps like a monkey, too. I'm surprised it doesn't just run down his leg."

It felt like the process was going to take a while, so Root put his headphones on, closed his eyes and tilted his head back.

The bathroom door rattled once in its frame, the same sound it always made when someone opened the French doors to the back yard. Root figured Warez or Brony forgot something over at the Hack House and came back for it. Or Lulz crapped his pants and came back to change. Root laughed and took another drag of sweet weed.

* * *

168   Mark Boss

Greater Kwan

Kwan checked the fit of the sound suppressor on the end of the bangstick, and then slipped down the hall and stood at the closed door. In the dark hallway, a thin strip of light touched the carpet at the bottom of the door, and he listened and heard an exhaust fan running.

The toilet flushed.

Greater Kwan burst through the door.

The air was thick with smoke. A fat man with a mop of brown hair sat on the commode with his pants around his ankles. He wore lime green headphones. The man's mouth opened in surprise and a lit joint fell into his lap.

Kwan shoved the bangstick into the man's forehead. The .44 Magnum bullet drilled into his skull, followed by an expanding wave of gas that blew his brains out through his ears. The man's eyes burst from the sockets, and blood erupted from his mouth. Even with the sound suppressor, in the tile-floored bathroom the gunshot was loud.

The hacker's ruined head drooped onto his chest, and his brains oozed into his beard.

One enemy dead.

Kwan took a cartridge from his pocket and reloaded.

The next door on his left led to the garage, and the right hand door lay open to a small laundry room. A pile of clothes sat on the floor, with an empty banana peel on top. After that was a circular stairway, a tiny foyer and the front door.

One Bullet 169

The big Korean took a second to lock the front door to slow down whoever might respond, and then went up the stairs. The house looked less than ten years old, but the stairs still creaked beneath his weight.

Kwan held a bangstick in each hand, with the flashlight in his pocket and the spear and hatchet tucked in his belt. The second floor had a kitchen, dining room, family room and another bathroom, but no enemies. The heat clicked on and warm air blew from the vent above his head. Sweat trickled down his neck beneath his bandage and he shivered.

The third floor was the master bedroom and a huge bathroom with a deep tub. An empty beer keg sat in the tub, and there were red, plastic Solo cups all over the floor. Like the second floor, the third floor was empty.

Kwan wondered if one of the hackers had heard him and was hiding, but there were few closets and not many places big enough for an adult to hide. He lowered the bangsticks and went downstairs and out the back door.

He started across the yard for one of the gas cans, but paused. Depending on the number of enemies, it could take him several minutes to clear the Hack House. If he lit the Sleep House on fire now, it might burn fast enough for neighbors to notice and call the fire department. So he left the gas cans at the edge of the ditch and went across the yard to the Hack House.

There were fewer options at the rear of the Hack House. Possible entrances included one large window, a set of French doors, and a small balcony on the second floor. A drain pipe ran next to the balcony, but he doubted it would support his weight.

There were lights on all over the Hack House, yet with the blinds closed he couldn't see which rooms were occupied. Kwan wondered again if any of the hackers owned a gun. Then the French doors opened and a skinny kid stepped out, head down and hands cupped as he lit a cigarette.

Kwan dropped the bang sticks and pulled the hatchet as he sprinted forward. Just as the kid got the cigarette lit, Kwan brought the rusty hatchet down like he was serving a tennis ball. The dull blade didn't chop, it smashed.

The kid's knees folded and he fell so fast Kwan almost struck his own leg. He planted one foot on the side of the enemy's head and whacked into his neck. When the head separated from the body, Kwan stepped back, panting.

He retrieved the bangsticks, wiped the hatchet in the grass and went to the French doors. Listened and heard music, probably from upstairs, but no voices. Kwan eased one of the doors open and looked in. Cold air blew out, even colder than the January air outside.

The room was probably meant to be a bedroom, but instead it held a metal rack of computer servers. The servers sat humming loudly, green and red lights blinking, wires trailing in fat bundles that someone had taped to the carpet.

Kwan closed the door behind him and hurried to the open door across the room. On his left he could see all the way down a long hallway to the

One Bullet 171

front door, with three closed doors along the way. To his right was an open door to another bedroom turned office.

In the office, two desktop computers and one laptop sat tangled on a long banquet table. Two widescreen monitors rested on the table, one showing lines of computer code and the other a pornographic movie.

Movement on his left brought Kwan's head around too fast, and the wounds in his throat burned. A hacker in a red hoody sat with a tablet computer in his hands. "Who the hell are you?"

Kwan lunged with the bangstick in his right hand. The hacker blocked with the tablet and the bangstick fired. The bullet punched through the tablet and into the wall.

The kid swung the tablet and knocked the bangstick aside and the loose suppressor fell off. Kwan jabbed with the bangstick in his left hand and shot the kid through the ribs. The hacker fell into his chair and shrieked.

While he dropped the empty bangsticks and grabbed for his hatchet, the kid sprang out of the chair and ran for the door. Kwan couldn't believe the hacker could even stand. He tripped him and drove the hatchet into his skull. The hacker collapsed.

But the shot from the second bangstick had been loud, and Kwan knew he'd lost the advantage of surprise.

As he took two more cartridges from his pocket, he heard footsteps on the stairs.

When he peeked into the hallway, a hacker leaned out from the stairs with a pistol. In the well-lit house, Kwan recognized the square nose of a Glock. He ducked back into the office as the hacker fired a stream of bullets. The bullets hit the door frame and flew right through the drywall.

Kwan lay flat on the floor until the shooter paused, then bounded up and into the hall. He ducked into a laundry room, and got down behind a clothes washer as the next burst of bullets flew. The hacker yelled something, but Kwan couldn't hear with all the noise. He took a moment to load both bangsticks, and waited.

The gunfire stopped. He hadn't counted the shots, but even with a full-sized Glock 9mm, the hacker could only fire 17 rounds before reloading. Kwan poked his head out and a bullet took off his left earlobe.

He jerked back, and clapped a hand to his stinging ear. Blood spilled down onto his shoulder.

The bangsticks only worked at contact range. Same for the hatchet. His enemy had a superior weapon and a better position, and Kwan knew he needed a new tactic. He pulled the pipe bomb from his back pocket.

His brother had made the bomb from a section of metal pipe crammed with black powder and nails, and rigged with hobby fuse. Kwan shook his cheap, plastic lighter and lit the fuse.

The fuse didn't catch fire.

Bullets punched through the drywall above his head. Kwan tried again and the fuse lit. He watched the fuse burn down, and wondered if the

One Bullet 173

metal washing machine he hid behind would protect him from the shrapnel.

When the flame was just short of the pipe, he threw the bomb down the hall, then crouched behind the washer and covered his ears.

The pipe bomb hit the front door below the stairwell and exploded. A wave of overpressure rolled outward in all directions. Roofing nails and chunks of pipe blasted into the stairwell and the hacker screeched. Kwan didn't wait for the smoke to clear. His ears rang as he ran down the hall and jumped onto the stairs.

The hacker lay on his back. His face was shredded. Kwan couldn't see the gun and wondered where it went. As Kwan stepped over him, the hacker's legs moved. He shoved a bangstick into the hacker's chest and fired. The hacker jerked once.

Kwan went up the stairs with the other bangstick ready. He heard glass break and something heavy hit the floor, so he charged up the last steps. At the top step, he looked across the hall into a bedroom. A chair lay sideways on the floor and a short hacker knocked out the glass along the bottom of the window with his shoe.

The hacker saw Kwan and launched himself out the window. Kwan heard a thump, rushed forward and looked out.

The short hacker rolled off the roof of the car in the driveway and ran down the street, screaming, "Call the cops, call the cops!"

It was time to leave.

174 Mark Boss

Kwan held his lighter to the curtains. As soon as they caught fire, he went down the stairs and out the French doors. When he reached the back yard and saw the dead hacker who'd gone outside for a cigarette, Kwan stopped.

He slipped the spear from his belt, took it in both hands and drove it into the hacker's chest so it stood upright. Kwan looked down at the spear and nodded.

Message sent.

* * *

Hax

Hax left the radio off and perhaps The Finn slept, and soon they climbed the steep bridge into Fort Walton and turned east toward the bay. When he reached his neighborhood, his shoulders sagged and Hax smiled. Root and Lulz were dicks, but Phishbait wasn't too bad and he was pretty good friends with Brony and Warez. He figured living in the Sleep House was like rooming in a fraternity house at a small college.

All things considered, he'd probably miss it.

A police car blew past him, lights flashing, and going way too fast on a residential street. The Finn opened her eyes and sat up. Hax turned onto his street.

There were cars parked in the middle of the road. Neighbors stood on the sidewalk under the street light, pointing. The Hack House was on fire. Two fire trucks were already there, but the house was fully engulfed and black smoke and flame belched from its windows. Next door at the Sleep

House, paramedics rolled a gurney down the driveway toward their ambulance. A white sheet covered the body on the gurney, and Hax couldn't see who it was.

Hax stopped the car and gaped.

"You have serious enemies," The Finn said.

* * *

Chapter 33
Vlad

After Ernesto left his house, the first thing Vlad did was reload his H&K 9mm pistol. Then he loaded a Benelli tactical shotgun and stood it inside the shower in the bathroom. Last, he stripped off his clothes and shoes, wadded them up and put them in the fireplace in the living room.

He crouched and stacked three pieces of dried wood in the grate with the clothes. A metal pail of pinecones sat next to the hearth, and he lit one and used it to get the fire going. As he pushed his shoes and belt into the rising flames, he felt a cold nose on his bare back.

Vlad turned and Amber nuzzled against him. The mastiff's eyes were still glassy from the tranquilizers, but when he patted her flanks, she was steady on her paws. Genghis trotted past them, through the open glass door and out into the grass.

"Come, Amber," Vlad said, and led her to the door. Genghis stood at the back fence, urinating. Amber gave him a shoulder bump as she jogged by, and then went about her own business. Vlad watched the two mastiffs, and then slid the glass door shut.

He got halfway down the hall to the shower before he stopped. The Cartel had drugged the dogs while they were outside in the back yard, and entered his house unopposed. Leaving the dogs outside again was foolish. Vlad went back to the door, whistled for the dogs and brought them both

One Bullet   177

inside. He left Amber at the back door, watching the fire, and put Genghis at the front door.

In the shower, he used a bar of Lava soap to wash Lesser Kwan's dried blood off. As he lathered up a second time, Vlad thought he heard voices in the bedroom. He turned off the tap, grabbed the shotgun and looked out, but no one was there.

He crept to the foyer, leaving a trail of wet footprints, but it was empty except for Genghis. The big dog sprawled by the front door and chewed one of Lacey's sandals, and then looked up at him.

"Good dog. Keep watch," Vlad said, and headed back to the shower. When he finally dried off and dressed, he was starving. He went to the kitchen and put a bowl of leftover beef stroganoff in the microwave. While he watched the bowl rotate inside the microwave, Vlad turned the small TV on the counter to the local news.

Two thick-necked men in green uniforms stood side-by-side at a press conference. Vlad listened as the sheriff of Bay County described a furious gun battle between his investigator and unknown gang members at Bay Medical Center. Then the sheriff of Santa Rosa County stepped forward to discuss a case of murder and arson at two houses in Fort Walton. The sheriffs seemed to think the cases were related, but they were vague on details.

After the clip from the press conference, the news ran footage of a house in Fort Walton in flames. Vlad stared. The burning home was the Syndicate's Hack House. Next, the news ran a distant shot of the Sleep House while EMTs brought out a body on a gurney.

178 Mark Boss

The microwave dinged and Vlad flinched.

He stood at the counter and mechanically shoveled the stroganoff into his mouth, but he didn't taste it. Amber wandered into the kitchen and poked her nose into the back of his knee. Vlad set the bowl on the floor and muted the TV.

His phone sat on the counter. Who to call first? Call the rest of the Syndicate and warn them that...what? Greater Kwan might have attacked the Hack House, or maybe the Cartel did, or hell, maybe Joe Barrow and Carly? But no, Hax said he saw Joe and Carly at the hospital.

Vlad drank a bottle of water and switched channels. The second station had coverage of the same news conference, shot from a slightly different angle. There was talk of FBI or DEA involvement, the possibility of a joint task force among the counties, and speculation that the Mexican drug wars had spilled into the streets of northwest Florida.

He snatched up his phone and called Ernesto.

The Cartel lieutenant answered on the first ring. "Hola, Vladimir. What can I do for your Syndicate this evening?"

Vlad caught the 'your' and couldn't help but smile. Cypress was dead, and the Syndicate was his to command, but his first day as the new boss wasn't going well. "I saw the news about the fight at the hospital. One of my men said they spotted your gunmen there."

"Really?" Ernesto asked. "Did your lookout also mention seeing Joe Barrow and his chica...ah,

One Bullet 179

what is her name? A buxom woman, with generous hindquarters, like a racehorse."

"Carly," Vlad said. "Yes, he saw them." Vlad felt his pulse beating in his temples, and he pictured different ways he'd like to kill Ernesto. Most of the ways were slow and involved a great deal of screaming. "What are you doing?"

Ernesto took a sip of something, and then cleared his throat. "We search for our money, just as I told you we would. Calm Ruben has ordered it found, so it will be found."

Vlad hated Ernesto's reasonable tone. "Your gunmen shot at a Sheriff's investigator in a hospital. The news said a nurse died, and a patient was found murdered in his bed." Vlad watched Amber lick his dinner bowl clean and tried to keep from shouting. "You woke the police. Between you and Joe and crazy Kwan, you've left a trail of bodies from Fort Walton to Panama City. Are you insane?"

"I don't appreciate that," Ernesto said. "I am a simple servant, following Calm Ruben's orders to my best ability. But when you disrespect me, you disrespect the Cartel." He stopped and let that statement hang.

Vlad squeezed the tablespoon in his hand. He slid his thumb into the bowl of the spoon and bent the entire thing in half. "There are cameras around hospitals. People with phones may have photographed your men."

"My men?" Ernesto laughed. "These are not Cartel members. These 'gunmen' as you term them are fresh from the back of a stinking truck, with the soil of Mexico still on their boots. They are 'illegals.' Throwaways. They are not in any law enforcement database. If they are captured, they know nothing. If they are killed, we replace them."

The Cartel lieutenant chuckled again. "Vladimir, you Europeans always think Mexicans are fools. I assure you we are not. Instead of calling to berate me, you could have called to share intelligence and help us recover what is ours."

Vlad examined the bent spoon in his hand. He wondered if telling Ernesto how he'd like to scoop his eyes out would help. "You should not have involved the police. We could have handled this quietly."

"I'll express your concerns to Calm Ruben," Ernesto said. "He's outside, soaking in the hot tub with your friend Lacey. They appear to be getting along very well."

Vlad walked out of the kitchen and stared at Genghis snoring by the front door. He'd seen Lacey's sandal when he first entered the house, but thought nothing of it because she never picked up her things. Now the Cartel had her.

"If you find our money, be sure to call us before dinner time tomorrow," Ernesto said, and then hung up. Vlad set his phone down on the counter. He flicked one corner of the phone and watched it spin on the smooth marble until it pointed back at him.

Then Genghis growled, and the doorbell rang.

* * *

Chapter 34
Carly

The traffic light where Highway 231 crossed Martin Luther King Boulevard turned red, and Carly stopped her stolen Ford. She reached down and pulled the lever to scoot the seat forward, and then lit a cigarette.

Across the street at a shopping mall, a small, white security truck drove a slow loop around the building.

Carly's hands shook.

While she waited for the light to turn green, she tilted the rearview mirror to check her makeup. But when she caught sight of her eyes, she looked away.

Joe was probably dead, shot down by the Cartel. Dwayne was very dead. Hell, the wounded nurse she'd passed in the hallway was probably dead, too. Carly thought about a movie she'd seen where a girl woke up and the city was empty and everyone had disappeared.

The light turned green, and she drove north toward the city of Lynn Haven. If everything went right, in 45 minutes she could reach the airport. Carly laughed. If everything went right. She tried to remember the last time anything went right, but it seemed like everything had gone wrong since she had her first period.

Wrong and more wrong. No matter what she did. Until she saw an opportunity to break free, to get away from all the cavemen in her life and live how she wanted. If Joe hadn't woke up in the airport and taken the money back from Dwayne. If Dwayne hadn't betrayed her with a bag of counterfeit money. If....

Carly stopped at the intersection with Highway 390. An old pickup truck sat up high on knobby tires in front of her. Beneath the red glow of the traffic light, Carly saw the silhouette of two heads in the truck. The driver wore a baseball cap. A girl sat beside him, not on the passenger's side, but in the middle of the bench. She tilted her head and rested it on the boy's shoulder.

Carly squeezed the steering wheel as hard as she could, but the tears started anyway. She thought of her childhood a thousand years ago. Thought of her father, who always smelled like sawdust, and who always kept her safe...until he left, and her mother started bringing home a new boyfriend every week. Most of them were losers. A few of them didn't care that Carly was underage.

After that, there were always men in her life. Some with money, some with muscles, all with problems. Like Joe, who trusted too much and thought he could solve everything with his fists. Or Dwayne, who talked big and lived fast, but betrayed her and screwed up the best deal he'd ever see in his short life.

She watched the couple in the pickup truck drive away and Carly threw her cigarette butt out of the window into the cold air. Dabbed her eyes, bit her lip and drove north.

North to get her money.

* * *

One Bullet   183

After that, Carly drove without really reading the road signs or seeing the other cars. But she watched for cops, and saw a lot of them. Far more than usual for the area. Up through Lynn Haven, across the bridge at North Bay, and a left turn took her west toward the airport.

She'd stolen the rental car from Pono, but the Ford subcompact wasn't the type of car anyone would notice, and the farther she got away from the hospital the less she worried about it. She had more important things to worry about.

The pine trees formed a dark wall on both sides of the narrow, two-lane road, and she drove with the high beams on and the windows cracked so the January air swirled around her face and kept her alert. She knew the damp air would wreck her hair, but she had to feel the wind or the small car would close around her like a coffin.

She spotted the sign for the airport and slowed for the access road. When she thought about all that had happened, it seemed impossible that she'd been at the airport with Joe just that morning.

She passed the long-term parking lot and cut her speed even more. Thanks to the damn terrorists, there were always cops at airports, bored and looking for someone to arrest. The short-term parking area was half-full, and people wheeled their suitcases down the long sidewalk toward the terminal.

As she cruised the row nearest to the terminal, Carly wondered what to do with the gun in her lap. She could wipe her prints off it and leave it in the car, but when the cops found the stolen Ford, they'd match the gun to Dwayne's murder. Still, she'd be long gone. Or she could dump it in one of the trash bins on the way inside. Maybe no one would find it.

Carly saw a minivan up ahead back out of a good parking spot. While she waited to take the spot, she looked down the row. A tricked out Honda sat nose out, with two men inside. The passenger lit a cigarette, and in the two-second glow of the lighter she saw a young man with a goatee and tattoos on his throat.

The minivan drove away. Instead of pulling into the empty spot, Carly slumped down in the seat and rolled past the two men in the Honda.

Maybe they were Cartel, or maybe they were just two rough-looking guys waiting to pick up a friend. But she was too close to the money now to be reckless. Carly reached into her purse, pulled out the airport locker key, and put it in her pocket. She tucked the pistol under her shirt, in front where she could reach it easily.

When she turned to go around to the next parking row, she saw the taxicabs and hotel shuttles waiting in a wide lane right outside the terminal doors. There were also a few civilian cars pulling up to let people pop out and dash inside.

She realized the Ford she drove was rented to Pono, so it had no connection to her. Instead of parking, she could drive right up to the terminal and leave the car with the keys in it. Drop the gun in a trash bin on the way inside, then go to the counter and buy a plane ticket. Pass through security, stop

One Bullet   185

at the lockers to grab the bag of cash, then down the hall to catch her flight.

When the airport cops found the Ford, they'd page the owner to move it, or move it themselves. Either way, it'd keep them busy for a while.

Carly smiled. It was a good plan. Maybe she'd learned a few things from Joe, after all.

She slowed down and unbuckled her seat belt. It'd be great to smoke one more cigarette before she went inside, but if the guys in the Honda were Cartel, she couldn't risk it.

She pulled into the drop-off lane across from the taxis and stopped the car.

The sliding glass doors to the terminal opened and Fergus walked out with two bottles of Coke in one hand and a bag of burgers in the other.

Carly stared at the Syndicate soldier. Fergus had sat many-a-night at the bar in Vlad's restaurant where she worked. But seeing him here was wrong. Like finding one of her own dresses at a yard sale.

Fergus walked toward her car, the white, paper bag swinging from his hand.

Carly tipped her head down so her hair fell across her face. She gripped the gun in her lap. Her right foot pressed the brake to the floor.

Fergus stopped.

He tucked the Cokes under his arm, reached into his pocket and pulled out a phone. Squinted at the screen, then put the phone to his ear and listened.

Carly let go of the gun, put her right hand up to cover her face and let off the brake. The car rolled forward.

Ahead on her left, a woman pushed a baby stroller toward the crosswalk. A man holding a toddler by the hand walked a step behind her. The toddler took tiny steps.

An airport cop walked between the shuttle vans, talking to a taxi driver. The cop had his thumbs hooked on his gun belt.

Carly gripped the wheel.

Fergus looked up from his phone and saw the cop.

The cop on her left, Fergus on her right, and Carly trapped in between.

The mom pushed the baby stroller down the smooth ramp into the crosswalk. Carly accelerated. She swerved to the right and went around the family before they could block her escape.

She looked in the rearview mirror, but Fergus wasn't watching her. He was talking into his phone and walking away from the cop, toward the parking lot.

The Cartel, the Syndicate, the cops. There was no way she'd make it inside the airport. She hammered the passenger seat with her fist. "Shit, shit, shit. I'm this close. I'm this fucking close," she screamed in the empty car.

She pulled off the access road into the entrance for long-term parking, and stopped. It took her three tries to light a cigarette, but finally she inhaled, sat back in the seat and waited for the shaking to stop.

Carly realized she was on her own against two criminal gangs and the big, blue gang of cops. She knew what she needed--a man. Because there was

One Bullet 187

always a man. A hard man like Joe, or Dwayne. Someone she could control. Use.

She smoked the cigarette slowly, and touched the cold, steel frame of the gun nestled between her thighs. Who could protect her from the Cartel and the Syndicate? Who was strong enough to help her get the money?

"Vlad." She heard herself say it and almost dropped the cigarette. It was crazy, but it made sense. She'd been with Vlad plenty when she first started hostessing at his restaurant, and even a few times after she began dating Joe. Vlad was strong, and more vicious than Joe. He could call off the Syndicate, fight off the Cartel, and pay off the cops.

Vlad didn't trust her, but he would help her because he wanted the money, too.

Carly ran her fingers through her hair. She'd have to stop on the way to Vlad's house and fix her makeup.

* * *

Chapter 35
Vlad

Vlad heard Genghis growl, and the doorbell rang.

Someone knocked on the door, three hard raps, and said, "Bay County Sheriff's Office."

"Genghis, sit. Quiet." He touched the mastiff's nose and the big dog hushed. In Russia, assassins often dressed as police to get close to their target. "Just a moment," he called. Vlad tucked his pistol beside his spine and pulled his shirttail out over it.

He bent to look through the peephole in the front door.

Two burly men stood side by side, both wearing shirt and tie beneath a windbreaker. They looked like cops, and the Southern accent was difficult to fake, so Vlad opened the door.

Genghis growled and the two men stepped back.

The one on the left, with a graying goatee, spoke. "Are you Vladimir Turgenev?"

"Yes."

"Do you own a silver Lexus?" Goatee held a small notebook, but rattled off the license plate number without looking down at the book.

"Da, that's my car," Vlad said. "One of my cars." He meant to say 'yes,' but Vlad knew when he was stressed his accent got heavier and his English got worse.

The younger investigator on the right snickered at Vlad's accent. Goatee glared at him, then

One Bullet 189

continued. "Sir, could you put your dogs away so we can come in?"

Something brushed his knee and Vlad glanced down. Amber stood next to him, showing her teeth. Genghis stood on his other side.

Vlad rested his fingertip on Genghis's nose and said, "Sit." Amber sat, too. Then he stepped out into the cold, night air and pulled the door shut behind him. "Is nice night. Let's talk out here." He spread his hands.

"Okay, we are investigating a murder," Goatee said. He squinted under the yellow porch light. "Found your Lexus at an auto shop over in Santa Rosa. There must have been a heckuva fight. Several victims present, bunch a shell casings, even a durn machete. You know anything about that?"

Vlad knew enough not to look away from the investigator, or to hesitate too long in answering. If he told them Joe Barrow borrowed his car, that might put the cops on Joe's trail. But it would also open up a whole new line of questions about who Joe was and what he was doing with Vlad's car.

"My Lexus burns the oil too fast, so I took it to Fred's Garage for repairs. What happened?" Vlad asked.

"Guess you haven't seen the news," Goatee said. "Was Fred a friend of yours?"

"No."

"Hmm. Well, he's dead. Both his mechanics, too, along with some other fellahs we're still identifying. So far, every one of them has turned up in our database. We figure a drug deal gone wrong, but we're contacting the owners of each car we found on the premises."

"Okay." Vlad nodded. "When can I get my car back?"

Goatee stared at him for a long moment, and then shrugged. "I'm not sure. It's an active crime scene." The other investigator was already half way to the car. Goatee took a business card from his shirt pocket. "If you think of anything that might help us, please call."

The investigator stepped back and Vlad reached for the doorknob.

Goatee paused, and his gray eyebrows rose and met on his forehead. "Say, I almost forgot. One of our techs mentioned you have a sizeable dent in the front end of that Lexus. Possible blood stains on the front bumper. Airbag deployed, too. You run into anybody lately?"

Vlad blinked. "No. Perhaps the mechanic took it for a test drive and struck a wild animal."

"Yeah. Perhaps." Goatee waved. "We'll be talking with you, Mr. Turgenev."

Vlad watched the investigator walk to his car, and memorized his gait and the set of his shoulders, and the sound of his voice. When the unmarked Dodge Charger pulled out of his driveway, Vlad went back inside.

Amber and Genghis still sat in the foyer, watching the front door.

The mastiffs followed him into the kitchen, where he drank a can of cold coffee from the refrigerator. He went into the bedroom and took off

One Bullet 191

his shirt so he could drop a ballistic vest over his head and secure the Velcro tabs.

He still had Lesser Kwan's H&K pistol, but he wasn't sure where the Kwans had acquired the gun, and he didn't have spare magazines for it. Still, he could use it and then toss it away if necessary.

Vlad clipped a holstered Sig Sauer .45 to his belt and slid a lightweight snub-nosed .38 Special revolver into his pocket. Took two extra magazines for the Sig Sauer, plus the small bag of $20,000 in cash he'd taken from Cypress that afternoon. Last, he went into the closet and pushed a loose piece of drywall away from the ceiling. He reached up between the beams and lifted down a Kalashnikov AK-74 with a folding stock, and four spare magazines.

In the living room, Vlad sat with one of his phones and sent text messages to his half dozen Syndicate soldiers. He ordered Simon and Lars to watch Carly's apartment, and Jorg and Manila Tommy to Joe's apartment. Hax had seen Joe and Carly at Bay Medical Center in Panama City, so the two were obviously still in the area.

He wondered why.

If Joe and Carly had the Cartel money, why weren't they on a plane to Fiji?

He picked up the phone and texted Fergus and Arturo to see if they'd seen Joe or Carly out at the airport. A minute later, Fergus replied, "nothing yeti." Vlad assumed Fergus meant 'yet.'

What kept Joe Barrow here?

The longer Joe lived, the better chance he'd have to tell his story to other Syndicate members,

192   Mark Boss

and Vlad's lies about who killed Mr. Cypress would unravel.

When they'd talked on the phone, maybe Joe had told him the truth about the ambush at the airport, but not about recovering the money. Joe said he took out the attacker and recovered the bag of Cartel money and the password envelope, but maybe he hadn't.

While he considered this, Vlad methodically loaded magazines for his AK, pushing the stack of cartridges down with his thumb and sliding the smooth brass shells in one at a time. The activity was familiar, and soothing.

The Cartel deadline was dinnertime tomorrow. If he didn't return their money, they would come for him. He wondered if the Cartel had started early by grabbing Hax at the hospital. Or if the Cartel, not Greater Kwan, had attacked the Hack House and the Sleep House in Fort Walton.

He could run. Abandon the organization he had helped Cypress build and crawl back to Russia. But it wasn't safe there, either. Powerful mobsters in St. Petersburg had ordered a hit on his younger brother, Alexander, because he served in a special army unit tasked with rooting out organized crime. Vlad used the $700,000.00 he stole from the overseas account to pay off the mobsters and keep his brother safe.

So now he had no way to pay off the Cartel, unless he found Joe and the missing bag of money.

He gave Amber's neck a squeeze, and carried his weapons to the garage. Vlad wrapped one of Lacey's beach towels around the AK and put it in

One Bullet 193

the back of his Porsche Cayenne SUV. The handguns tugged on his pants as he got into the Porsche, and it was hard to buckle the seat belt around them, but the weight felt good.

As he waited for the garage door to rise, Vlad revved the Porsche. He wasn't going to run. Not after he'd worked so hard to build the Syndicate, and risked his life to seize control of it. No way.

* * *

Chapter 36
Carly

On her way from the airport to Vlad's house in Panama City Beach, Carly stopped at a Circle K minimart. The stolen Ford still had half a tank of gas, so she pulled past the pumps and parked in front of the door.

When she opened the door, the kid at the counter barely looked up from his phone, but as she walked by, he smiled and said, "How's it going?"

"Restroom?" she asked without breaking stride.

"Back left," the kid called out, but she was already walking down the aisle.

The women's restroom was relatively clean, and it didn't stink, but the light above the mirror flickered so much she had to look away from it.

She locked the door, put her purse on top of the paper dispenser, took out her makeup bag and faced the mirror. The wind and rain had wrecked her hair, but she started there anyway. After she dealt with the tangles, she washed tiny, black flecks the size of crushed pepper from her cheeks and hands--gunshot residue from shooting Dwayne dead. Then she worked on her face, going top to bottom to fix her eyes, cheeks, and lips.

As she remade herself in the shaky, yellow light of the tiny bathroom, Carly wondered how everything had gotten so screwed up. But putting on her makeup was like putting the pillow over Dwayne's face before she shot him. You did what you had to do, and you moved on.

One Bullet 195

She finished applying lipstick, winked at herself in the mirror, and unlocked the door.

Carly put her purse over her shoulder, and tucked her right hand inside to grip the gun. The last time she'd walked out of a minimart bathroom, Joe was stomping two idiot robbers to death.

The kid at the counter stroked his patchy goatee. "You thirsty? Need a pack of smokes?"

She scanned the store but there were no other customers, or robbers, or Cartel hit men. And she was thirsty. Carly pulled a bottle of Diet Coke and a bottle of water from the cold case and plunked them down on the counter with a five-dollar bill.

"You been out clubbing?" the kid asked.

She pictured Joe beating one of the robbers senseless with his own shotgun and smiled. "Yeah. Clubbing."

In the reflection from the glass door, she watched him watch her as she walked out. She gave him a little wiggle, and smiled. Men. They were all so simple.

With her face fixed and a cold bottle of Coke, she felt better than she had all day. Carly drove through the deserted streets of wintertime Panama City Beach until she reached Vlad's house. The lights were off, the garage door was shut, and there were no vehicles in the driveway. No way to tell if Vlad was home or not.

She rolled past the house, turned onto the next block, and backed the stolen Ford into an empty driveway. Carly put both bottles in her purse, looked around the car to make sure she had not left anything, and then walked back to Vlad's house.

There were no suspicious cars on the street. No Cartel gunmen with machine guns. Just a quiet, upper-middle class neighborhood with big houses on small lots, brick mailboxes, and half-grown Sago palm trees.

She dug in her purse for the key to Vlad's house and realized she'd kept the keys to the Ford. When she started at his restaurant, Vlad gave her the house key so she could bring the bank deposit bag by the house each night. Vlad counted the money from the restaurant, and always took a cut for himself.

Carly knocked on the door and heard the dogs bark from the back yard. If Vlad was home, the dogs would have been inside with him, so she knew he wasn't there. She used the key, went into the dim foyer and tripped over a sandal.

She flipped on the foyer light and picked up the sandal. It was a size smaller than hers, and probably belonged to the latest girl in Vlad's endless parade. She'd marched in that parade for a while, until she met Joe.

The dogs kept barking, so she went through the house with her hand on her gun, all the way to the sliding glass door to the back yard. Before she opened the door, she called, "Genghis, Amber, hush. Come inside." Then she opened it.

Amber gave her a sniff as she ran past, but Genghis shoved his head into her stomach until she petted him. The mastiff rolled over on his back so she could scratch his belly. "That's it. Just like a man. I touch you and you're helpless," Carly said to the dog.

One Bullet

She heard Amber in the kitchen, crunching dry dog food. In the months she'd dated Vlad, Amber tolerated her but never took to her. When Genghis finally got curious enough to go see what Amber was eating, Carly switched on a few lights and went into Vlad's bedroom.

There was a lip gloss and a Bic lighter on top of an issue of "Cosmopolitan" on the nightstand. More sandals on the floor, and one pair of running shoes that looked like they'd never been run in. A slinky, black dress, Size 0, hung over the headboard. Two toothbrushes in the bathroom, and long, blonde hair in the sink. She wondered how long the latest girl had been around. The skinny bitch was obviously a pig.

Which reminded her that her own clothes were disgusting, and that she needed a shower, or better yet, a bath.

She dropped her purse on the bed, and took off her shoes, but kept the gun. Carly went down the hall, through the living room, where Amber and Genghis sat by Vlad's recliner.

"Come on, you just ate. Time to go out," she said to the dogs. Amber hesitated, but when Genghis went to the glass door, she followed. Carly let them out to do their business, and locked the door behind them.

She went into the washroom, and set the washer for a small load on the delicate cycle. Carly stripped off all of her clothes, and dropped them one at a time into the water.

With the roar of water filling the washer, she didn't hear the dogs bark, or the garage door open. * * *

Chapter 37
Hax

Hax and The Finn sat in his Mustang and watched the Hack House burn. While firefighters carried bodies from the burning house, the fire crept across a tree and onto the roof of the Sleep House next door.

"This is bad. This is very bad," Hax muttered. The smell of smoke drifted in through the air conditioning vents, and he switched the climate control to 'recirculate.' "They keep hauling out dead people. Have you seen anyone come out alive?"

"No. All corpses," The Finn said. "I suppose your action figures will melt."

"Uh. Yeah. Extreme heat. Plastic. Yes, my collection will melt. Who cares? Some of those guys were my friends. Lulz and Root were jerks, they put my inhaler in the microwave. But Phishbait was just kinda weird, he wasn't an ass or anything. Warez and Brony are my friends. They grew up in Eastern Europe, but we had a lot in common. One time, we went to this hacker conference in--"

"Sir, we need you to move your car."

Hax turned and saw a cop approach on foot, holding a long-handled flashlight. Hax rolled down his window. Smoke rolled in, and the air was hot.

"Sir, you have to move this car off the street. We have more emergency vehicles on the way," the cop said.

"Okay, no problem." Hax glanced at The Finn and saw she had one hand inside her jacket, and he knew she was holding a gun. "Be cool," he said, and then started to cough.

He took the Mustang through a tight U-turn and went up the street to the stop sign. The Finn watched the cop in the side mirror. Hax drove south toward the Brooks Bridge. The cold January air blew the smoke from the car, and he took slow, deep breaths to clean his lungs. "So, what's the plan?"

The Finn unbuckled her seat belt and at least two different, equally unlikely fantasies shot through Hax's head.

She knelt and reached into the back seat for the guitar case she'd captured from the gunmen at the hospital.

Hax stared at her rear end until the Mustang hit a pothole and his eyes jumped back to the road.

The Finn laid the guitar case along her lap and his, and popped the clasp on her side of the case. "First rule of survival is to take stock of your equipment."

"Okay..." Hax looked down as her left hand trailed across his lap to find the clasp on his end of the guitar case.

"Mind the road," she said.

"Right. Driving the car. Moving east at 45 miles per hour." Hax tried to focus while she lifted a variety of weapons from the guitar case. "Their band must have played some rough bars." He laughed, but it came out high-pitched, almost hysterical.

The Finn held a giant pistol with a suppressor the size of a can of Red Bull. "Are you well?"

"Sure. I am dandy. You're the one with the snakebite. How are you? Because my workplace just burned down, and my house is burning right now and my friends are dead and my computers are slagged and the action figures I've collected for the last 14 years are melting and a drug Cartel is trying to kill me and..." Hax gasped for air. The Mustang swerved and The Finn grabbed the steering wheel. He let off the gas and she maneuvered them into the parking lot of a CVS drug store that was closed for the night.

He put his head on the steering wheel and shut his eyes and breathed. "All my money was in that house. What am I gonna do?"

"You kept your money in your house?" The Finn asked.

"Yeah, I hid it in a hollowed-out hard drive."

"Why didn't you keep it in a bank like everyone else?"

"A bank?" Hax lifted his head from the wheel. "I'm not putting my money in a bank. Banks get hacked."

He stopped. The Finn smiled. They laughed.

The Finn flipped the lid of the guitar case shut and Hax stopped laughing. She sat back in her seat and said, "We must return to Vlad's house. He owes me the remaining fifty percent of my fee for Cypress."

"He owes me my paycheck for this month. It'll be all the money I have." Hax touched the top of

One Bullet 201

the guitar case, his hand near hers. "What if the Cartel is there?"

She squeezed his hand. "We will be cautious. Besides, now we have equipment. You drive, and I will check the weapons."

"Okay."

They drove east, back through Destin and San Destin, and past the turn for the string of small beach communities along State Road 30A. It was late and traffic was light, but Hax saw three Highway Patrol troopers and two Sheriff's Office cars on the way. He kept his speed just below the posted limited, and finally they left the highway and cruised through the side streets of Vlad's neighborhood.

When he slowed to turn onto Vlad's street, The Finn touched his arm. "No, keep going. The next block."

He took them around the block and stopped so they could look between the houses at Vlad's back yard. There were a few lights on in Vlad's house, but they couldn't see anyone. "You think he's home?" Hax asked.

"The garage is shut, so we can't see if his car is there. We could call him, but the Cartel or the authorities may be monitoring his phone." She lifted the big SOCOM .45 from the guitar case and checked the magazine and the fit of the suppressor. "Leave the car here, and we'll go through the back yard."

"No. He has dogs. Big, scary dogs that look like bears. We can't go through the back yard." He looked at the dark houses around them. "This is a decent neighborhood, but I hate to leave my car on the street. Let's park in the garage and go in through the door there."

The Finn tilted her head. "How?"

Hax held up his smartphone. "I have hacks." He drove slowly back to Vlad's house and stopped in the driveway. Then he went through his phone for the right app. Pointed the phone at the garage door and smiled. "Check this out."

The garage door didn't move.

The Finn blinked. "Should I get out and push?"

He poked the phone and aimed it again. "There are a lot of different models of garage door openers, so sometimes it takes a few tries. Wait, did you just make a Star Wars reference?"

The garage door rumbled and rose.

The Finn slipped out of the car. "I will check before you pull in." She held the SOCOM in both hands, and her head swiveled to survey the street and yard.

As she crept up the driveway, Hax's phone rattled. He wasn't sure if the phone was supposed to rattle after the hack app successfully opened a garage door. Hax held it up in the dark car and read the screen.

The call was from Brony.

Brony is dead, Hax told himself. He was at the Hack House, or maybe the Sleep House, but either way, he's dead. He wondered if the call was a trick, but then shrugged and answered. "Hello?"

"Dude, can you talk? Have they found you?" Brony asked.

One Bullet 203

Hax sat up in the seat. "You're alive? I saw the Hack House on fire, and maybe the Sleep--"

"Yeah, that burned, too," Brony said. "Listen, the Syndicate is at war. One of the Kwan Brothers, I'm not sure which one, attacked us and killed everyone and he tried to kill me but I jumped out a window and landed on Lulz's car like in a movie and..." Brony stopped and took a breath. "I'm leaving the country. I'm on my way to Atlanta to get a flight."

"Going where?" Hax remembered Brony was from Romania or Bulgaria or one of those Dracula countries.

"I have friends in Copenhagen. They operate a dairy farm. I'm going off the grid. Going to milk cows, smoke weed, and stay the hell away from computers."

Hax looked up. The Finn stood in the garage, and waved him forward.

He looked away from her. "That sounds like a good plan," he said to Brony.

"Dude, why don't you come with me? No one will find us on a farm. On weekends we can go into the city and chase femmes and drink beer."

Hax stared at The Finn, a small woman holding a big gun. What if he did run? His hand was on the gearshift. He could hit 'Reverse,' floor the gas pedal and be gone in five seconds. Would she shoot him?

But all his money burned in the Sleep House. He needed Vlad to pay him his final month's salary. And his family and friends were here. But... And... Hax shook his head. The Finn tilted her head and looked at him. She held the gun down by her side.

Did she need his help? No. Did he want to help her? Yes. Hax didn't give a damn about Vlad or the Syndicate, but there was something about this cold, young woman. "Brony? Yeah. Good luck, man. I mean it. I hope it all works out. If I'm not dead or in jail, I'll come visit you some day." Hax hung up.

The two-car garage was empty, but he parked the Mustang close to the wall in case Vlad came roaring in with his Porsche Cayenne. The Finn darted past the car and hit the switch on the wall to lower the garage door.

Hax watched in the rearview mirror as the door rolled down behind him. That was it. The door shut, and he was committed. There'd be no running away now.

When he turned off the car, he heard dogs barking in the back yard.

He got out and followed The Finn to the door leading into the house. "I don't think my smartphone will open this one."

She turned the handle. "Don't worry. It isn't locked." She crouched and went inside, and Hax bent his long legs and tried to mimic her commando style.

The dogs continued to bark, but a dim, green glow on the wall caught his attention. He trotted to the alarm unit and stared at the small screen and keypad. "The alarm isn't set. We're cool."

"Shhh." The Finn held one finger to her lips. "I hear something."

Hax knelt next to her and listened. "Sounds like a washing machine."

One Bullet

205

She nodded and went down the hall. Hax watched her for a moment, mesmerized, and then went after her.

The light was on in the utility room. He heard water filling the washing machine, then it stopped, and the noise changed as the machine began its wash cycle.

The Finn stepped into the utility room, moving fast, gun raised. Hax poked his head around the corner.

Carly stood at the washing machine, staring into the swirling water.

When she saw The Finn, Carly snatched a gun off the dryer.

Hax wanted to pull his head back out of the path of the gun, but he couldn't. Carly was naked. Completely, gorgeously naked.

His eyes roamed over her lush body. "Oh. My. Goddess," Hax said.

Both the women said, "What?" at the same time.

Hax raised one hand very slowly and waved. "Hey, Carly. How's it going?" He grinned.

Carly stared at him. "Aren't you that hacker?"

"Yeah. Hey." He stared until The Finn drove her elbow into his ribs. Hax coughed. "Uh, Carly, meet The Finn. The Finn, meet Carly."

* * *

Chapter 38
Greater Kwan

Greater Kwan got into the bland Toyota he'd stolen from Vlad's hired assassin and drove away from the burning Hack House. As he navigated the dark streets of Fort Walton, he heard more sirens, but he reasoned they were fire trucks headed for the burning houses and not cops looking for him.

If the houses burned fast enough, it might even be tomorrow before the cops and the fire marshal realized it was a homicide scene.

He climbed over the steep bridge, and rolled into the busy parking lot of a nightclub. Kwan switched the dome light on, dug the Syndicate phone out of his pocket and re-inserted the battery. After the phone booted up, he went through his Syndicate contacts list.

Killing the hackers would cripple the Syndicate's intelligence gathering and surveillance, but they weren't...worthy. The fat one he'd killed in the bathroom was soft and weak and stoned. Not a warrior. But the Syndicate had a handful of warriors, and it was time to consider how he would destroy them.

In the military, his instructors taught him the value of information. In the Syndicate, Mr. Cypress taught him the value of disinformation. Lies.

Kwan scrolled down the list and smiled. Manila Tommy. Tommy was a sawed-off gossip with muscles and a bad attitude. He drank too

One Bullet — 207

much, drugged too much, and best of all--talked too much.

A low-rider truck with a thumping stereo cruised by, rattling the Toyota's windows. Kwan typed a text message to Manila Tommy, "i didnt kill cypress!! vlad did. joe wasnt there. vlad is bringing in new soldiers. doesnt need u anymore."

He read the message and hit 'Send.' The 88 characters of the text were better than 88 bullets because they contained some truth, and two big lies. Vlad had no plans to bring in new soldiers, but if Tommy thought he did, he would worry about it. Tommy would tell the other Syndicate soldiers, and soon they'd have questions for their new boss. Right when Vlad needed them most, his soldiers would doubt him.

While he took the battery out of the phone, Kwan considered Joe, the bagman. Joe Barrow was an unknown. He'd come to the Syndicate with solid references from past jobs, but like the hackers, he was a specialist who did one thing--money exchanges. Kwan wondered what Barrow was doing, and if he would run, or stay and fight.

Kwan put the phone away and drove east toward the Panama City area. His wounded earlobe dripped blood on his shoulder, his throat hurt and he was thirsty.

He considered returning to the quiet house in Panama City Beach he'd broken into. It wasn't too far from Vlad's house, with easy access to the Syndicate businesses in town and on the beach. But spending a second night in the same location was risky.

Along the quiet stretch of highway between San Destin and Panama City Beach, Kwan cracked the windows and let the winter air cool the cabin. Sweat ran down his shaved head, and when he cleared his throat, he tasted blood. He'd kept the expired bottle of Tylenol from the beach house, but he didn't have a drink to swallow the pills with.

Up ahead, he saw the sign for Highway 395 that veered south to Seaside and Seagrove on the coast. It also led along State Road 30A to Mr. Cypress's condominium in Rosemary Beach. Kwan slowed the car and turned. Who would look for him in Cypress's condo?

The coastal communities were quiet and he kept his speed low and watched for law enforcement. At Rosemary Beach, he turned right and crept through the narrow, twisting streets to the condo. Lesser Kwan's Jeep still sat in front of Cypress's place.

Greater Kwan braked and stared at the Jeep. After a minute, he drove down a few blocks and left the car in front of an empty unit. It might be towed away, but he didn't care. Vlad's assassin wouldn't be calling the police to report a stolen car.

He flipped through his large ring of keys to all of Cypress's houses. Kwan took his equipment from the car, and searched the backseat for the spear. Then he recalled he'd left the spear in the chest of one of the dead hackers. His message to Vlad.

Kwan wiped sweat from his forehead and walked slowly to the condo. His legs were stiff from the after effects of the adrenaline-fueled fight

One Bullet 209

at the Hack House, plus sitting in the car. He felt like the wind might knock him over.

He opened the front door and went in with a bangstick ready. The condo was dark and still. Kwan put his things on the floor, held the bangstick at chest level, and yanked open the closet door. The closet was empty. He went down the hall to Mr. Cypress's room and crouched outside the bathroom. Ducked in low, ready to slam the bangstick into Vlad's pet assassin.

But the bathroom was empty, except for the scent of Cypress's arthritis ointment.

Kwan went room to room, turning on lights and checking closets and under beds, but it was hard to maintain his intensity as each room proved empty.

When he was satisfied no one was in the condo, he got a bottle of water from the refrigerator and swallowed four Tylenol. There wasn't much to eat in the kitchen, but the cabinets had dry and canned goods. He dumped three bags of instant oatmeal into a bowl and heated it in the microwave.

He went into the living room with the bowl and another bottle of water, and stopped. For a moment, he thought he saw Lesser Kwan sitting in the rattan chair and loading a gun.

Kwan blinked. No. That was this morning--a hundred years ago this morning. Lesser Kwan had sat in the chair and loaded his weapons while Vlad talked to Cypress and planned to betray them.

The TV was still on, set to the weather scan channel with the sound off. The green, rubber ball he liked to squeeze sat on the couch. He eased down next to it. The first spoonful of oatmeal burned his throat. Kwan gagged, and guzzled water. Set the bowl on the floor to let it cool and watched the weather scan. He could almost hear the robotic voice that went with the channel, calling out the tides and the chance of precipitation.

Kwan squeezed the hard, rubber ball and weighed the value of his brother's life against the four hackers he'd killed in Fort Walton. He found the hackers meant nothing. They had no value to him. His brother was glorious, a young warrior with unlimited potential. The hackers were weak, lifeless men who sat slaved to their machines, grinding out dollars.

Killing the hackers felt pointless. Kwan thought destroying the organization Vlad had worked so hard to build would be thrilling, but it was empty. As tasteless as the now cold oatmeal.

The only thing that would satisfy him was killing Vlad. Kill Vlad.

* * *

Chapter 39
Vlad

As Vlad drove from Panama City Beach east into Panama City, he considered what Joe might do. If Joe didn't have the Cartel cash, then he needed money to run. As the Syndicate bagman for the last year, Joe knew the locations of all the Syndicate businesses. If he needed money fast, robbing a Syndicate business made sense.

Vlad began his hunt with a Syndicate-owned pawnshop in nearby Lynn Haven that held not only cash, but guns. He figured it was a prime target for Joe, or for Greater Kwan. The pawnshop was a block off Ohio Avenue and had closed hours ago. The front was well lit, but the small parking area in back was dark.

The Porsche Cayenne bumped over the old pebble-and-concrete street as Vlad circled the block. He switched the headlights off, took his boot off the gas and let the vehicle roll. But there was no sign of Joe or Kwan. He parked and waited in the dark for half an hour, then drove fifteen minutes to a self-serve laundry in Springfield.

The laundry was a good money machine, and probably a better target for Kwan than for Joe because Kwan wanted to destroy the Syndicate, while Joe wanted to escape it. Vlad had worked with Mr. Cypress to acquire or start a series of small, cash-based businesses along the Emerald Coast from Pensacola to Port Saint Joe. Cash businesses that were perfect for laundering the

Cartel's drug money, mixing bad money with good before it reached the US bank system.

Although it was closed for the night, the laundry kept the interior lights on to prevent break-ins. Vlad shook his head. Some of his places had been robbed. The Syndicate kept their ownership so quiet, even other criminals didn't know which businesses were theirs.

Vlad pulled into the parking lot of a tattoo parlor across the street from the laundry to keep watch. A Sheriff's Office car cruised by. Ten minutes later, a black Charger with plain wheels and a crash bar on the front bumper turned into the parking lot. Those clues, plus the spotlight mounted above the driver's side mirror made Vlad certain it was an unmarked police car.

He pulled his phone from his pocket, pressed it to his ear and spoke, pretending to have a conversation.

When the Charger's headlights swept over Vlad's Porsche, the unmarked cop car slowed.

Vlad held one hand up to shield his eyes, and continued his imaginary conversation, but the Porsche felt cramped and hot. Vlad forced himself to keep talking, and then realized he was speaking in Russian. He smiled and looked at his phone.

The cop car made a sharp turn and pulled out onto the road, activated its discrete light rack and took off, heading north toward some unknown emergency.

Vlad rolled his shoulders and blew out a long breath. Took the Sig Sauer off his lap and put it on the passenger seat next to him. He tipped up the

One Bullet 213

can of coffee, but only one lukewarm sip dripped out. Vlad threw the can against the front windshield and it bounced all the way to the back seat.

He dialed Simon, who was watching Carly's apartment. "Listen. Thanks to the Cartel, the cops are everywhere. Don't sit in one spot too long, and don't attract attention."

"Got it," Simon answered.

Vlad hung up and drove to a check cashing business a few miles away in Millville. With the ridiculous rates the check cashers could legally charge, Vlad couldn't see the point of criminals bothering with loan shark operations anymore.

The check casher was in a square, cinderblock house near Sherman Avenue. When he steered the Porsche into the oyster-shell parking lot, a security light above the house's front door snapped on. Vlad nodded, glad the manager had remembered to activate the light.

There were metal bars over the windows and a simple alarm system, but he knew that wouldn't stop Joe. And Kwan would just burn the whole thing down. Other than a gun under the front counter, the only thing the business had was cash. Vlad had instructed the check cashers to make daily bank deposits to avoid leaving money inside, but he knew they sometimes held the money until Friday.

He hid the Porsche in the shadow of an oak tree behind the house, and sat with the windows down, lights and engine off. The arms of the oak above him creaked in the breeze, and Vlad tilted the seat back and stretched. The coffee worked its way through him, and he reached up and clicked off the interior light in the SUV. Then he eased the door open and stepped down.

While he stood beneath the oak, listening to the patter of his urine on the roots, Vlad heard footsteps.

He paused, and then zipped up.

Heard a scraping sound as someone's shoe kicked an oyster shell loose in the parking lot.

Vlad reached for the Sig Sauer, then remembered it was on the passenger seat.

A long shadow fell across the lot on the other side of the tree.

He grabbed the snub-nosed .38, but the hammer snagged on his pocket. The cloth tore and he brought the gun up as a man rounded the tree.

Joe or Kwan? Vlad thought. Which one?

The short-barreled gun was horribly loud, and he knew cops were blanketing the area. A gunshot would bring them swarming.

As the man came around the tree, Vlad took a long step and swung the gun at the man's head.

The man stumbled, causing Vlad to miss.

He hit the man in the shoulder.

"What the hell?" the man yelled, and twisted around.

The man was tall, as tall as Joe or Kwan, but longhaired, and he stank of beer and cigarettes.

The drunken man stumbled, lost his balance and fell to one knee. He flailed his arms, and tried to get up.

Vlad aimed the gun at his face just to get him to shut up, but in the dark the drunk couldn't see the gun.

One Bullet 215

"Get off me," the drunk yelled. "I don't have any money. Why don't you go rob a--"

Vlad cracked the man across the pate of his head, and he collapsed.

"Shut up," Vlad said.

He stood in the darkness, hands trembling with adrenaline, ready to fight Joe and Kwan and the entire Cartel at the same time.

Ready to bash and bite and kill.

But the stupid drunk just lay there, as still and brainless as the oyster shells beneath him.

"Shit." Vlad kicked the man in the ribs, got into the Porsche and drove away.

* * *

Chapter 40
Vlad

Vlad drove across town to check Joe's apartment. When he reached the complex, he looked for Manila Tommy's white BMW, but couldn't find it. He looked for Jorg's Acura, but didn't see it, either.

He drove slowly around the parking lot, then pulled into an empty space and called Manila Tommy. The pimp's phone went straight to voicemail.

"I'm at Joe's place. You are not," Vlad said, and hung up. For the last few months, Manila Tommy had become less reliable, but he didn't think Tommy would fail at something this important. What if none of the Syndicate soldiers had followed his orders?

Vlad whipped the Porsche out of the complex, and drove as fast as he dared to Carly's apartment. Simon and Lars sat in a spotless Chrysler 300 with fancy wheels across from her building.

There were no empty parking spaces near them, so Vlad pulled into the next row and walked over. His legs were stiff from sitting in the car. The Chrysler's window went down before he reached them.

Lars leaned out and dropped a handful of pistachio shells on the ground. "No sign of Joe."

Vlad nodded and looked in the car. Simon sat amid a pile of empty cans of Monster energy drink, and both men were alert and armed. "How about Greater Kwan, or Carly?"

One Bullet 217

"No, sir. We watched. Hell, Simon won't even let me go piss in the bushes," Lars said. "I had to go in a bottle. Remember how Mr. Cypress used to carry that plaid Thermos around and--"

"Yes, I remember," Vlad said. He stared at the unlit window of Carly's apartment. Checked his watch. "It's almost dawn. Call the others and tell them to meet at the pizzeria on Thomas Drive. I have one more place to check, then I'll see you there."

He walked back to the Porsche and climbed in.

Vlad checked the waffle shop he and Joe had breakfast at that morning, and then drove toward the Syndicate-owned pizza restaurant on Panama City Beach. As he came down off the Hathaway Bridge, he saw a Florida Highway Patrol trooper parked, watching the trickle of cars.

He yanked his boot off the gas pedal and checked his speedometer. The Porsche slowed, but at that hour there wasn't much traffic to hide in. Vlad rolled past the trooper, going just under the speed limit, and slapped the steering wheel. "Damn Cartel. Those bastards screwed up everything."

Ten minutes later, he reached the restaurant. The pizzeria was a narrow place in a run-down strip mall on Thomas Drive, which paralleled the white-sand beaches. At dawn on a January morning, when half the businesses on the beach were shuttered for the winter, it would look strange to have several cars parked at an unopened pizza place. So Vlad pulled around back and parked beside the other Syndicate cars. Manila Tommy's

BMW was there, along with Lars's Chrysler and Arturo's pickup truck.

Before he got out of the Porsche, he clipped the Sig Sauer to his belt beneath his jacket, and tucked the H&K next to it. The front door was locked, so he tapped on the glass and Jorg opened the door for him and stepped back. The ex-kickboxer looked away.

Vlad stopped half way through the door and stood close to Jorg. "Why weren't you and Manila Tommy at Joe's apartment? If he needed money, guns, or his passport, he'd have to go there."

Arturo, Fergus and Lars sat at a table, eating cold pizza out of the box. Simon stood at the front counter, fixing a pot of coffee. Everyone looked away from him, except Simon, who rolled his eyes.

"What?" Vlad asked. He marched into the room and stood with his back to the side wall, facing the men. Fergus turned sideways in his chair to listen, but didn't make eye contact.

Jorg shut the door and locked it. "I can explain."

"Do so," Vlad said.

The ex-kickboxer rubbed one of his cauliflower ears. "I went to get Manila Tommy and go to Joe's place, like you said, but Manila said he needed to make a stop...then a guy called him, and we went by a package store, and...." Jorg spread his big hands. "I told Tommy. I told you'd be mad, but he's senior to me, like Mr. Cypress's left hand man, and he ordered me to take him to this chick's place in Laguna Beach and--"

One Bullet

"Enough excuses." Vlad looked at the front window of the pizzeria, and noticed the blinds were closed. His fists tightened, and Jorg stepped back. "Did anyone else see Joe or Kwan?"

The soldiers shook their heads.

"Where's Manila Tommy now?" Vlad asked.

Jorg glanced toward the back of the restaurant.

When Vlad went to the front counter, Simon held up one hand. "Tommy's back there with a girl. He's coked up. Drunk, too."

Vlad growled.

Fergus muttered, "We're fucked, boys."

No one replied.

Simon put down his coffee cup. "Been hearing some odd shite. Tommy said you called him when Cypress got dead." Simon's left hand was next to the coffee cup. His right was under the counter, out of sight.

Vlad nodded. His right hand rested on the countertop, and his left drifted back to the checkered grip of the H&K. "I called Tommy. Told him I needed a ride home because Joe and the Kwans shot holes in Cypress's Panamera, so I couldn't take it on the road. Tommy never came. I had to get one of those hackers from Fort Walton to drive me."

"Tommy has some crazy ideas. He thinks maybe you took down Cypress." Simon's shoulders bounced up and down once, and he frowned. "Our boy Tommy's been going heavy on the coke lately, but..."

Vlad breathed in through his nose and got a sure grip on the H&K.

A woman laughed, loud, from behind the swinging metal door that led to the kitchen.

Simon stepped back. Picked up the pot and poured himself another cup of coffee.

Vlad went around the counter and stopped. He stared at the kitchen door for a minute, trying to recall the layout of the place. If he stepped through the swinging door, he was certain there was a tall refrigerator on the left, and the pizza oven straight ahead, but he couldn't remember what was on the right. If Tommy was waiting with a shotgun, it would be hard for him to miss.

"Tommy, come out here," Vlad called. Then he stepped back and put the counter between him and the kitchen door. "Tommy, hurry up."

The woman's laughter stopped. Tommy pushed the door open, and came out grinning, one hand tugging at his zipper. "Hey, what's the rush?"

Vlad examined the former smuggler turned pimp. Tommy was half Filipino and half African American. He had the muscles of his Navy father, and the height of his tiny, bar girl mother. His eyes darted, and it was clear he was jacked up on something.

Tommy strutted over to the counter and reached for the coffee.

"I told you to watch Joe's place," Vlad said. He eased around the counter.

Tommy bobbed his head, saying, "Ah yes, boss, yes yes," in a bad, imitation Asian accent.

Vlad ran his tongue around the back of his teeth, and felt his pulse thumping in his ears. He'd spent all night in the car looking for Joe. Not like

One Bullet   221

Cypress, who always sat at home in the hot tub and ordered people around. No, he'd set the example for his soldiers by going after Joe himself, dodging cops and beating the hell out of a random drunk.

He looked around. Jorg stood by the door like he was ready to run. But Fergus, Lars and Arturo watched him from their table, the pizza forgotten. Simon tossed his coffee into the sink and walked toward the others. "Fucking amateur night is what."

"What?" Tommy said, and turned toward Simon.

Vlad erupted. He shoved Tommy into the side of the sink and drove three hard right hooks into the shorter man's ribs.

Tommy howled. Came around with a right hook of his own and caught Vlad on the temple.

Vlad rocked back, and shook his head to clear it.

Tommy raked the heel of his cowboy boot down Vlad's shinbone.

The pain was hot, immediate. Vlad's knee buckled, and Tommy snatched a pizza cutter off the counter and swung.

Vlad got his forearm up to block, but the cutter sliced the outside edge of his hand.

He stepped back, extended his longer arms, and finger jabbed Tommy in the eye. Grabbed Tommy's wrist and squeezed, but the shorter man wouldn't let go of the cutter. Tommy got one knee up into his gut before Vlad drove him back and smothered the knee strikes.

The two men swayed, hands locked on wrists, chest to chest.

Tommy snapped his teeth at Vlad's face, and Vlad smelled his breath. Vlad pulled his right hand loose and punched low, aiming for the liver. He missed, but the punch still lifted Tommy up on his toes. The shorter man grunted.

Tommy stomped on Vlad's instep, but Vlad's padded hiking boots saved him a broken foot.

They slid from the edge of the sink and down along the counter, still wrestling for the pizza cutter. Simon jumped out of the way.

Their feet got tangled, and Vlad tripped and went to one knee. Tommy whipped the pizza cutter up but only ripped Vlad's jacket. Vlad lifted with his back and legs, and smashed Tommy into the cabinets above the counter. A cabinet door popped open and stacks of paper plates fell out. Tommy dropped the pizza cutter and shoved Vlad away.

Vlad lost his grip on Tommy and stumbled. When he planted his right hand on the counter to catch himself, it landed on an electric can opener.

Vlad slammed the can opener into Tommy's head. Tommy kicked and bit and thrashed. Vlad kept swinging. Three times, five, six, seven. Lost in his rage, Vlad couldn't hear anything except the blood pumping in his ears. Couldn't see anything except Tommy's glassy eyes. Bam, bam, bam, over and over.

Finally the blood-slick can opener slipped from his aching hand. Vlad stepped back, panting.

Tommy lay on his side on the floor. His eyes were shut. A bubble of blood formed on his lips, then popped.

One Bullet 223

"Lesson one," Vlad rasped. He cleared his throat, turned to his soldiers and tried again. "Lesson one. When I tell you to do something, you do it."

The five men nodded. Jorg had his fingers on the door lock.

Vlad rolled his shoulders. Noticed the lapel of his jacket hanging loose. The Sig Sauer was still in its holster, but the H&K was on the floor. He picked it up and walked around the counter to the nearest table. Pulled a wad of napkins from the dispenser and held them to his bleeding hand.

Behind him, the door to the kitchen creaked.

He turned and saw a skinny girl in a short, leather coat and a miniskirt creep across the kitchen to Tommy.

Simon pulled a chair up to the table with the others, and peeled a slice of pizza off the cardboard box.

Despite the burning pain in his shin, and the cut on his hand, and the ringing in one ear, Vlad smiled. "Jorg, when Tommy wakes up, you take him to the hospital and get him fixed. I've got money in the car for the medical bill. Don't go to Bay Medical, the cops are there. Take him to Gulf Coast, then you go to Joe's apartment and wait."

"Yes, sir," Jorg said.

"He's dead," the girl said quietly.

Vlad blinked. Lowered the bloody wad of napkins. "What did she say?"

"He's dead," she said again. She raised her bloody hands from Tommy's face, stared at her fingers and started screaming.

"Shut that bitch up," Simon said with his mouth full of pizza.

The girl stumbled back from Tommy's body. She turned to Vlad and shrieked, "You murdered him. I saw you from the doorway. You did it."

"Calm down," Vlad said. He took one step toward her, and she jumped back.

The girl ran toward the kitchen door.

Vlad raised the H&K 9mm and aimed at her skinny back. Hesitated. No, a man--a real man-- would not shoot a woman in the back.

He'd grab her, slap some sense into her head, and let her go. He could fix this.

A barrage of gunfire exploded behind him.

Vlad flinched. Expected to feel hot lead strike his back.

Instead, the girl arched as the bullets tore through her and punched holes in the kitchen door.

For a half second, she danced, a puppet to the bullets. Then she fell.

Vlad looked over his shoulder.

Jorg, Simon, Lars, Fergus and Arturo stood in a cloud of gray smoke, each holding a smoking pistol. Lars coughed and waved at the smoke.

Vlad lowered his cold gun. His finger was on the trigger but he hadn't fired.

Simon brushed past him. Stood just beyond the spreading pool of blood and kicked the woman. "This bitch is extra dead."

Vlad turned to the Syndicate soldiers.

Jorg looked at the door.

Lars glanced away. Arturo made the sign of the cross.

One Bullet 225

Fergus wiped a ribbon of sweat from his face. "Never shot a bird, before. Shit."

Vlad heard Simon call from the below the counter. "She was right. Tommy is done. Now we got two to dispose of."

"Boss?" Jorg called from the front door. "I hear sirens."

* * *

Chapter 41
Joe

When I wake up in the boathouse, the first thing I feel is the weight of the pistol cradled on my chest. Oh right, my gun with one bullet. Maybe I'll change my name to Joe 'One Bullet' Barrow.

But my head is propped on a seat cushion from the boat, and with the roof and the walls of the boathouse keeping the wind out, I feel pretty good. Cold and stiff as a corpse, but pretty good.

I sit up and rub some blood flow into my arms and legs. It's too dark to see the bruise on my shoulder where I ran into the truck mirror, but I bet it's a beauty. The barnacle cut on my finger stings, too.

There are shelves along one side of the boathouse, so I take a look while the feeling returns to my legs. My wet shoes squeak, but there's a big yard between me and the house, and I don't think anyone will hear me. The shelves are stacked with life vests, extra seat cushions, a coil of nylon rope, a spare anchor and a bunch of other sailor stuff. There are three huge, white ice chests on the floor. Two are empty, but the third has a half dozen bottles of water rolling around the bottom.

The water tastes stale, but I drink two bottles anyway. I step around some fishing poles, a mop and a long paddle, and peek out of the boathouse. Across the bayou toward the hospital I can see a lot of lights, but no swirling blue lights. A loud

One Bullet 227

droning sound bounces off the water between the trees.

I look up and see a Sheriff's Office helicopter coming down the bayou, its searchlight shining a fat beam of white light. I don't know if those things carry heat detectors or whatever, but they must. How else do they always find people hiding in the woods?

The copter drops down until it's just a few hundred feet above the bayou. I grab the edge of the boat and step off the wooden walkway between it and the wall of the boathouse. Plunge feet first into the cold water. The searchlight from the copter hits the water outside and I take a gulp of air and slide under the boat.

My shoes touch the shallow bottom and I put my palms on the hull to keep from bobbing back to the surface. My heart is racing, and even under the water I can hear the helicopter, but I've got to stay down as long as I can. Maybe the cold water and the hull of the boat will hide me from the heat detectors.

After a while, I'm not sure if I'm hearing the copter or the sound of my own blood pumping in my ears. I let a little air out through my lips, but I'm starting to see bright flashes and my eyes are closed. I've got to breathe.

So I slide up the hull. My aching head breaks the water and I draw in a huge breath of air that tastes like barnacles and rotting fish. I can still hear the helicopter, but it's faint.

Getting back to the hospital to meet Carly will be tough. The Cartel guys are insane, running around shooting everyone like they're in Mexico City. Now the cops will be all over this neighborhood. But the copter is gone, so I climb back onto the walkway to get my gun before I swim back to the hospital.

There's something odd about the paddle against the wall and it takes me a second to realize it's got a scoop at both ends. It must be the kind you use with a kayak. I look up and see a stubby kayak not much bigger than I am hanging from the rafters.

It's not easy to release the ropes and lower the kayak to the water without splashing and making noise, but I know it's worth the trouble. Paddling across the bayou will take a lot less energy than swimming, and I won't freeze my ass off.

I put the gun and the paddle on the edge of the walkway and manage to get into the kayak without tipping the thing. Grab my stuff, and then push off and just glide out into the bayou. As soon as I'm clear of the boat house the breeze picks up and I shiver, but it still beats being in the water.

There's a slight current tugging me out toward the bay, but the copter is gone and I don't see any cops with lights on the far bank. The kayak is tricky to steer because it turns so easy, but I keep the nose more or less straight and aim for the big tree behind the house, where I took the gun from the Cartel goon.

Pretty soon the paddle hits bottom, and the kayak grinds over the mud below the bank. I step into the ankle-deep water and wade ashore like the world's loneliest Marine. The dead goon is still beside the tree, tangled in the exposed roots. I'm surprised the cops didn't spot him, but then again, he wasn't making much noise.

For some reason I don't want to touch him, so I use the paddle to push him farther out into the water. The current should take him out to the bay and the sharks.

As I creep across the road into the woods behind the hospital, I listen for cops. But there is no squawk of radios, no sirens, no bloodhounds barking. From the edge of the trees, I can see a few Sheriff's cars and some black-and-white Panama City PD cars near the lobby entrance. But even at this distance, I can tell their posture is relaxed. They're standing around, probably swapping stories about what happened inside.

It looks like the gun battle is long over.

Damn, how long did I sleep in the boathouse?

That's when I realize it's not as dark as it should be. I don't have a watch or a phone, but I know what that dim glow in the east is. It's almost morning. Damn it. When I left, I told Carly I'd meet her at the truck in two hours, not the next morning.

I don't know how she could have waited that long beside the truck without drawing the attention of the cops. It's not possible, not with all the law enforcement types that must have swarmed this place. But I have to check. Besides, the truck is my ride out of here.

I pat my front pocket and somehow the keys are still there, so I sneak across the lot, going from cover to cover. The SUVs and full-sized pickup trucks are plenty big to hide behind, and in northwest Florida, there are lots of them. This time I'm careful not to run into any side mirrors.

None of the cops are looking my way when I slink up to the bubba truck, work the key into the door and climb up into the cab. I put my seat belt on and wait. If a cop comes to check the parking lot again, I'll speed out of here, but if not I'll wait for a diversion.

It's bad to hope some drunk bastard is getting into a car wreck right now, but I need an ambulance to come roaring up and distract these cops. While I wait, I start to understand why the rednecks love these big trucks. From up high you can see everything, and if you have to go over curbs or off roads, you have plenty of clearance.

After a little while I hear a siren, and sure as hell an ambulance slows down just enough to take the turn off Highway 77. When it pulls up to the hospital entrance, the cops run over to open the back doors. While they help the EMTs lift the gurney out of the back, I crank the truck and roll to the edge of the parking lot.

I take the long way around the hospital out to Business 98. Turn left and head down into the old neighborhood locals call The Cove. The nice thing about The Cove is they have alleys behind the houses--something you don't see much in this area.

It's not hard to make a few turns, then kill the headlights and coast down an alley and stop. The houses on either side of me don't have their lights on yet, so I figure it's safe to sit here a few minutes and think.

One Bullet 231

Carly first. I was late to our meeting, so maybe she took a cab. Or maybe she bolted right after I led the Cartel boys away. I don't think she's still at the hospital. Hopefully that girl, Pono, is okay, too. Her brother is a scumbag, but if the Cartel tried to kill him, they'd have a tough time getting by her. She's loyal, and I hope she's not laying on a slab in the morgue.

Vlad and the Syndicate didn't show up, which is something. But why not? If Vlad thinks I took the money, then where is he? I thought he and the Kwan brothers would be all over me. It's worse not knowing what they're up to, because Vlad is a smart guy.

With the Cartel it's simple. They will hunt me down until they get their money back. Even if I return the money, if they think I killed their bagman, they will kill me. That's fine. I like simple.

What I don't want is for my mess to get Carly killed.

I may not know what Vlad is up to, but I know the Cartel sent a flood of gunmen, and they have plenty more. I have to get the money Kid Sasquatch stole from me and return it to the Cartel. Then I'll find Carly, and work things out with Vlad.

Kid Sasquatch is in a coma, but Pono isn't. I want to believe she isn't involved in all this, but I've got to talk to her again. She said she came to the mainland days ago, so it makes sense she'd stay at her brother's place.

I reach over and get Sasquatch's laptop off the passenger seat. Open the lid and switch it on. I know his name, so I just need to look up his address. I'd use a real phone book, but you can't find a payphone anywhere these days. They took them out to hurt the drug dealers, but it doesn't seem to have slowed them down.

The Syndicate hackers would laugh, but I'm not too sure how this Wi-Fi stuff works. I know I need an Internet connection to look stuff up because Carly told me that. The laptop says it found five different networks. Four of them are secured or locked or whatever, but one called ChimpWithPencil is open. So I click on that and in a minute I'm on Google.

Google says Dwayne Kimura/Kid Sasquatch lives in an apartment. That's good because with apartments you have a lot of people coming and going, and you can mix in with all the rest.

I guess the Internet is good for something other than terrorists and perverts.

There's not much traffic this early. Some workmen heading to job sites, their trucks loaded with tool boxes and ladders. I hit the drive through at the McDonalds on Harrison Avenue for three egg McMuffins and two cups of coffee. The sweet old gal in the window hands me a thick wad of napkins with my food.

It's cold but at least the rain has stopped and the sun is out for now. The hot coffee helps a lot. Most mornings I'd be at the gym and standing outside the door when the employees got there. But somehow today, or I guess yesterday, everything went to hell.

I try to go over it all in my mind as I drive to Sasquatch's apartment, but it's too much and I'm not

One Bullet 233

that smart to begin with. The apartment sign is ahead and I take the turn a little fast and the bubba trucks sways, and then I'm stopped at a stupid gate. There must be some kind of pass key or card, but I don't have one.

Here I'm sitting in a truck the size of a tank, and this flimsy, little wooden arm is in my way. I should turn the truck around and look for another way in, but I'm sick of this stealth mode crap. I put the truck in Park, jump down and grab the wooden arm.

I give it one good yank, straight up, like snatching a barbell off the floor. Something in the hinge snaps, a bolt hits the asphalt by my feet, and the arm is free. I push it all the way to vertical, and get back in the truck.

No one saw me. Hell, there's no one awake this early.

The apartment complex is big, but I finally find his building. There are enough empty parking spaces in front for me to park. I reach behind the seat, move my jacket aside and root around for tools. There's a tire tool with a flat tab at one end for popping wheel covers off. Perfect.

I slide the tire tool into my front pocket and cover it with one arm. My clothes are a wreck. I look like a guy who got in a fight and swam across a bayou. But there's nothing I can do about that, so I walk up the stairs like I belong here.

Rap once on the door, then wait. If Kid Sasquatch has a girlfriend sleeping over, I'd rather her answer the door. But no one answers, so I go to work with the tire tool. The fit between the door

234   Mark Boss

and the frame is pretty tight, and I have to muscle the flat tab in. Apparently Kid Sasquatch locks his doors. Hell, maybe whoever his partner is stashed the money here.

The lock gives a loud squeak, then it gives and the door swings open and I have to jump in to catch it by the knob. There are wood slivers from the frame on the floor of the stairwell, and I don't want the neighbors to notice them. I kick the slivers inside, close the door and stand with my back to it. I look at the apartment, but mostly I listen.

The heater is running. Warm air gusts out of the vent above me. But there's no sound of a radio or a TV or a person dialing 911.

There is a weird, burbling sound. Like somebody face down in a ditch.

With the tire tool in both hands, I shuffle forward. The open door on my left lets into a tiny utility room. Up ahead, there's two doors on my right. Straight on is a dining room and the kitchen.

When I get into the dining room the noise is louder, then I see the fish tank in the corner. It's one of those tanks that's shaped like a clear pillar, where the fish can dive really deep. There's some tiny, big-eyed fish darting around inside it. On the bottom there's a whole village of little ceramic houses that look like those grass huts in Hawaii. One of the fish peeks out at me from a hut.

Then the other fish see me and race to the surface. They look hungry and there's a plastic shaker of food on the table, so I drop some funky-smelling flakes in the tank. The flakes float on the water, and the fish shoot up and hit them and take

One Bullet   235

out a tiny chunk at a time. Like a shark tasting a surfer. It's fun to watch, but I need to find the bag of money Sasquatch took from me.

The apartment has two bedrooms, two bathrooms, and a living room. Searching each room takes a while, but there are only so many places you can hide a 15-pound bag of cash. When I peek through the blinds at the little balcony, I see a door off of it that must be a small closet.

There are people down in the parking lot now. Kids going to school, parents going to work, a guy from a pest control company mixing a canister of chemicals. I don't like stepping out on the balcony, but I snatch open the door to the outside closet and get behind it quick. The closet is four shelves of empty. Not even a dead roach.

I shut the door and step back into the living room and there's Pono, holding a phone in one hand and a baseball bat in the other. I didn't hear her come in.

She's a big girl, and she has a wild look in her eyes.

"Wait," I say. "Just wait." Put up my hands to show her they're empty. And they are, because I forgot my one-bullet gun in the car. Not that I'd shoot a girl, but forgetting it entirely is sloppy. I guess McDonald's coffee isn't strong enough to make me smart.

"If you're looking for Dwayne's drugs, they aren't here," she says. She doesn't shout, she says it quietly. Then she puts down the phone and takes up a batting stance. I bet this girl can knock a softball over the fence. Or my head off my shoulders.

"I don't deal drugs." My left shoulder aches where I ran into the damn mirror. I want to put my hands down but she's right on the edge of attacking.

"Then you must want his money. Too bad. If there's any money here I'm using it to bury--"

All of a sudden she chokes up. Her eyes flood with tears. She blinks them away and keeps the bat ready, but now she looks like a 19-year-old island kid who's in way over her head.

I put my hands down. "Pono, the money was never his. It's not mine, either. The bag of cash belongs to the Cartel. The money in the overseas account belongs to the Syndicate." I sit on the couch and rub my sore, unshaven face. "Do you know what a bagman is?"

Pono is trying to sniff but she needs a tissue and she clearly doesn't want to put the bat down. I wonder if she dialed 911 before she dropped the phone? She sniffs hard, then says, "What's a bagman?"

"A bagman is the only guy other criminals trust with their money. I'm a bagman, and I work for an organization called the Syndicate that--"

"Commits crimes."

I spread my big hands. "Yeah. Commits crimes. The Cartel sells drugs and they make a lot of cash. Too much cash to hide or spend. So the Syndicate launders it for them. But they need someone to make the exchange, and that's my job. I deliver an envelope with the account number and a password to an overseas account. The Cartel bagman brings a bag of cash, and we swap. The

One Bullet 237

Syndicate gets cash to spend, the Cartel gets their money cleaned. It's good business for everyone."

She lowers the bat and sinks into a recliner. Sitting there with one hand on the bat and a scowl on her face, she looks like some warrior queen from ancient Hawaii.

Pono waits, so I keep talking. "Your brother jumped me during a delivery at the airport. He killed the Cartel bagman before I got there, then attacked me. When I woke up, the password envelope and the bag of cash were gone, so I chased him down in the parking lot and took them back."

Her hand tightens on the bat and I wonder if I can get through this without admitting I ran the big bastard over with a car. I go on, "Everyone thinks I took the money, even my own guys. If I don't return it, either the Cartel or the Syndicate will kill me, so yeah, I came here looking for the cash."

I lean forward and try to make eye contact, but she's looking out the glass door at the balcony. "If your brother would just wake up, I could ask him where he hid the money and I'd be out of your lives. You can take him home and maybe...I don't know, but doctors can do amazing things these days. He'll probably learn to walk again."

Her dark eyes stop and swivel back to me. "No, he won't walk again. Or answer your stupid questions, or help you find your filthy drug money. Dwayne is dead. Your girlfriend murdered him."

"What?" It doesn't come out loud. I'm not sure I made a sound at all. I thought it, but I'm not sure I said it, so I try again. "What?"

Pono locks eyes with me. "That bitch you brought to the hospital murdered Dwayne. When you ran out on us, it sounded like they were having a war in the hallway. So I grabbed a chair to block the door."

She wipes her eyes. "While my back was turned, she hit me with something. When I woke up, the door was open and she was gone. Dwayne had a pillow over his face, and four holes in his--" She starts crying hard, big, deep sobs that start in her belly and yank her forward like she's gonna vomit.

I feel sick. Dizzy. Carly killed Kid Sasquatch? I didn't even know she owned a gun. There's no way. But...

"Why?" I get up and Pono tenses, but I go to the glass door and look out at the winter morning. Close my eyes and rest my forehead on the cold glass. Something burns in my stomach. Not sure if I'm gonna throw up or crap myself. What the hell is happening?

Pono says something, but it's soft and I can't hear her because the blood is pounding in my ears the way it did when I hid beneath the boat in the bayou. But there's no helicopter in the sky outside, just a solitary crow hopping on the ground, picking at a soda pop can. The crow caws and I get a shooting pain behind my right eye.

I sit straight down, like dropping onto the stool in your corner after the eleventh round of a fight you know you're losing.

One Bullet 239

"It was Carly," I say without looking over my shoulder. Pono may take the bat and bash my brains out, but I don't care. Shit, I deserve it.

"I just said that. She killed Dwayne," Pono says.

I sit there and take some deep breaths, and bite my lip and don't cry. But it's close and I sit there for a while.

Until it's time to turn around and face Pono and face reality.

"I knew Dwayne had to have a partner," I say. "Someone who knew where I was meeting the Cartel bagman, and who knew what time the exchange would take place. I thought maybe it was a guy from the Syndicate, named Vlad, but it was Carly. She must have told Dwayne about the exchange. She went with me to the airport yesterday morning, but she wouldn't go inside. Dwayne went in the bathroom, took out the Cartel bagman, then ambushed me. He and Carly must have worked out a deal to split the money."

I thought about the look on Carly's face when she realized the money in the bag I retrieved from Sasquatch was counterfeit. She was furious. He betrayed her, hid the real cash and switched it out with fake money. That's when she knew he'd ripped her off. Her partner betrayed her.

Like she betrayed me. Only worse, because I love Carly.

"When the Cartel finds out Dwayne is dead, what will they do?" Pono asks.

"They'll keep looking for their money." I look at her and the warrior queen is a scared kid again. "If they find you, they'll--"

"I don't know anything," she shouts.

"It doesn't matter. They won't believe you until Calm Ruben has asked you a hundred times. Calm Ruben doesn't stop asking until you're dead."

She holds the bat between her knees and rests her head on it. Takes a deep breath and puts her shoulders back and sits up straight in her brother's chair. "Will you help me?"

* * *

Chapter 42
Joe

I'm sitting on the floor in Kid Sasquatch's apartment and Pono is looking down at me from her brother's chair when she asks, "Will you help me?"

I don't know what to say.

It's hard to wrap my head around all this. Carly is gone. I don't know where the money is. I ran over Pono's brother with a car and I think my girlfriend shot him dead. Pono should kill me, or at least turn me in to the cops, but instead she just asked me to help her.

The only thing I know for sure is that Calm Ruben and the Cartel won't quit until they get their money. And Vlad and the Syndicate won't quit until they get me.

The pain behind my right eye is bad. The dawn light from the glass door behind me is too bright and my breakfast sloshes around like melted ice and warm beer at the bottom of a cooler. "Can I use the shower?"

"What?" Pono looks at me and her puffy eyes come back into focus.

I got in four fights yesterday, swam a bayou and slept in a boathouse. I need a hot shower. "Please?"

"Yeah." She points at the master bedroom. She must be using the guest bath.

Sasquatch's bathroom is slightly cleaner than a truck stop. He has threadbare beach towels and a bottle of body wash that smells like rotting

242 Mark Boss

pineapples. The hot water finds every stinging cut I didn't know I had, but by the time the hot water gives out, I feel almost human.

My hair is too short to worry about combing, and a squeeze of toothpaste and my finger do a pretty good job of rinsing the taste of the bayou out of my mouth. I should ask first, but instead I go through Sasquatch's closet until I find a decent suit. The legs of the pants are too long, so I roll the cuffs. The jacket is okay through the shoulders, but the arms are too long. Nothing I can do about that.

He must have been wearing his only dress shoes and I won't wear his sneakers, so I wipe my own shoes down with a towel and put them back on. In the foggy bathroom mirror, I look like an unshaven, bleary-eyed thug, but a well-dressed thug. It's got to be wishful thinking, but I swear I smell coffee from the kitchen, so I square my shoulders and march out to face Pono.

She looks up from the counter, where she's pouring two mugs of hot heaven.

This girl is a saint.

"There's no milk," she says while she spoons sugar into both cups.

"That's okay." The first sip almost burns my tongue, but it tastes fantastic. "Damn, that's good. Thanks." I go out to the living room, and she follows me, walking slow with a full mug in her hands.

"It's Kona coffee. Hawaiian," she says.

"I like it."

One Bullet 243

"You ran over my brother, didn't you?" She asks it straight out, no quiver in her voice, no bat in her hand.

Heat from the coffee mug soaks into my sore hands, and for the first time since yesterday I don't feel cold. I don't want to break this--this quiet minute where no one is shooting at me and I'm just standing in a warm apartment drinking a cup of good coffee and the sun is up and maybe something good could happen for a change.

"Yeah." There's no way to explain it away so I shut up and wait.

"He survived. The doctor told me the coma was temporary and Dwayne would wake up in a day or two. You didn't kill him."

"I'm glad. Whatever you think about me, I'm not a murderer."

Pono shrugs her big shoulders. "Dwayne made some bad decisions, but he was a good big brother. He looked out for me when we were little. Family is everything in the islands." She looks away, then back. "But he's gone and we're still here, stuck with his mess."

"I have an idea. You any good with computers?" I ask.

"I guess. We use them in school."

"I'll be right back." I put down my empty mug and go down the stairs two at a time. Unlock the bubba truck and find Sasquatch's laptop and the envelope with the password instructions, and take them back to the apartment.

Put the laptop on the kitchen counter and flip it open. Then I spread the password instructions out

244 Mark Boss

next to it, and smooth the wrinkled paper with my palm. "This is your brother's laptop, and these are directions to access an overseas bank account."

Pono stands next to me at the counter. "I've never seen this laptop before. Dwayne wasn't into computers, but he always has the latest phone. Had the latest phone."

Maybe I've never planned a bank heist or hacked a computer, but as a bagman I carried out eleven jobs without losing a penny. Until this one. Maybe there's a way to fix that.

"To help the Cartel launder its drug money, the Syndicate loads an overseas account and then gives the Cartel instructions on how to access it. We give them the account number, the password and all that. In exchange, the Cartel pays us the same amount in cash."

I tap my finger on the wrinkled sheet. "We may not have the Cartel's bag of cash to give them, but this account gives us access to the same amount. $700,000.00. Maybe we can use this to get the Cartel off our backs."

Pono swivels the laptop toward her and types in the address of a bank on some island where the cruise ships never land. While I get another cup of coffee, she works her way through the instructions. She can type fast, and she uses all her fingers.

Getting money from a numbered account isn't like hitting the ATM on your way to a movie. There are numbers, multiple passwords, security questions. There's even a bunch of pictures that pop up and you have to pick the one that matches the

One Bullet 245

account. I point to a picture of a big dog with drool on its cheeks and wise eyes.

"You sure this is correct?" Pono asks.

"Yeah, it's one of Vlad's dogs."

She clicks on the picture and an 'Account Home' screen opens, and her shoulders sink. "It's empty," she says.

"What?" I put down my coffee and squint at the screen. "Account balance. Zero. What the hell?"

I read it again, but she's right. The account is empty, cleaned out. I think hard about yesterday. "In the airport your brother sat down with this laptop and the instructions. He must have tried to access the account, but the cops made him move before he could finish. After that, I followed him the whole way to the parking garage and he never stopped. There's no way he had time to empty the account."

"That means somebody took the money before they gave you the envelope," Pono says.

"Before?" I step back fast and my elbow hits the coffee maker. The glass carafe tumbles into the sink and shatters. "Vlad."

"Who is Vlad?"

"Vlad is the second-in-command of the Syndicate. We met for breakfast yesterday. He gave me the envelope. Even loaned me his Lexus because my car is in the shop." Behind me, coffee drips onto the empty hot plate and hisses.

"The whole thing was a set up. Vlad stole the money from the overseas account and sent me to that meeting with a worthless envelope. Carly told your brother about the meeting, and he stole the

246   Mark Boss

cash and the envelope. Carly betrayed me. Vlad betrayed me. Everybody."

I look up and Pono's eyes go big and she backs away from me. "I wasn't in on it. I didn't--"

"I know. I know." I hold up my hands, palms out. "It's just a lot for me to think about, you know?"

"We should go to the police," she says. "Tell them everything. They'll protect us. Or if you don't want to go, I will. I didn't do anything wrong."

"Pono, that's sounds good right now. And the cops will try. They'll protect you and grab as many of the Cartel and the Syndicate guys as they can find. But you'll go back to Hawaii and one day a month from now, or six months from now, a Cartel guy will put a gun in your face. And when you can't tell him where their money is, he will pull the trigger."

She clicks off the coffee maker and pulls the plug out of the wall. Tears a paper towel off the roll and pushes the splashed coffee into the sink. It still smells good.

"Why are you helping me?" she asks.

"Because you're the only person in this whole mess that doesn't deserve it." It's weird, but I didn't have to think before I answered her, because it's true. Maybe this is what it's like to tell the truth.

I swivel the faucet to the other side of the sink and rinse my hands. "The banks open at nine. I've got a safety deposit box with some money in it. Not a lot, but enough to buy you a ticket home to Hawaii. Once you're in the air, I'll start fixing this."

"How?"

One Bullet

I remember what Vlad said to me yesterday on the phone. He said, 'You're a bagman, not a hitman.' He's right. I've never plotted someone's murder before today.

"Joe, how will you fix it?" Pono asks.

"I'm gonna kill them all."

* * *

Chapter 43
Joe

I go back to the bathroom in Kid Sasquatch's apartment and finger brush my teeth again. The Kona coffee was good, but strong. When I come out to the living room, Pono is sitting on the couch with her cell phone in her hands. A nylon suitcase is on the floor by her feet. It's January, but she's wearing flip flops and her big, brown toes poke out from under her jeans.

"Who you calling?"

"No one," she says. "I'm looking at pictures." She turns the phone around and it's a photograph of her and her brother. Her dead brother, Dwayne. In the picture, she's smiling. His face is flushed and he's holding a bottle of beer, and he looks happy.

Last night, Carly shot Dwayne in his fat, happy face. I can't make sense of that. I mean, I know it had to be about the money, but the idea of Carly shooting anyone is too big a jump for me.

While I stand there thinking about Carly, Pono gets up and points at the clock on her phone. "It's almost nine. Should we try the bank?"

"Yeah. We'll hit my safety deposit box, get the cash, and I'll drive you to the airport. The sooner you're on a plane, the safer you'll be."

"I should have bought a round-trip ticket, but I was going to stay for a while," she says. "At least until Dwayne either came back with me, or got his life together and found a regular job."

I go to the door, but she doesn't move.

One Bullet 249

"Just because I don't have the money right now, doesn't mean I won't pay you back. I've got a job on campus in the cafeteria. I'll send you the money," she says.

I smile. The money doesn't matter, I just want my girlfriend and my life and my reputation back. But she cares, so I nod. "That's fine. We'll work it out."

Crack the door and take a peek at the parking lot below, but the only things moving are two ladies walking laps and talking loud. "All right, we're good." I grab Pono's bag in my left hand and she reaches for it, then smiles and lets me carry it.

When I open the bubba truck, a wave of stench that smells like the bayou I swam pours out. The driver's seat is still damp, and I roll the windows down and let the winter air blow the stink out.

Pono sits with her bag between her feet and says nothing while I drive south to 23rd Street. Twenty Third Street is one of the main drags in Panama City, four lanes of strip malls, fast food joints and banks. Lots of banks. It seems like there are cops and sheriff's deputies everywhere on the road, probably because the Cartel shot up the hospital. I guess some of it is my fault, too.

Pono opens her bag and slides Sasquatch's laptop out and puts it behind the seat. "I know that overseas account is empty, but you might need this."

"Are you sure you--"

"I don't want it." She stops and takes a breath. "Dwayne used that for crimes. He sold drugs. I know that, and I don't want anything to do with it."

"Okay." There's nothing to say. I pull into the bank. It's not easy finding a spot wide enough for the bubba truck, and I'm not used to parking the thing. Finally, I put it in an empty row, open the door and climb down. "It's cold out here. You want to come in?" I don't say that a man and a woman together attract less notice than a big thug by himself. Carly hated that.

Reach under the seat and find the gun I took off the Cartel guy and look at it in the daylight. It's an old Browning Hi-Power 9mm that looks like it was used to pound nails.

Pono's eyes get big. "You're not going to rob the bank, are you?"

"No. I'm just gonna open my safety deposit box. That's it." I hold up my key ring and show her the box key. "I'll have to show my driver's license, but it's no big deal."

"Then why do you need the gun?"

I take a slow look around the parking lot. Some cars, but not crowded. No obvious threats. "A lot of what the Syndicate does is financial."

"Crimes."

"Yeah, financial crimes. Money laundering. It easier if you have help from the banks. So Vlad or Manila Tommy will find some college kid who's strapped for money and encourage them to get a job as a bank teller. The Syndicate pays the kid's bills, and now and then, they ask for a favor. Like an account number, or a special deposit. Easy stuff."

Pono gets out of the truck and comes around to my side. Tilts her head toward the bank. "You're

One Bullet 251

worried there might be one of those Syndicate kids inside?"

"Yeah. If someone spots us, all it will take is one phone call to the Syndicate. And when we walk out, it'll be straight into a trap."

She pushes her big shoulders back. "I'll come inside with you. I can watch for the Syndicate while you get your stuff."

This nineteen-year-old kid has guts. "Okay." I put the gun under the seat. "It's only got one bullet, anyway, and I'm not planning a suicide. Let's go."

The wind whips my suit jacket and my too-long sleeves, but I'm walking next to a brave girl and I have the start of a plan in my head and I feel strong. This is what I do. I will make this work.

We walk in and there's a line, people leaning on the brass posts between the velvet ropes, staring at their checks or their phones. The long counter is on my left, with four tellers working, three girls, one guy. On the right is Member Services and a sunny, little lady asks, "Can I help you?"

"Yeah, I need to get into my safety deposit box. Please." I hold up the box key like it's evidence.

"Of course. Let me just call a manager to take you over there." Desk Lady gets on the phone and I take the opportunity to look around some more. The safety deposit room is back over my shoulder, at an angle to the tellers. The big metal door is open, but there's a metal gate across the opening that looks like one of those shark cages you see on TV.

Pono is turned sideways, watching people.

A cop marches toward us. She's wiping one hand on her uniform pants. Holding a white envelope in the other.

Pono elbows me. Raises her eyebrows all the way to her hairline.

I shake my head 'no.' Behind the cop is the sign for the restrooms. She isn't looking at us. There are dark rings under her eyes, and she probably just finished a night shift. The cop gets in line between the velvet ropes and I hear Pono breathe out.

"Okay," Desk Lady chirps. "Mr. Chubbuck will be right with you."

I'm not sure whether to sit on the chairs with the people waiting for auto loans or what, so I stand there. A side door opens and a guy about my age comes out smiling and sticks out his hand. "Brian Chubbuck, how are you? Is this your daughter? No, your wife? Lucky fellah."

Brian Chubbuck talks fast. He's wearing a suit with fat pinstripes. His hair is slicked back. He's squeezing my hand like it's a contest. And he's wearing a pinkie ring.

The stupid bastard is lucky I didn't bring the gun in with me.

Pono stands behind him, trying hard not to laugh. She coughs, and he looks back at her.

"Yeah, I need to get into my box." I hold up the key again.

"Safety deposit box? Fantastic. I never know what I'll find in those. Like visiting a dying aunt who always liked you. Am I right?" Chubbuck asks.

One Bullet 253

What the hell is this clown talking about?

Pono is turning red now.

"Right over here. Right this way." Chubbuck leads us to the cage and stops. "First, I need an ID-- driver's license, military ID, arrest record, anything with a picture." Chubbuck laughs.

I dig through my wallet and give him my Florida driver's license.

He squints at it. His lips move. "Birth date? You sure this is you? No way you're this old. You could pass for twenty nine, thirty, tops. Hey, you ever do any modeling?"

Pono snorts.

Chubbuck tucks my license into the top of a clipboard, just like a cop making a traffic stop. I wonder if he's going inside the box safe with us.

He writes down my name, the date and time, and the box number. Taps the pen against my chest. "Just need the old John Hancock. Put an 'x' if you have to." He laughs, and his Adam's Apple bobs up and down.

I print my name without driving the pen into his throat.

Chubbuck pulls out a key on a lanyard and opens the cage door. He stands in the doorway and waves us through. I step back to let Pono go first. When she turns sideways to squeeze by, he leans in and brushes up against her.

Creep.

I stand there but he doesn't move.

"Can we have some privacy?" I ask.

"Oh right, right." He winks at me as I go in. "I have to close the cage behind you. Don't let me find you kids fooling around in here. I'll be back in ten." He holds up one hand and mimics smoking a cigarette.

He shuts the cage door and it's way too much like a cell door in prison. I'm not worried about prison, though, because chances are I'll be dead before this is all over.

Pono whispers, "That guy is a perv. If he touches me again, I will break him."

"No argument from me." I open the lock, slide the safety deposit box out and set it on the table. There are two chairs. Pono sits, but I stay standing. "You see anyone checking us out back there?" I nod toward the lobby.

"Not sure. One of the tellers, the girl with the fake red hair, was watching you while your back was turned."

I look through the bars and check out the red head, but don't recognize her. "Did she pick up the phone?"

Pono shrugs. "Not that I noticed, but it was hard to focus with Chubbuck in my face."

"Let's get this done and get out of here." I open the box, and take out two padded mailing envelopes. Open the first one and spill out a skinny brick of cash--$5,500 in dirty twenties and tens. The second envelope is a lot heavier. I remember what I put in it, but I have to check.

Raise the flap, reach in and pull out the gun. It's a fat, steel nightmare. A Ruger Alaskan in .480 caliber, made for guys in Alaska who argue over their fishing spots with grizzly bears.

"Wow." Pono stares at the silver gun.

One Bullet 255

Even in my hands, the gun looks huge. "Honestly, I've never even shot the thing. I won it in a poker game. Guy gave it to me as a marker, and didn't come back for it." At the bottom of the envelope are half a dozen loose cartridges. I spill them out and load the big revolver. Try to tuck it in my waistband, but it's just too wide. Finally, I put it back in the envelope. "Let's go."

I put the box away and we go to the gate. Chubbuck is nowhere in sight. The line in the lobby is longer now. I lean to my right and check out the tellers until I spot the girl with the fake red hair.

She's staring at us.

There's no customer at her window, the other three tellers are busy, and there's a line of people, but she doesn't turn on her desk light to indicate she's open.

Fake Red looks away fast and picks up a phone. Not her desk phone, but a cell phone.

"We might have a problem."

Pono squeezes in next to me to watch. "Where's that perv?"

A lady in a suit walks past and I call to her. "Hey, could you get Mr. Chubbuck? We're ready to leave."

"Certainly." She starts toward the block of offices.

I call after her, "I think he went outside for a smoke." She doesn't hear me.

* * *

Chapter 44
Vlad

Vlad stood at the counter of the pizzeria, looking down at Manila Tommy's cooling corpse. Blood dripped off Tommy's head onto the cold, tile floor and it was quiet enough to hear it splat.

Tommy's phone rang.

Vlad flinched.

At the front door, Jorg pushed the blinds apart and stared out. "I hear sirens. Can't tell if it's fire or police."

Arturo rattled his key chain. "Why wait to find out? Let's get the hell out of here."

"Wait," Vlad said. He pulled Tommy's phone from the dead man's pocket and read the screen. It read, "Redkitty21." Vlad shrugged, and answered. "Speak."

"Tommy?" a young woman asked.

Vlad looked down at Tommy. "He can't answer. Who is this?"

"It's Natalie. Where's Tommy?"

"He's busy. So am I. What message shall I give him?" Vlad asked.

"Well...it's kinda private, but Tommy said to call him if I saw this guy and--"

"What guy?" Vlad pressed the phone to his ear. Jorg said something, but Vlad ignored him. Simon laughed and spun his pistol on one finger.

"Tommy said if I spotted this guy, he'd take me out on his boat and we'd go to Firefly for dinner," Natalie said.

One Bullet 257

Vlad squeezed the phone. "Natalie, listen. Tell me who you see and where you are, and I'll put a thousand dollars in your hand this afternoon. Now who?"

"Joe Barrow," Natalia said in a whisper.

"Describe him."

"Big guy, middle aged, busted lip. He looks strong. I bet he works out a--"

"Where are you?"

"First Southern Bank on 23rd Street, by the--"

"I know it." Vlad looked around the pizzeria. Gun smoke still hung in the air. Tommy and the girl whose name he didn't know lay dead at his feet. Jorg and his remaining soldiers stood watching him. Even if they left now, they'd never make the drive from Panama City Beach to 23rd Street in town before Joe left.

Vlad grabbed the electric can opener and flung it against the wall. It left a spray of Tommy's blood on the drywall. He took a breath. "Natalie, I want you to give Joe your phone and--"

"My phone? But it's brand new. It's the new--"

"I don't care. Give Joe your phone. I'll buy you ten phones. Give him the phone before he leaves or I will take you out on my boat and I won't bring you back. Understand?"

Natalia sniffled. "Yeah. Okay. Could you tell Tommy to call me?"

"I'll tell him," Vlad said.

She hung up.

* * *

Joe

"Where is that Chubbuck creep?" I put one hand on the middle bar of the cage door and squeeze. It looks like aluminum, but it's steel.

The cage door swings open. It wasn't locked.

Across the lobby, I see Chubbuck coming toward us.

"Come on," I say to Pono and we head for the exit.

Chubbuck comes over with his arms out. "Hey, that was fast. Did I forget to lock that door? Shame on me. Say, you didn't grab anything in there, did you?" He points at the two envelopes under my arm and laughs.

Fake Red Hair Girl comes through a side door and stops. Looks at Chubbuck and hesitates.

"Hey sugar, what's up?" Chubbuck asks.

"Are you Joe?" she asks me.

Up close, I realize she's young, college age like Pono. But small. Too much makeup, too tight clothes. Her bottom lip quivers and she holds out a phone. "He told me to give you this."

I take the phone, and look at it. It's in a rubber shell the color of bubble gum. "Who told you?"

"Say, is that the new model? What's it called?" Chubbuck reaches for the phone and I turn my shoulder into him and bump him back.

"Am I supposed to keep this?" I ask Fake Red.

She nods. Her eyes are full of tears.

"Okay, thanks." I turn aside and walk, Pono a step behind me. The doors look a long way away.

Chubbuck is asking something about a signature loan but I can't hear him.

I look through the sliding glass doors at the sunlight outside, bright on the white concrete sidewalk. Squeeze the envelope and feel the gun.

Stop.

Pono stumbles into me. "What?"

"Not this way. Not out the front door. The Syndicate may be here already, but there may not be enough of them to cover both sides." I turn and march past Chubbuck and Fake Red toward the back exit.

Stop and look out, but I can't see anything except a lot full of cars. "Pono, I'm going for the truck. Wait here. When I pull up, you come out fast and jump in. Okay?"

She nods. "Okay."

I hand her the envelope of cash, then slide my hand into the second envelope and find the rubber grip of the gun. If I have to shoot, I won't waste time trying to pull off the envelope, I'll just shoot through it.

I take a step forward and the doors slide open.

* * *

Chapter 45
Vlad

Vlad stood in the narrow pizzeria. He put one hand over the phone and said quietly, "It's the teller at First Southern Bank. She spotted Joe Barrow, and I told her to give him her phone."

He raised the phone to his ear and took a breath, ready to unleash a torrent of curses and threats. His Syndicate soldiers watched, eyes wide.

Instead, Vlad touched the phone's screen and ended the call. Set the phone down on the counter, and then ran hot water in the sink. He methodically soaped up his bloody hands. The hot water stung, but he washed them while his men watched. Finally, he leaned on the counter and dried his hands with a rag.

"I guess we're not going after him," Simon said to the other soldiers. He went around the counter and knelt next to the nameless dead girl, and took a phone and a pack of cigarettes from her beaded purse.

Vlad continued to dry his hands. His Sig Sauer pistol was on the counter within easy reach. "Simon, find a clean cup and pour me some coffee," Vlad said.

Simon looked up from under his long hair, then stood up and walked in his easy, boneless way to the cabinets along the side wall. "You want sugar and all that shite?"

"Of course." Vlad examined his army. Jorg stood by the front door, fingering his cauliflower

One Bullet   261

ear while he peeked between the blinds. Lars sat at the table, licking grease off a slice of cold pizza. Fergus stood with his back to the wall, his gun still in his hand. And Arturo stood jingling his car keys.

The siren they'd heard drew closer, right outside on Thomas Drive, and then it sped past.

"It was an ambulance," Jorg said. He laughed. "Just an ambulance."

But Vlad wasn't listening. He was thinking about Joe. What was Joe doing in a bank? Why was Joe still in town? Any sane man would have run.

Simon passed him a cup of coffee with a plastic spoon in it. "If Joe is at that bank, what are we waiting for? Let's go fix the bastard."

Vlad shook his head. "He will have left by the time you get there, but I know what he's doing. Joe is a bagman, a money guy. He must have stashed money in a half dozen different accounts around town. Simon, take Lars and Jorg and cross the bridge. Start checking the banks on 23rd Street. At each bank, one of you can go in and look for Joe, while the other two wait outside and watch the doors."

"Finally some action," Simon said. He marched to the door. Jorg and Lars fell in behind him.

Lars stopped halfway through the door and looked back. "What do we do if we find him?"

Vlad smiled. "If Joe has the money, kill him and bring me the money. If he doesn't have the money, bring him to me."

Lars squinted, and his lips moved. "So, uh..."

"I want the bag of money," Vlad said. He needed the money to get the Cartel off his back. Ernesto had given him until tonight to return their $700,000 or Calm Ruben would torture and kill him. "Kill Joe."

Lars nodded. "Okay, get the money, kill Joe."

The three soldiers left, and Arturo started to follow them. "You want us to check the banks here at the Beach?" he asked.

"No, I have an important job for you two," Vlad said to Arturo and Fergus. "Arturo, you worked in a pizza shop, yes?"

"In Dallas when I was a kid." Arturo nodded and looked at the front door.

Vlad walked back to the swinging door to the kitchen and held it open with one hand. He held his pistol with the other. He pointed at the big, brick pizza oven. "How hot do these ovens get?"

Arturo shrugged. "Much hotter than a regular oven. Up to 1,000 degrees."

"Okay." Vlad went back to the counter, picked up Tommy's phone, and brought up a search engine. He poked the screen and scrolled.

Fergus glanced at the front door. "Maybe we should leave? Go look for Joe?"

"It says here that cremation chambers cook at 1,400 to 1,800 degrees, and do the job in two to three hours," Vlad said. He kicked Manila Tommy's corpse. "You may have to cut him and the girl up to make them fit in the oven. And with the lower temperature, it will take an hour or two longer, but it should work."

One Bullet 263

Arturo stepped back and made the sign of the cross.

Fergus stared at the dead girl on the floor. "You want us to cremate Tommy in a pizza oven?"

"Exactly." Vlad clapped him on the shoulder. "Cypress always said you were the clever one. If you chop them up, they'll cook quicker. Get the oven warming up, and once you have them both inside, start cleaning up this mess." He pointed at the blood spatter on the walls, the broken can opener and the paper plates spilled across the floor.

Arturo rubbed his hands up and down his arms and chewed his lip. Fergus muttered to himself, but Vlad couldn't tell if they were curses or prayers.

Vlad tugged on his bloody shirt. "I'm going home to shower and change clothes. I'll come by later and check on your progress." He clapped his hands. "Get to work!"

The two men flinched, and went through the swinging door to the kitchen.

Vlad looked between the blinds to check the parking lot, and then stepped out and locked the front door.

* * *

Chapter 46
Joe

I stand at the back entrance to First Southern Bank with my hand inside an envelope, gripping the huge Ruger revolver. I need the keys to the truck, but they're in my right pocket and my right is holding the gun, so I reach over and fish them out with my left hand. It has to look awkward to people.

Take one step toward the exit, ready to fight my way through the Syndicate to get Pono safely to the airport.

The automatic door slides open.

There's a guy in my way--a skinny kid pushing a dolly full of soda pop. He must be here to re-stock the drink machines.

Which reminds me of Pudge Loomis. Pudge drives a supply truck for Coin and Vending. He goes all around Bay County re-stocking snack machines. Now I know how I'm going to get Pono into the airport without the Cartel or the Syndicate spotting us.

I let the kid go by and then march out fast. The first thing I gotta do is get out of here alive. The teller with the fake red hair called someone and they told her to give me her phone. It must be the Syndicate because Cypress has people in the banks to help with his money laundering.

Outside, I'm walking fast, head up and looking for trouble.

The lot is crowded with people hurrying in and out of the bank, and cars sitting bumper-to-bumper

One Bullet 265

at the drive-through windows. I know most of the Syndicate faces, but I don't know all their cars so I'm not sure what to look for.

Unlock the bubba truck and climb up into the cab. One good thing about a truck cab is that no one can hide in the back seat and surprise you. I drop Fake Red's phone and the envelope of money on the floorboard, but keep the Ruger in my lap. Crank up and back out fast.

As soon as I pull up to the sidewalk, Pono bolts out of the bank and jumps into the passenger's seat. She's agile for a big girl. Being young helps, too.

"Did you see anyone?" Pono asks. Her eyes are big again.

"No, I think we're okay, but I'm gonna drive around and make sure." I take the turn onto 23rd Street too fast and the truck leans like it might tip over. Some moron honks at us and whips his SUV into the next lane to pass. With all the cops around, I should slow down.

The bubba truck is tall, and I have good visibility with its giant side mirrors, but it's hard to spot people following you if they're careful. Maybe the Syndicate is hanging back, waiting for us to stop somewhere quiet. Up ahead, a king cab truck with a toolbox on the back turns into the Lowe's hardware store.

I follow the king cab. On any morning, the parking lot of Lowes is packed with contractors, house painters and construction workers. And they all drive big bubba trucks. I park and the truck blends right in. I leave the engine running, and sit and watch to see if anyone is following us.

But the people coming in all get out of their trucks and go inside. Nobody just sits there, like we're doing.

"Did you need something here?" Pono asks.

I look over and she's holding the teller's phone in its bubblegum-colored shell. "No. I just want to be sure no one is following us."

"Why did that girl give you her phone? This is brand new." Pono shows me the phone but I can't tell one model from another. "She looked really scared."

"I don't know that kid, but somebody ordered her to give me the phone. Probably Cypress or Vlad." I lean forward and tuck the gun under the front seat where I can reach it fast if I need to. "Hey, does that tell the last number she called?" I point at the phone.

"Sure." Pono's big fingers dance over the touchscreen. "Says she called somebody named 'Tommy' and it has his number."

That has to be Manila Tommy, which means she called the Syndicate, not the Cartel. I'm not sure if this is better or worse, but it feels good to know something. "We have to get you to the airport. Getting there shouldn't be a problem, but getting inside might be. The Syndicate and the Cartel will have people waiting for us."

Pono nods. "That makes sense. They both want the money. Can't I just take a cab or an airport shuttle? Once I'm inside, I'll be safe. No one kills anyone inside an airport."

I look at her.

One Bullet   267

Then she remembers what I told her earlier, about how Dwayne killed the Cartel bagman in an airport bathroom, and damn near killed me, too. Just because you think a place is safe, doesn't mean it is.

She says, "Oh," in a small voice.

"Yeah. We can't risk it. Getting you killed before you board the plane isn't part of my plan."

"You have a plan?" She leans forward and I see hope mixed with fear, and I know I have to do this one thing right. I have to save this girl.

"I got a plan. May I?" I reach for the phone and she hands it over. I dial Pudge Loomis's number from memory. For normal people, their 'Contacts' list in their phone is full of friends. But when you're a criminal, law enforcement calls your 'Contacts' list 'known associates' and 'co-conspirators.' So you learn to memorize phone numbers.

Pudge Loomis answers on the third ring. "Yeah-lo?"

"It's Joe. Where are you?"

"Why you want to know?"

Pudge is crunching ice in his teeth. Old-school country music plays in the background, and I can hear people talking. I know where Pudge is, so I turn the key and crank the truck.

"Pudge, I need to borrow your delivery truck for a few hours. Meet me at your place. We'll need two extra uniforms."

"My delivery truck, huh? Yeah, uh, lemme think...no. Hell no!" Pudge hangs up.

Hmm. Pudge has worked for the Syndicate for years--cash businesses like vending machines are a great way to launder money. I know he's been skimming a little extra each month to pay for his gambling habit. Knowing that gives me leverage.

Pudge just needs reminding.

I pull out of Lowes, cut down Wilson Avenue, and onto 19th Street. No one leaves the lot at the same time we do, so I don't think the Syndicate has found us yet. The country music in the background while Pudge talked gave him away. He's at Mr. Leo's bar for his mid-morning constitutional. Some people end the day with a drink. Pudge starts it with one.

The morning rush is over and traffic thins out, making it easy to notice all the cops on the road. It's like the President is coming to visit, and there are Sheriff's cars and PCPD on every other corner. Pono keeps tugging at her seat belt, and I know the poor kid is nervous.

I should say something to reassure her, but what? 'Hey kid, I've got two guns and seven whole bullets now, so we'll be fine. It's just a half dozen Syndicate soldiers and an entire Mexican drug cartel. Plus the cops. No problem.'

I suck at pep talks.

"I just gotta talk to this guy named Pudge Loomis. He's our way in to the airport," I say.

"Did he just hang up on you?" she asks.

"Yeah, Pudge is kinda paranoid." I shrug. "He gambles, so he's used to people looking for him." But it pisses me off that he hung up on me. I never

One Bullet 269

told Cypress about Pudge stealing, and he owes me for that.

I put my blinker on to turn in at Mr. Leo's. Leo's is a cinderblock building with a low roof and a dirt-and-grass parking lot. The sign out front says, "Dart tournament Thurs nite. Ninjas welcome."

As soon as I'm inside, I'll drag Pudge out back and convince him to help us.

The problem is, he's pulling out of the lot just as we turn in. Pudge doesn't recognize the bubba truck I'm driving, and he's probably half drunk anyway. He wheels his "Coin and Vending" delivery truck out onto Highway 390 without even checking for cars.

"Hell."

"Is that our guy?" Pono asks.

"Yeah. We'll get him." I pull out to the light and have to wait to make a left turn. Pudge is three cars ahead, but his big, gray truck is easy to spot. The bubba truck is stout, but it isn't heavy enough to push Pudge's delivery truck off the road, and there are too many cops around anyway. I have to be patient. But we don't have all day.

We follow him out to 23rd Street and I have to drop back so he won't spot us. As we're heading west, I see a white Chrysler 300 flying east-- Simon's car. As the Chrysler blows by, I duck down behind the wheel, but the Syndicate soldiers don't even notice us.

They must be heading for the bank we just left.

Up ahead, Pudge turns right and then takes a left into the south side of Gulf Coast State College.

270 Mark Boss

He guides the truck through the crowded lot and parks it. Damn, I guess he's actually working today.

Gulf Coast is like those colleges you see in movies, with broad sidewalks and old oak trees. Everyone should be tan and wearing flip flops, except it's January. So instead it's hoodies and sneakers, and everyone looks sleepy.

I reach for my door handle, but there's lots of kids walking to class, standing around smoking and monkeying with their phones. If I try to follow him, Pudge will spot me in a heartbeat. Pono, however, is an actual college student.

"I don't really fit in here but I need to know which building he goes in. He's the key to getting into the airport."

Pono stares at the big delivery truck for a minute. She tugs on her seatbelt again. "You want me to follow this guy?"

"Just until we know what building he's going into. It'll be okay. There's people all around. I'll watch for you."

She unbuckles her seatbelt and picks up her brother's laptop computer. "Joe, did you go to school?"

"High school. Part of it, anyway."

She nods at the truck. "Is this Pudge guy dangerous?"

The delivery truck's door pops open, and Pudge tumbles down with all the grace of a horse falling out of a tree. He's five feet tall, and at least five feet wide. Even from here, I can see him stagger. He rolls up the back door of the truck, and wrestles out a yellow dolly. While we watch, he loads the dolly

One Bullet 271

with boxes of snacks. Despite the cold January weather, sweat stains his gray uniform shirt.

A ripple runs through Pono all the way to her shoulders, and she bursts out laughing.

"I'm pretty sure you can take him," I say.

Pono laughs so hard she snorts. Then she gets out and goes down the sidewalk with her brother's laptop under her arm like she's been a student here for years. Up ahead of her, Pudge wheels his dolly toward a big building and stares at the college girls. He says something to one of them and she flips him her middle finger. Kids.

I tuck the Ruger in my belt under my jacket, lock the truck and follow from a distance. It's tricky to gauge the right distance. People look around them, but they don't look very far. It's a caveman thing. They don't look any farther than someone can throw a rock or a spear at them. So I can't go near Pudge. But if Pono is near enough to see him, and I can see Pono, this can work.

Some polite kid holds the door for him, and Pudge wheels the dolly into the cafeteria. Pono goes inside, too, and I find a bench outside where I can watch through the wide glass windows. I didn't think to bring the bubblegum cell phone and I don't smoke, so it's hard to just sit here without drawing attention.

Down the sidewalk I see a cop, and it's not some rent-a-cop with a radio and pepper spray. It's a real cop with a badge and a gun. I look up and Pono is by the windows inside, signaling me. Time to go.

I hurry inside the cafeteria and slide into a chair next to Pono. There aren't many kids in here yet because it's too early for lunch, but there are a few studying in groups at round tables. It seems like all the kids have tattoos now. Across the long room, Pudge is re-stocking the vending machines along the wall. He works slowly and it gives me time to think.

I guess Pono can read the look on my face. "There are people around," she says.

"Yeah. It'd be better if we could catch him in another building. Somewhere quiet. But we don't have a lot of time to fool with this. Besides, I just need to talk him into helping us."

"I bet you're very convincing," Pono says. I look over but she isn't smiling. She's serious. And she's right.

The Ruger is digging into my back in the little plastic chair. I look through the window behind us to make sure the cop has moved on. Then I check for cameras above the vending machines. Pudge is unloading his last box of snacks, and he shoves shiny bags of chips into the vending machine.

Over to my left is a sign for restrooms, and the doors are back off the main room in a sort of nook. It looks like a quiet spot. "Back in minute," I say and smile like everything is fine.

I march across the room, walking fast. Pudge looks up and I grab the collar of his shirt and herd him toward the men's room. The last time I went in a public restroom I got the hell beat out of me, but this is Pudge Loomis and my only worry is that he'll scream.

One Bullet 273

"Joe, what the hell?" is all that comes out of his mouth. That and the stink of rum.

I hustle him into the bathroom and let go of his shirt. He backs up until he runs into a sink. "You shouldn't hang up on people, Pudge. It's rude."

"Joe, Joe, listen, man." Pudge holds up his fat little hands and they're filthy. I mean dirty like he cleaned a septic tank barehanded. "Just take it easy."

There's no one at the urinals and I check the three stalls and they're empty. I have to make this quick.

"Pudge, I need your delivery truck and a couple of spare uniforms for two hours. That's it. You can take a siesta at your house, and I'll bring the truck right back. Your boss at Coin and Vending will never know."

Pudge shakes his head, and his beady little eyes dart at the door. I step between him and the only exit. "Don't be stupid. I'm asking nice here."

"I can't. I can't even be seen with you, Joe. Everyone is looking for you. The Syndicate, the Cartel, hell, probably the cops, too. You are radioactive, man. You're gonna get me killed." Pudge puffs out his chest. "You can beat me senseless, but I ain't giving you the keys to the truck. Vlad will kill me slow if I help you."

I nod, and pretend like I'm thinking it over. "When I found out you were skimming money from the machines, did I tell anyone? Did I tell Coin and Vending, or Vlad, or Mr. Cypress? No. Now I thought I could ask a favor and you'd do it, but no.

So it's like this. You help me, or I call Mr. Cypress and tell him you've been stealing from him."

Pudge stares at me, then starts laughing. He doubles over and slaps his knees and his laughter echoes off the tile floor. He must be drunker than I thought.

"Cypress? I ain't afraid of Cypress," Pudge says. "Because he's dead! You gonna tell him to come haunt me?" Pudge laughs and his nose runs a ribbon of mucus down his lip.

Cypress is dead? So Vlad...is the new boss. Things are worse than I thought, but they make a lot more sense. Cypress was a mean old bastard, but he kinda liked me. Or at least trusted me enough to handle his money. Vlad is another kind of animal.

"It doesn't change anything," I say. "If I tell Vlad you stole from the Syndicate, he'll come after you. Vlad is worse than Cypress." It sounds good, but Pudge is still shaking his head, so I step into his space and look down at him. "I need the truck, Pudge. Just for a few hours."

"Okay, Joe. You win." He sticks a dirty hand under his belly and into his pants pocket. "Here's the keys. The gas tank is half full."

I reach for the keys. Pudge's hand whips up, and he's holding a blackjack--a lump of lead covered in leather, with a strap for your hand. I try to lean out of the way, but he slaps me with it.

A blackjack can shut your lights off quick. I turn into a plank and just tip over. It's weird. I watch the sinks, the mirrors, then the ceiling go by as I fall on the tile floor.

Pudge runs for the door. He's laughing.

One Bullet 275

He yanks the door open.

Pono is there. She hits him with the laptop. Not swinging it flat, like most people would. She uses the edge and nails him between the eyes.

Pudge falls on his ass, cradling his face.

Pono steps inside the bathroom, closes the door and leans against it. "I was listening outside. So we're going to use his delivery truck and some uniforms to sneak inside the airport?"

I try to answer but my brain is scrambled and it comes out a grunt.

"Hey, are you okay?" Pono goes around Pudge and leans over me. Her hair dangles in my face and it tickles.

I sit up and rub my head. "Yeah, I'm okay." She helps me up, and it scares me that I need the help. But the fog is wearing off, and now I'm pissed.

Pudge holds his face and moans. I fish in his pocket and pull out two big key rings. "We're taking the truck. I'm going by your place for a few shirts, and I'll bring the truck back later. Take a cab home."

"You can't do this to me, Joe." Pudge squirms like a turtle on its back. "The moment you go out that door, I'm calling Vlad."

I draw the Ruger and show him the gun. His eyes pop. I shove the barrel into his throat and lean on it. Pudge gasps for air.

"If you call Vlad, or the cops, or your bookie...if you even use a phone before I bring that truck back, I will murder you."

His beady eyes focus and he's foolish enough to look at me. He looks away fast. Tears leak out and roll off his fat cheeks onto the tile. "Don't kill me, please. Don't kill me."

His phone is sticking out of his shirt pocket. I yank the phone out and tuck it in my pocket. Scoop his blackjack off the floor and see that the old leather split when he hit me, so I drop it next to him. Hold the door open for Pono, Warrior Princess, and we leave.

* * *

Chapter 47
Fergus and Arturo

"Will there still be bones?" Fergus asked. "I mean, after we cook them." He stood at the stainless steel sink in the kitchen of the pizzeria. Manila Tommy lay on the counter with his legs dangling in the sink. Fergus unlaced Tommy's shoes and set them on the floor.

Across the room, Arturo squinted at the brick pizza oven. "Yes. There will be bones. I think they crush them after they cremate."

Fergus sawed at Tommy's right leg, just below the knee. Some of the blood ran into the sink, but the rest poured off the counter and splashed his jeans. "Bloody hell, I forgot how much blood is in one man."

The leg came free and Fergus dropped it into a five-gallon stew pot on the floor. "This is going to take all damn day." He stepped back and ran a paper towel over his sweaty face. Tiny bits of white lint clung to his unshaven chin.

Arturo came over, but stood outside the puddle of blood. "Tommy had a lot of blood for a junkie."

"Gallons." Fergus dropped his bloody steak knife in the sink. "You don't suppose there's beer around, do you? I could use a pint."

"Good thinking." Arturo turned to check the refrigerator, but the dead girl lay in front of the door. He gently rolled her to one side. She was still flexible, not stiff yet. When he rolled her onto her

278   Mark Boss

back, they saw the dozen exit wounds on her chest. Arturo flinched.

Fergus shook his head. "We shot a girl. What is she? Twenty years old, maybe? We'll burn in Hell for sure."

"My father killed three men in his life. One was his best friend," Arturo said as he searched the refrigerator. He pulled out two bottles of Heineken and passed one to Fergus. "My father told me never to harm a woman. He said God would not forgive."

Fergus leaned on the counter and opened his beer. He raised the bottle to Manila Tommy. "You were a man of infinite jest, old Tom, but a damn fool." Fergus drank half the beer.

Arturo sat on a step stool and sipped his bottle. "I can't do it." He pointed the toe of his cowboy boot at the dead girl on the floor. "I can't chop her up."

"It's not right, Vlad leaving us his mess," Fergus said. "Look at this place. Blood everywhere. Tom and the bird both dead. What if one of the pizza boys didn't get the message about this place being closed? He'll come look in the window, shit himself, and call the cops."

Arturo leaned forward and lowered his voice. "Tommy said that Vlad killed Mr. Cypress, not the Kwan brothers."

"So Vlad killed Cypress and Tommy knew it, and Vlad killed him?" Fergus threw his bottle against the wall, and glass rained onto the floor. "Vlad! Where is he? Going home to take a shower and eat a hot breakfast, while I'm covered in Tommy's blood. It isn't right."

One Bullet 279

Fergus picked up his gun and went to the front door. He pushed the blinds apart with his thumb and forefinger and watched the cars passing on Thomas Drive. "Arturo, you ever visit Thailand?"

Arturo shook his head, and set his empty beer bottle next to the dead girl. Then picked it back up.

"I know a fellow owns a bar over there," Fergus said. "The beer is piss, but the girls are pretty, and you can get football on satellite. Bet he could use two men like us, you know, to mind the door. Crack the odd head now and then." Fergus walked back and stood in the center of the bloody kitchen. "I say we leave this mess for Vlad and go to Thailand."

Arturo stood up and rattled his car keys. "I like this plan."

* * *

Chapter 48
Vlad

Vlad shut the front door of the pizzeria and locked it. He went around the side of the building to where his Porsche Cayenne was parked in back. The blood on his shirt had cooled but was still wet, and the cotton stuck to his chest.

He opened the driver's door and put the H&K pistol on the seat. Took a careful look at the loading docks behind the strip mall, and then pulled off his suit coat and shirt. He wadded the clothes up and tossed them onto the floorboard.

Vlad stood still for a moment. He shut his eyes and let the morning sun soak into his shoulders. It was a weak, January sun, but it had rained for days so he welcomed the feel of it. He opened his eyes, expecting to see an SUV full of Cartel gunmen, or a half dozen cop cars, or Greater Kwan parachuting out of the sky with a machine gun in each hand.

Vlad laughed. Let them come. He'd outsmart them all. Out fight them all. He cranked the Porsche and whipped out of the lot, gravel crunching beneath the tires. With the windows open to the salt smell of the Gulf of Mexico, Vlad drove to the far western end of Panama City Beach and turned off into his neighborhood.

When he reached his street, he drove around the block to check for the Cartel, but saw nothing more than retirees digging in their dead, brown yards and a Postal Service truck starting its morning route. He went up the street to his house, bounced

One Bullet 281

over the lip of the driveway and clicked the garage door opener.

A new Ford Mustang sat cooling in the garage. Vlad blinked, and then remembered Hax had taken The Finn to the hospital for her snakebite. He eased the Porsche in next to the Mustang, but left the garage door open in case he needed to get out in a hurry. Vlad took the wad of bloody clothes in his left hand, and his gun in his right, and went inside.

He heard Genghis and Amber bark from the back yard, but it was a greeting bark, not a warning. "Hax, are you here?"

"Yeah. Yes, sir. In the kitchen," Hax called.

Vlad went down the hall to the kitchen. "Get me a garbage bag to throw these clothes..."

The Finn sat on the countertop. She'd obviously showered and changed her clothes. The sun through the window made her hair shimmer. Vlad smiled and took a step toward her.

The toaster popped.

Vlad swung the pistol up.

Hax stood at the toaster with a Pop-Tart in his hands. The hacker dropped the Pop-Tart, and it hit the granite counter and crumbled. He blew on his fingertips and licked them. "They were in the cabinet. I'm really hungry. She said it would be okay." Hax pointed at The Finn.

"Of course. Eat all you wish," Vlad said and smiled at The Finn. He stood with his shoulders back so she could admire the breadth of his chest and arms. "You look well. The bite of one snake was no match for you."

"It was a small snake," The Finn said.

282   Mark Boss

Vlad's eyes drifted down to her snug jeans, and he imagined her muscular thighs wrapped around him.

"I'm fine, too," Hax said as scooped broken bits of Pop-Tart into his mouth. "A truckload of Cartel thugs tried to murder me at the hospital, but I'm good. Just ducky."

"You should return to the Hack House. Work at finding Joe and Greater Kwan," Vlad said to Hax.

"Yeah, uh, Kwan found us. He killed everyone and burned the house down. Both houses probably." Hax pulled a bottle of Sunny D orange drink out of the refrigerator. He read the date on the bottle, nodded and opened it.

Vlad gripped his pistol. "Kwan killed my hackers and--"

"You have a house guest," The Finn said.

"Lacey is back?" Vlad asked. Had Calm Ruben already grown sick of her? Outside of the bedroom, Lacey was needy and irritating.

"Nope. Carly," Hax said with his mouth full.

"Carly is here?" Vlad shook his head. What the hell was happening? He stood in the kitchen and squeezed the wad of bloody clothes. He wanted a hot shower. He wanted breakfast. He wanted to take The Finn to bed. And then murder Joe and Greater Kwan and return the money to the Cartel before they tortured and killed him. "Shit."

"Yeah," Hax said. "Some mornings it's just not worth getting up."

"I did not sleep," Vlad murmured, then raised his voice. "I will speak with her. Where is she?"

One Bullet 283

The Finn pointed toward his bedroom, and she wasn't smiling.

Vlad dropped the wad of clothes in the sink, squared his shoulders and went down the hallway.

His bedroom door was shut and he almost knocked.

When he flung the door open, the first thing he noticed was that the room was clean. When Lacey was there, it was a mess.

The second thing was Carly.

Carly lay on his bed, wearing his bathrobe. Her hair was wet, but her makeup was fixed. She rolled over on her side and the loosely belted robe hung open. Vlad took a long look at her cleavage and grinned.

"Hey," Carly said. "I brought you something." She reached into a pocket and pulled out a stubby key. She twirled the key on her finger, and hung one foot off the bed. "It opens a locker at the airport. Guess what's inside?"

"My money," Vlad said, but his throat was tight.

"Our money." She dropped the key inside the robe and arched her back. "Why don't you come get it?"

Without taking his eyes off of her, Vlad reached behind him for the door. His hand found the knob and he pushed it back to close it, but it hit something.

Vlad looked down and saw a boot. A heavy, tanker style boot--the kind you can stomp someone to death with.

The Finn leaned on the door jam. "Am I interrupting?"

"Yeah, why don't you go oil your gun," Carly said.

The Finn glared. "Maybe I'll take target practice first."

Vlad glanced at The Finn. "We were about to negotiate."

"Is that what you call it?" The Finn crossed her arms. And waited.

Vlad sucked in a breath, prepared to sigh. But sighing was for weaker men. Instead, he called out, "Carly, get dressed and come to the kitchen."

Carly swung off the bed. "I guess I'll get dressed." She went into the master bath and slammed the door.

Vlad turned to walk past The Finn, and for a moment they were very close. She smelled clean, but cold, like a laboratory. A shiver crept from the scar at the base of his spine all the way up to his hairline. Vlad went down the hall.

In the kitchen, Hax stood at the counter eating Life cereal straight from the box. Vlad thought of lab rats and food pellets and shook his head. The Finn went to the glass door and watched the dogs chase a squirrel around the back yard.

Vlad looked at his truck tire and the sledgehammer leaning against it in the dead grass. Perhaps he had time for a quick workout and some fun with the dogs. He reached for the sliding door, but heard footsteps behind him.

Carly came out in yesterday's outfit, but the clothes were clean and carefully ironed. Vlad

One Bullet   285

thought about it a moment, trying to remember if he owned an iron or an ironing board. "Carly, why are you here?" he asked.

She sat in his recliner and crossed her legs. "I need your help."

"You don't need any man's help."

Carly smirked, but her eyes were hard. "The Cartel is sitting on the airport, waiting for Joe, and probably to make sure you don't leave town. If I can't get inside, I can't use this." She held up the locker key.

"You're certain the money is in the locker?" Vlad asked.

"It has to be." Carly looked at the glass door. Amber stood with her nose pressed to the glass, watching her. "My partner, Dwayne, betrayed me. He was supposed to bring me the cash, and keep the envelope with the password to the overseas account. That was the deal. Instead, he stored the money in a locker and switched it out for a bag of counterfeit. But Dwayne didn't have time to give me the bag of counterfeit, because Joe took it from him. Dwayne tricked me."

"He tricked you? Like you tricked Joe?" Vlad laughed. "Did this Dwayne really beat Joe in a fight?"

"Yeah, in the men's room."

Maybe Joe isn't as tough as Cypress said, Vlad thought. "So with the Cartel watching the airport, you can't get inside. You want me to help you get the money?"

"Duh, yeah," Carly said.

"And you want a portion?"

"It's $700,000. Give me $100,000, you keep the rest," Carly said. She sat forward in the chair. Outside, Amber's head swung back and forth, watching the humans talk.

Vlad pretended to consider her proposal. He knew the moment he had the cash, he'd be on the phone to Ernesto to hand it over to Calm Ruben. What was left of the Syndicate was no match for the massive Cartel. "You get $50,000, and you leave town. That's it."

Carly opened her mouth, then closed it. Nodded.

The Finn turned away from the glass door. "There is the matter of my fee. You paid me fifty percent up front for the hit on Cypress. I want the remaining half before I agree to any future operations, such as killing this Joe."

Vlad blew out a lungful of air.

Hax leaned over the kitchen counter. "Yeah, uh, I didn't get paid this month. And since Kwan killed everybody and burned the house down, I'm thinking of...well, looking at other opportunities. " Hax leaned his head over, and his neck popped. "I might take my talents to Europe."

Everyone, including Amber, stared at him.

"Hey, programmers are sought after. I got skills," Hax said.

"Hmm," Vlad said. Fifty percent of The Finn's fee, a month's salary to Hax, and fifty thousand to Carly meant he'd be going to Calm Ruben with half of what he needed.

He wondered what would happen if he yanked open the glass door and commanded the dogs to

One Bullet 287

attack. He'd never set them on anyone. Plus he had the H&K in his belt. He could put Carly and Hax in the pizza oven with Manila Tommy, but The Finn was far more dangerous. She was certainly armed and might kill him. He was outnumbered, and it would be smart to wait until he had the advantage.

After Carly, Hax and The Finn helped him kill Joe and take the cash, he wouldn't need them anymore. It was a shame to waste extraordinary women like The Finn and Carly, but leading the Syndicate meant making hard decisions.

So what to do next? If he went to the airport, the Cartel would grab him and take him to Calm Ruben. Vlad watched Genghis play with a soccer ball and thought about it.

"Give me the key." He put his hand out to Carly. "I'll call Joe, and send him to the airport with the key. He's a bag man. He can figure out how to get past the Cartel and bring us the money."

The Finn shook her head. "Why would Joe bring you the money? The moment he has it, he'll flee."

"You obviously don't know Joe," Carly said. She looked at Vlad and smiled. "I think I know what Vlad has in mind. Joe will bring the money, because he'll think Vlad has me."

"Exactly," Vlad said. "I'll call Joe and arrange a place to meet him." He turned toward the bedroom. This could work. Joe would handle the dangerous part of getting past the Cartel into the airport. Vlad would get the money, and then kill everyone. A simple plan usually worked best.

288   Mark Boss

But first he wanted a hot shower. Vlad got three steps down the hall before he heard Carly say, "We're not sending you with the key to meet Joe."

Vlad marched back to the living room. "Sending me? No one sends me. I send--"

"She's right," The Finn said.

"What?"

Carly crossed her arms. "If you and Joe meet, it will be a race to see who loses their temper first. You'll kill each other. No, I should go."

"Absolutely not," Vlad said. "We can't trust you. If you meet Joe, you'll get the money and run away together. I'll go."

"No, I should go," The Finn said.

"Why? So you can grab the other half of your fee and jump on a plane back to Russia?" Carly asked.

"Russia?" The Finn glared at her. "I'm from Finland. Thus, the name."

"Whatever, I'm not giving you the key, bitch," Carly said.

The Finn stepped toward Carly, and Vlad jumped between them. "Stop." He held up his palms. "I know what to do. We need to send someone Joe has seen before. Someone he won't view as a threat. Him." He pointed at Hax.

Hax choked on his Sunny D. "What?"

* * *

Chapter 49
Hax

The orange-flavored Sunny D went down his lungs instead of his throat, and Hax turned to spit into the sink, but Vlad's wad of bloody clothes blocked the drain. Hax swallowed hard and cleared his throat. "This is a bad idea. I'm not a bag man, or a gun man, or a hit man. I'm a hacker."

"It's simple," Vlad said. "Just do what we tell you. Like a robot." The big thug tucked his gun in his belt. "I'll be in the shower. Then we'll call Joe and set up a meeting." Vlad went down the hall.

Hax looked across the bar into the living room. Everyone looked mad, except for Amber, who stood panting at the glass door. A halo of fog on the glass surrounded her head.

The Finn put one boot on the edge of the fireplace, leaned forward and stretched her hamstrings. Hax watched and even Genghis came over to the door to see.

"All she needs is a pole and some bad music." Carly looked at Hax and rolled her eyes.

The Finn straightened and looked at Hax. "While you are meeting Joe, I must prepare for the second meeting."

"Second meeting?" Hax asked.

"The one where Joe hands the money over to Vlad, genius," Carly said. She held up her cell phone at arm's length, with the camera facing toward her. Her entire expression changed--her eyes went soft and wet and worried. She tapped the screen to take a video of herself, and spoke like she was out of breath from running.

"Joe, you have to help me. Vlad says if you don't bring the money, he'll...he'll hurt me. Please, Joe, I never betrayed you. I don't care about the money, I just want us to be together. And I--" Carly whipped the phone away from her face and stopped the video. She looked up at Hax and The Finn. "What? Joe will want proof Vlad has me."

Hax recalled the times he'd seen Joe and Carly together and how much he envied the big man for having a hot girlfriend. He shook his head. The Sunny D turned to acid in his stomach.

"I need your car keys," The Finn said.

"Why? Are you leaving?" Hax asked.

"No. I need to retrieve the guitar case we placed in your Mustang."

"Oh. Yeah, sure. I'll help." Hax followed The Finn down the hall to the garage. He watched the way she walked, quiet and purposeful, like a ninja. She opened the door and he stepped out into the garage. After the tension inside, the big garage felt freezing.

He unlocked the Mustang and wrestled the long guitar case out and onto the hood. The Finn popped the clasps open and flipped back the lid. A half dozen guns, several knives and a pair of yellow nunchaku sat nestled in foam inside.

The Finn whistled softly and ran her hands over the weapons.

Hax took a breath. "You think Vlad will send you ahead to set up an ambush for Joe?"

One Bullet 291

"Yes, that would be smart." The Finn held up a pistol with a long magazine. "The Glock Model 18C, fires three-round bursts. Excellent. Hard to acquire."

"I noticed when Carly held up the locker key that the key ring has the locker number on it. In case people forget what locker they rented," Hax said.

"Yes." The Finn checked the edge on a Gerber sheath knife with a skull crusher pommel.

"When Vlad sends you to set up the ambush, why don't you come to the airport instead and meet me?" Hax asked, and his words spilled out faster and faster. "I'll have the key. We can get the cash and leave. Go anywhere. That kind of money will pay for a lot in some countries. We could get a house--a beach house--and make margaritas and go fishing and...be happy." Hax reached for her hand, but she stepped back.

"Vlad owes me the remainder of my fee. I wish to collect," she said. Her eyes were flat. No expression on her face.

"You can take that out of the $700,000."

The Finn said nothing.

Hax looked away, then looked back at her. "It's not just the money, is it? It's Vlad."

"Yes. It is Vlad." The Finn shut the guitar case and slid it off the hood of the Mustang. The weight of it made her lean to one side as she went into the house.

* * *

Chapter 50
Joe

Maybe it's because college fills your head with ideas and information and all that, but the kids in the cafeteria don't notice a big girl and a bigger guy come out of the men's room together. Pono is frowning, and she looks ready to use the laptop on someone's face again. I'm walking slow, like a tired, old man.

When we reach the vending machines, I shut the glass front of the candy machine and grab hold of the dolly. With the dolly rolling in front of us to clear a path, we walk along the crowded sidewalk down to the parking lot and Pudge's delivery truck.

I haven't driven a big truck since I was a kid running untaxed cigarettes, but I'll figure it out. I swing the dolly up into the back of the truck. Pono grabs a nylon strap bolted to the frame, heaves herself up, and grabs the door and rolls it down. She's more nimble than you'd think for a girl her size.

We pile into the delivery truck and I flip through Pudge's huge key ring for the right key. The truck cranks on the first try, and I take us out of there slow and easy as I get used to the steering and brakes. At the stop sign leaving the lot, I realize the mirrors are adjusted for someone Pudge's height. I spend a minute with the windows down trying to get them straight, until some kid in an old Camaro rolls up behind us and beeps.

One Bullet 293

I pull out and the delivery truck bucks almost as hard as the bubba truck, but without the acceleration. Damn, I kinda miss that truck already. Flip the sun visor down, turn Pudge's talk radio station off, and think what to do next.

"So we're going to Pudge's house for some shirts and hats, then we'll dress up like vending machine people and sneak into the airport?" Pono asks.

"That's the plan."

"It's a good plan. Who notices vending people?" Pono digs between the seat cushions for her seat belt. I guess Pudge never has passengers. "My mom worked as a janitor in a shopping mall, and no one noticed her. Hundreds of people passed her every day and never said 'Hello.' At first, she said it made her feel like crap, but after a while she stopped caring."

I've never talked to a mall janitor, so I guess I'm one of those people who walked past her mother. But that doesn't mean I don't notice janitors. Some janitors are undercover cops, or gang informants, or ex-convicts. So I always watch them.

People in the South eat lunch early, so the traffic is heavier now. I'm extra careful with the big truck when I change lanes. "Pudge's trailer is just over in St. Andrews, so we'll be there in a few minutes."

"Joe, I'm not from here. I have no idea where St. Andrews is," Pono says.

"Oh, right. Sorry. I'm not from here, either, but I learned my way around for my job." My job.

Taking bags of cash back and forth between criminals. It doesn't sound very cool when I think about it. I tote cash like a mule drags a plow. Big deal. Everything feels dirty now.

We veer off 15th Street onto Beck Avenue and into St. Andrews, an old part of town with a mix of rundown trailers and waterfront mansions, coffee shops and one strip club. But it's got a nice marina, and good restaurants, and there's always people around, even in the winter.

"So after we get inside the airport and I get on a plane for Hawaii, what will you do?" Pono asks. "You said you were going to kill them all. Is that a good plan?"

While we sit at a stop light, I squeeze the steering wheel and think about her question. A guy rides through the intersection on a rusty bike. He has a little, black dog sitting in a basket between the handlebars. It's cold out, but they both look happy.

"It took five seconds."

Pono leans forward and looks at me. "What did?"

"My fight with your brother, Dwayne." I say his name. I think it's the first time I've said it out loud, and it reminds me that he's laying in a hospital with two broken legs. No. I rub one hand over my eyes. Dwayne is dead. Carly shot him to death on the floor of his hospital room. Put a pillow over his face and shot him.

"It's not really his fault," I say. "Because he didn't know me, and I don't know for sure who put him up to ambushing me. Maybe Carly, maybe Vlad. But when I lost that fight, I lost everything. I

One Bullet 295

lost my woman, my job, my reputation. As a bag man, I never failed. Not once. But yesterday, in five seconds, that all changed."

The light turns green, and we rumble forward. I lean over the wheel and look for the side street that will take us to Pudge's.

Pono is quiet.

We drive down the street into an old neighborhood of rundown houses and giant oak trees dripping with Spanish moss. Pudge's doublewide trailer is set back from the street. His yard is dirt and leaves--no grass will grow because of the shade from the oaks. I've been here before to pick up laundered money, but Pudge always met me outside. I really don't know what to expect inside. Does he have a girlfriend, or kids, or an elderly parent?

"Will there be dogs? He seems like the type to have a pit bull," Pono says.

"No. He bets on dogs, but he doesn't own any." I roll the truck up his empty, dirt driveway. Tree limbs brush the top of the truck and acorns rain down on the metal roof and they sound like the first raindrops of a bad storm. Set the brake, shut the engine off and we sit for a minute.

"I can't kill them all. That was stupid to say, but I was mad," I say. "The Cartel is huge and powerful. The only way to square things is to give them their money back. Which is fine by me. I didn't steal it in the first place."

"Why not call and tell them you're trying to get it back?"

"They won't believe me. Would you?" I look at her and she shakes her head. "No, actions are the only thing that count now. I'll get their money and give it back to them somehow. But Vlad, that's different. He set me up. He told the rest of the Syndicate I murdered Mr. Cypress, but he's the one that did it. It's either Vlad kills me and runs the Syndicate, or I kill him, and get my life back."

"Including your life with Carly?" Pono asks.

I'm not sure about Carly. I want her back. Want her so bad it's a need, like thirst, or hunger. Maybe I got it wrong? Maybe Vlad set me up at the airport, and Carly got caught in the middle. But why did she murder Dwayne? I don't know. Still, she deserves a chance to explain. I give Pono my default answer. "I don't know."

I pop the door open and step down from the truck with the Ruger in my hand. Check the windows along the trailer to see if the blinds move. Listen for a radio or TV or someone talking on the phone, but nothing. All quiet.

Pudge must have thirty keys on his key ring. I stand on top of a wobbly cinderblock step and try them one-at-a-time on the front door. Pono keeps looking back at the street like she's expecting the cops to roll up.

The sixth key opens the door, and I step in fast with the Ruger up and ready. The trailer is still, and warm. And...moist. Humid, even. In January.

Pono steps in beside me, picks a wrench up off the floor, and hefts it. "You think anyone else is home?" she whispers.

One Bullet 297

I almost say they'd have to be in a coma not to hear the delivery truck, but I think of her brother's last days and keep my mouth shut.

It smells like beer, but also like fresh wood chips, which makes no sense.

The kitchen is not what I expected. It's neat. There are three bins along one wall, with newspaper, cardboard and aluminum beer cans divided among them. Pudge never struck me as a save-the-Earth guy. Maybe there's money in the aluminum beer cans. There are plenty of them in the bin.

Pono goes past me into the next room. "There's a washing machine, but no clothes in the dryer."

"Must be in his bedroom. We just need two shirts and two caps." We go back through the living room. There's only one chair, a sagging recliner in front of an old, projection-style TV. An upended milk crate for a footrest. There are half a dozen ball caps on nails above the door. I grab two of them. They're gray colored and have "Coin & Vending" in curly letters on the front.

I pass one to Pono and she sniffs the hat and frowns. "I hope he washed his shirts, at least."

"Me, too. Let's check his bedroom." I start down the hall, but it's so narrow I have to turn my shoulders sideways. Pudge has homemade wooden shelving on both sides of the hall. Glass cases fill the shelves. There's no overhead light, and the hall is dim.

I stop.

Something on my left moves, but when I turn my head I don't see anything. The glass cases are stacked from the floor to just below the ceiling. "What is this?" My first thought is drugs, that Pudge must be making drugs, but you don't make meth in a glass fish tank.

And these tanks aren't full of fish.

They're full of snakes.

Pono says, "Ohmigod," and I hear her retreat into the living room. "Joe. Joe, I don't like snakes." She sounds out of breath.

I want to turn and look back at her, but I can't look away from the cases. Everywhere there are eyes. Hard, black little eyes looking at me. Above my head, beside me, in front of me. Everywhere.

On the floor by my right foot is a case full of tiny, white mice scrambling over each other in a pile of fresh wood chips. The mice, I realize, aren't pets. They're food for the snakes. Next to them is a case with little frogs clinging to the glass walls. More food.

It's very warm in here. Sweat starts under my hair and rolls down my forehead. "Pono, just stay out there. I'll get the shirts and be right back."

"Okay." Her voice sounds like a little girl's.

When I take a step, the floor creaks and a snake rattles its tail. That weird, saltshaker sound that makes your heart thud against your ribs. It's high, and to my right. I look up, but the cases have tree limbs and rocks and plants in them and I can't see the rattlesnake. But I can hear it.

Take another step, and another rattle starts. This time on my left.

I turn completely sideways and scoot along like a crab, with as much room between me and cases as

One Bullet   299

possible. While I'm trying to control my breathing, I notice the cases have plywood covers on top, with a rock or a brick holding them down.

That's good to know. I crab walk two more steps and I'm almost to the bedroom.

"Joe?" Pono calls.

I stop and look back. "Yeah?"

She points at the floor by my feet.

I look down and see a loose piece of plywood, about one foot wide by three feet long. There's a fist-sized rock on the floor, too. The case next to them has a piece of driftwood and a little plastic pirate in it, but no snake.

Hell.

With all the rattling from the other cases, I can't tell where the loose snake is.

This is bad.

I'd rather fight three guys than one rattlesnake.

The house phone rings.

I flinch and take a big jump forward and land in the bedroom.

"Hurry," Pono calls out.

I yank open the drawers of a cheap pressed-wood dresser, but it's all T-shirts and socks. Turn and see a laundry basket on the bed, full of folded gray shirts. I grab two off the top and they have "Coin & Vending" on the right pocket, and a decal that says "Pudge" on the left. "I got them."

Step into the hall. The rattling is so loud now it sounds like a bee hive. One of the snakes on my left, at shoulder height, rams his nose into the glass and leaves a smear. I can't help it, but I jump back and hit the row of cases behind me.

A case tumbles off the shelf. I don't try to grab it, and it hits the floor and shatters in front of me. It's between me and the living room.

The snake at my feet goes crazy, thrashing in the broken glass.

Pono throws the wrench at the wriggling snake and misses. I kick the thing aside, and run.

She flings the front door open and we both skip the cinder-block steps and just leap out. Run to the truck and climb up inside. I roll up my window, and crank the engine. Pudge's front door hangs open, swaying in the breeze.

I put the truck in 'Reverse' and the phone in my pocket rattles and I almost piss myself.

* * *

Chapter 51
Joe

As we roll down Pudge's dirt driveway to the street, the phone in my pocket rattles and I almost piss myself.

Pono sees me flinch and pulls her feet up on the seat. "Is there a snake in the truck?"

"No, it's that phone--the phone the red-haired girl in the bank gave me." It's still rattling, but with the bubblegum-colored rubber armor on it, the phone is hard to pull out of my pocket.

"Hello?" I hold the phone to my ear, but I can only hear a murmur. While I'm listening, I see a fat, speckled snake the length of my arm slither out of Pudge's trailer. It drops off the cinderblock steps and disappears into the leaves.

Pono locks her door.

The phone stops murmuring and I hold it out to look at the screen. It's a video of Carly talking. Then it stops. "What?" Press it to my ear. "Carly? Carly, don't hang up. Just tell me where you are." But no response.

I show Pono the phone. "Is it on video talk or something?"

She tries to take the phone but I can't let go. It's my link to Carly. Finally, Pono just pulls my wrist so she can see the screen. She pokes the touchscreen. "It's not video chat, it's a recorded video."

"I couldn't hear what Carly said."

"Let me jack up the volume." She taps a button, and then pushes my wrist back. I prop the phone against the dash so we can both watch.

In the video, Carly sits in a leather recliner, and she looks scared. Her face is flushed and she's out of breath. She says, "Joe, you have to help me. Vlad says if you don't bring the money, he'll...he'll hurt me. Please, Joe, I never betrayed you. I don't care about the money, I just want us to be together. And I--"

Someone yanks the phone away from Carly, and the video stops. I'm rocking back and forth in the truck, hot blood pumping in my temples. I will kill Vlad. Beat him to death with my fists if he hurts her. I know Carly betrayed me, or I think she did, but she looked really scared. I want to watch it again, but I don't think I can handle it. It's hard to breathe and I roll my window back down and suck up lungfuls of cold air.

I know Carly set me up at the airport. I think I know that. But Vlad knew about the exchange, too. Was it really all Carly? Was it Carly at all? I clench my fists and the knuckles pop so loud I can hear them.

Pono takes the phone from my hand the way you take a gun from somebody when they have it in their mouth.

The back of my neck is hot. I scrub my fingers through my short hair and down over my eyes and breathe and listen to the acorns fall on the truck. My foot has been on the brake so long it's starting to cramp, so I take the truck out of gear and flex my ankle.

One Bullet   303

"In the video it doesn't look like a hotel," Pono says. "It looks like somebody's house."

"Mr. Cypress has about six houses around here, plus Vlad's place, and who knows where else."

She squeezes my bicep. "There's no reason to believe anything Carly said. People lie. Think about why--"

The phone rattles. I look down and the Caller Identification says 'Tommy,' so I answer. "Yeah, Tommy?"

There's a pause, then a sound--half growl, half chuckle. I know that sound. Vlad.

"Joe, did you watch the little movie I sent you?" Vlad asks.

I can't seem to talk, so I just grunt.

"Good. Carly is lovely, isn't she? What's the English word? Photogenic. For now."

"What do you want?" It's hard to get the words out because my throat is so tight.

"I need a bagman. Know any good ones?" Vlad asks.

"Three or four. Call them."

"Where's your professional pride? You're Joe Barrow, the bagman who never fails. What was it? Ten jobs or twelve?" Vlad laughs, then his voice changes. "I'm sending one of my hackers to meet you, a boy you've met before named Hax. He will give you a key to an airport rental locker. Then you go to the airport, retrieve the money inside the locker, and bring it to me. Simple."

Pono is leaning over, listening. I look at her and she shakes her head 'No.'

But it makes sense now. When Dwayne knocked me out in the men's room at the airport, he had a few minutes before I woke up and went after him. He must have already rented the locker and stashed the bag of counterfeit cash in it. All he needed was a minute to switch the bags. Smart. I guess he had it all worked out, except for the part where I ran him over with Vlad's Lexus.

"Here is how you'll receive the key. I'll send Hax to the old..." Vlad goes on but I'm not listening.

When I think hard, I realize he won't hurt Carly. Vlad is a murdering thug, but he has limits. Like me. Which is hard to think about, to accept that we're alike in anything. But I don't think he'd kill a woman.

I say, "You won't do it."

"What? Don't interrupt. Now when you get to-_"

"You won't hurt Carly. It's beneath you to harm a woman. You won't kill her, you're bluffing."

Vlad clears his throat. "Joe, listen to me. You're right. I would never hurt Carly. But you put me in a bad position. Here is what I will do. I will give Carly to Calm Ruben. And we both know what he does to prisoners."

It feels like he reached through the phone and punched me in the chest. That short, hard punch that makes your heart skip a beat. It's hard to breathe. I put my forehead on the steering wheel and close my eyes. Calm Ruben is a monster. I can't let him take Carly. "Okay. I'll get your money."

One Bullet 305

"Good boy, Joe. You're a bagman. Stick with what you know."

It could be a set up. Maybe Vlad has another way into the airport and the locker key is a lure. Or maybe he'll wait until I deliver the money and then kill me. Once I'm dead, Vlad can tell the rest of the Syndicate whatever he wants.

He's right. I'm a bagman. I know how to run an exchange, and I know better than to let someone else pick the location of a meet. Wherever he wants me to meet Hax, I have to change it to somewhere in my favor.

"No."

Vlad stops. "What? What part is wrong? The location? The time? You know Hax, he won't give you any trouble. Even you could snap him in half."

"If we set up a meet in town, I'll have to go early to check it out. I'm not walking into another ambush. No, send Hax to meet me at the airport. He'll have to go through security to reach the locker area. So will I. We'll all be unarmed. That's the only way I'm doing this."

"All right, Joe, I'll send him to the airport," Vlad says.

"And I'm not giving Hax the money."

Vlad laughs, and this time it's a genuine roar. "I don't want you to! Give a hacker $700,000 and you'll never see him again. Nyet. I want you to deliver the money personally, like a good bagman should."

"Then we agree. I'll look for Hax at the lockers in the airport in two hours."

"Agreed. But listen. You picked the location for this meeting, so I'll pick the location for the next one. When you get the money, call me and I'll tell you where to bring the money."

"We'll see."

"No, Joe, we won't see. Simon already has Carly in the trunk of his car. You'll meet where I say or she goes straight to Calm Ruben."

"Okay."

Vlad hangs up. I look at the phone for a minute and then put it on the dash.

"That didn't sound good," Pono says.

I nod. It is bad, but it's not Pono's problem. It's mine, and it's time for me to fix it. "Ready to go to the airport? You've got a flight to catch."

* * *

Chapter 52
Joe

I back the delivery truck out of Pudge's dirt driveway and we rumble slowly through St. Andrews back out to Beck Avenue. Driving north through Lynn Haven is usually the faster way to the airport, but in this case we're already near the bridge, so I take the route through Panama City Beach. It's winter and traffic won't be too bad. We can make it out there in forty-five minutes, and that will give me time to put Pono on a plane before I meet Hax.

Pono uses her phone and she's quiet for a while. I work hard at thinking.

There's no point in trying to buy a bunch of guns. With only two hours until the meeting with Hax, I don't have time to set up a gun buy. Besides, I won't be able to carry them into the airport, and I need the money I have left to buy Pono a ticket home.

The moment Hax and I open the locker, he'll call Vlad and tell him I have the money. The second meeting will be soon after that. Vlad is smart, so he won't give me time to stock up on weapons and set a trap.

I'll have to make do with the tools I have.

Over the bridge, then curve right onto Back Beach Road away from the Gulf, and follow the highway until we hit the intersection with Highway 79. When we stop at the light, Pono puts her phone face down on her thigh. "I found a flight that leaves soon. It's here to Atlanta, then L.A., then on to Honolulu. It's expensive."

I take the bank envelope out of my jacket and hand it to her. "Go ahead and take whatever you need. Take some extra for food and a cab when you get home."

"My family will pick me up. They better. My cousin drives an airport shuttle," she says.

"You have a big family?"

"Huge. More like a tribe."

"That sounds nice." I wonder what that's like. A family, a tribe. Like a gang but you're all related. You can quit a gang, but you can't quit a family.

After the intersection, we pick up some speed on the highway and the delivery truck shakes. Something in the storage area bangs against the inside wall. I should have tied the dolly down.

It doesn't seem long before I spot the sign to turn for the airport. We follow the long access road in, past the outlying parking area. There are cars and people and a few taxicabs, but it's not crowded.

I watch for Cartel gunmen. They'll be sitting in parked cars, as close to the terminal as they can get. But it's hard to guide the big truck and look for killers at the same time. I don't spot any, but I'm sure they're here. If they're smart, and they are, they'll have a couple of guys inside as spotters. Probably hanging around the restaurant, where they can linger without drawing attention.

"Keep an eye out. If you see any guys that look like thugs, tell me," I say.

Pono nods. She leans forward in the seat and puts on a Coin & Vending shirt. She buttons it up

One Bullet 309

and then picks up a hat. Sniffs it and frowns. "I'm not putting this on until we get out of the truck."

"It's just for a little while. Once we get inside, we'll buy your ticket. You can go through security and then ditch the disguise when you reach the gate area." I put the other cap on and it smells like chewing tobacco and sweat.

We take the truck up next to the terminal and park. I tug off my jacket and put on Pudge's work shirt. At least it smells clean, although it's tight through the arms.

"We'll do exactly what Pudge did when we were watching him at the college," I say. "Are you ready?"

Pono tugs her hat down low and under the brim her eyes change and she's a Warrior Princess again. "I'm ready."

I put the big Ruger and the beat-up Browning under the seat, and then we pile out of the truck. Go around to the rollup door in back. Pono throws the latch and rolls the door up, and I reach in for the dolly. It slid around during the drive here and crushed a box of candy. There's blue and red M&Ms all over the floor of the truck.

While Pono stacks boxes on the dolly, I look around. There are people getting in and out of cars, hugging each other hello or goodbye--it's hard to tell which. Everyone's luggage is the same sized airline-approved nylon bag with the wheels and the handle.

Cab drivers stand around across the lane, monkeying with their phones and talking. A lone Mexican sits on a bench, smoking a cigarette, but he isn't watching us. Probably just some dude. The terminal's automatic doors slide open and a cop comes out.

Not a Panama City Beach cop, but some kind of airport cop. He looks down the sidewalk, then walks toward us.

"Heads up," I whisper to Pono.

The cop stops and hooks his thumbs in his equipment belt. He must have thirty pounds of gear hanging there--radio, gun, baton, pepper spray, spare mags. The radio is the real danger. The gun doesn't bother me because I know I can take it from him.

"What are you doing?" the cop asks.

I point at the dolly full of snacks. "We're due to stock the vending machines." I hope he doesn't notice my pants don't match my shirt, and my shoes are too fancy for this work.

"Yeah, I see that," the cops says. "But why are you parked out here?"

I spread my hands. Shrug.

"It's our first day on this route," Pono says. "We've never done the airport before. Are we supposed to park somewhere else?"

"Oh? Okay." The cop looks at her and she's smiling. When Pono smiles it's hard not to smile back. He does. "You're supposed to take it around there." He points. "There's reserved spots for service vehicles."

Pono watches where he points. I'm watching his hands. She smiles and puts a box back in the truck. "We'll move the truck right now. Thanks for telling us!"

One Bullet 311

"Sure, no problem," the cop says.

"Hey, you want a bag of M&Ms? We have an open box," she says.

The cop pats his stomach. "I better not, but thanks." He walks away, and waves to one of the cabbies.

I breathe out. Pick up the empty dolly and slide it into the truck. We have to pull forward and circle around the short-term parking lot, but the cop was right. There's a sign for service vehicles, and the parking spots are extra long to handle big trucks.

In a minute, the two of us have the truck open and the dolly loaded so fast I think we could actually work for Coin & Vending. I take one more look around for the Cartel or the Syndicate, then we go inside.

"It feels weird not having any luggage," Pono says as we walk side-by-side across the clean, white floors of the terminal.

"If things work out later today, I could go back to Dwayne's apartment and get your clothes. Mail them to you in Hawaii." If things work out. The odds of that are not good, but there's no point in making Pono carry that weight. She's got enough on her shoulders.

She stops walking. "Dwayne." People circle around us, headed for their flights.

"What?" I look around, still watching for trouble.

"Dwayne's body. I didn't make arrangements to have it sent home. I can't go home without him. What will I tell my mom? That I left him here?"

She's shaking and her voice is too loud.

312   Mark Boss

I lean the dolly against my waist and reach out.
Touch her hand. "Listen, I'll take care of it. We
need to get you home, get you safe. When I'm done
with Vlad and the money and all that, I'll call you
and we'll make the arrangements. Okay?"

The Warrior Princess is gone and now she's a
college kid who just lost her brother and stumbled
into something ugly.

I tug on her hand. "The airline counters are
right over there. Go get in line for a ticket. I'll wait
here and watch your back. Okay?" Tug her hand
again.

She sniffs hard, once. Squares her shoulders.
"Okay. I can do this." Pono gets in line behind a
family with four very antsy kids, and I lean on the
dolly and pretend to do something with the
bubblegum phone.

The line takes ten very long minutes. It's hard
to continually scan groups of people going past,
looking for nervous, angry faces. My shoulders are
so tight they feel like they're right below my ears,
and I've got a headache coming on. If I actually see
a vending machine, I need some caffeine and sugar.

Pono comes back with a boarding pass in her
hand and passes me the bank envelope. It's a lot
thinner. "Thanks for buying my ticket. I hope
there's enough money left for...whatever you have
to do."

"It's fine." I push the dolly forward and we
blend in with the foot traffic. The funnel of people
leads to the TSA security line. I wave to one of the
TSA trolls. "Hey, we're restocking the machines by
the gates. Can we go around?"

One Bullet   313

"Nope, gotta go through the line like everybody else," she says. "You two new?"

Pono smiles. "Yeah, it's our first day on the airport route."

"Well, you shoulda asked your boss the proper procedure. Then you'd know," TSA lady says without smiling.

I hope I'm not frisked. I'm not carrying any weapons, I just don't want this bitch grabbing my crotch.

We pass through the cattle gates and get wanded. Some fat guy with a patch on his shirt gropes me while the robot voice over the speakers tells everyone in the terminal they have to get treated like a criminal for 'security purposes.' Chances are, I'm the only criminal here. Other than the Cartel. And the Syndicate. And...hell.

I'm surprised the TSA goons don't insist on tasting each bag of candy.

But finally, we're through and it feels good to push the dolly fast and take long strides. We find Pono's gate and she takes off the Coin & Vending shirt and wraps it around the hat and hands them to me. "I guess you should give these back to Pudge."

"Yeah." I just stand there because I don't know what to say. I ran her brother over with a car and put him in the hospital. Then my girlfriend stuck a pillow over his face and shot him. Are we supposed to hug now?

"Joe. Thanks for helping me. Thanks." She puts her hand out and we shake. It's formal and strange.

"Have a safe flight."

Pono turns away, and then looks back. "Joe, once you have the locker key, why don't you take the money? The Syndicate betrayed you. The Cartel tried to kill you. You don't owe them anything."

I tried to explain this to Carly yesterday and couldn't. "It's my...code. I'm a bagman. That means I deliver the money or die trying. I lost the Cartel's money because I didn't protect it. If I survive my meeting with Vlad, I'm going to give the Cartel their money back."

Pono squints at me.

"I know it sounds crazy," I say. And it does. But in my head, maybe even in my heart, it makes sense.

"Take care, Joe."

She walks away with her boarding pass in one hand. People are already lining up to board her flight. I wave, but she isn't looking. The airline lady asks for her pass, and Pono smiles and then she follows the rest of the passengers out to the plane.

I have to focus.

Focus on the four parts of my job here. Get Pono safely on the plane. Meet Hax and get the locker key. Use the key to get the money. Escape the airport.

I just did one of those four. The most important one. In this whole sorry mess, I did one thing right. I helped somebody. Somebody who isn't a Syndicate criminal or a Cartel killer, someone that doesn't have any leverage on me. Just a girl who needed help. I did that. And I think it matters.

* * *

Chapter 53
Joe

I wheel the dolly around and get it going. The box on top is labeled 'Snickers' and I'm tempted to rip it open and eat two or three, but that's too much like taking money from the bag during an exchange. A flight must have just landed, because people pour out of the door into the gate area and there are squeals and hugs and loud conversations.

It's hard to keep focused and watch for danger with all this happy going on.

Although it isn't quite two hours after I talked to Vlad, I head for the rental lockers. It's always better to arrive before the other guy and take a look around. This is a fairly small, regional airport and there are only two rows of lockers. A dozen people sit in vinyl chairs in the nearby gate area, probably all early for their flight. Half of them look like retirees, the other half are business types. And then there's one guy--Hispanic looking--sitting by himself, reading a paper.

He's wearing a faded jean jacket, and cowboy boots with worn-down heels. Could be Cartel, but he's not your typical, amped-up kid giving you the hard look and ready to fight. He looks like an old ranch hand, reading the local paper--the News Herald. Even from here, I can read the big headline of "Hospital Murder."

His position has a good view of the lockers, so I keep note of him. And he does feel familiar.

316   Mark Boss

I spot the computer kid, Hax, coming toward me. He's thin and gangly and underneath his mop of hair, his eyes are huge. He walks right by, so I guess this disguise is pretty good.

"Hax?"

He whirls around. Bends his knees like a frog about to hop. "Joe?"

"Yeah. Come on." I roll the dolly along and turn into the back row of lockers, so I have one row between me and the rest of the gate area. "Which locker is it?"

Hax holds the key out, and answers without checking the key ring. "It's 23. That's a prime number. Joe, I'm just the delivery man here. It's not personal. You were always nice to me," he rattles on out without stopping for air.

"I know. It's okay." I'd rather him open the locker while I keep watch, but he's shaking and looks ready to faint. So I take the key from him and stab it in the lock. The door swings open and there's a medium-sized, black nylon bag. A bag a lot of people have died over.

I pull it out and drop it on the stack of boxes on the dolly. Unzip it part way and take a quick look. Stacks of money, neatly bound with rubber bands. Now is not the time to count it. I zip the bag and look up, and there's the ranch hand.

He stands with his hands loose at his sides, like a gunfighter. His dark eyes are hard, and other than a brief twitch under one eye, he doesn't move.

And I remember where I saw him. "You were at my apartment yesterday. Waiting in a drain pipe while it rained."

One Bullet 317

He looks puzzled. Maybe he doesn't speak English?

"You saw me yesterday? Why didn't you shoot me?" he asks.

I tap the bag on the dolly. "This is the Cartel's money. I'm going to give it back, but first I need it to help a friend."

"I do not serve the Cartel," he says.

Hax is between us, and he flattens himself against the lockers. He's shaking his head like every bad thing he imagined might happen is about to.

If this ranch hand isn't Cartel, what's he doing here?

"My nephew worked for the Cartel. A bagman, like you. You met him yesterday morning in a restroom. You left alive, he did not." He stops talking. I guess he's reached his limit of words for one day.

His hands clench into fists and he steps forward. Hax moans.

"Wait." I put up my hands, palms out. "I didn't kill your nephew. When I went into the men's room, he was already dead. A man named Dwayne Kimura killed him and took the money."

The ranch hand stands still and weighs my words. He watches my face and I don't look away. The truth has a strange power to it--an assurance. I never knew that before.

"Where is Dwayne Kimura?" He says the name softly and with an accent.

"Dead. Shot dead in Bay Medical last night. You can check that out. I'm sure it's on the news."

The ranch hand reaches behind his back, and I wonder how he got a weapon in here as I get ready to tackle him.

But he comes up with a folded newspaper. He shakes the paper out and points at the front page. "Hospital Murder. Was it this man?" he asks.

"Yeah."

The ranch hand lowers the newspaper. His shoulders sag. He turns without another word and walks away.

"Oh shit, that was intense," Hax says.

'Intense' is right. That ranch hand had the look of a man that would kill without doubt or hesitation. "Hax, I'm going outside to call Vlad and set up a meeting. I'm trading this bag of cash for Carly."

I wish I hadn't said I'd give the money back to the Cartel in front of Hax. Maybe he was so scared he might not repeat it to Vlad. Or maybe he'll think I lied to avoid a fight.

"Yeah, okay. I'm supposed to call Vlad, too. When you leave," Hax says.

His color is a little better now and maybe he will make it outside without fainting. I know he's a hacker, which is just a fancy name for a thief who uses a computer, but he never seemed like a bad kid.

Maybe it's time to do a second good thing.

"Hax, when I meet Vlad tonight I'm going to kill him. And I'll kill whoever is between me and him. You don't want to be there. Understand?"

He nods hard enough to make his neck pop. "Yeah, yeah, I get you. I do. But I have to go back to them. There's this girl."

One Bullet

There is a girl. Carly for me. Some other girl for him. We're both fools. I should tell him she's not worth his life, but that's bullshit. Some women are worth your life. Worth dying for, and worth killing for.

"That's up to you." I get the dolly rolling. "So long, Hax."

* * *

Chapter 54
Joe

I follow the crowd out past the security checkpoint. Most of them head for the luggage area, but a few of the business types aim for the rental car counters. I go with them, still pushing my dolly of candy. No one looks at me.

Wait my turn in line at the Enterprise rental car counter, and finally a kid in a bad tie calls me up. I ask for a pickup truck, but they're all out, so I ask for an SUV and get the keys to a Jeep Grand Cherokee. There's a little holdup because I don't have a credit card, but a wad of cash plus a driver's license and an insurance card still does the trick.

The kid doesn't ask why a vending machine guy is renting a car, and I'm glad because I don't have a story ready. I take the key and packet of papers and head outside. Tug my cap low and try to stick with the clump of business travelers headed for the rental car lot.

If the Cartel gunmen are watching close, they might wonder why the vending guy isn't headed back to his truck. Or why he's renting a Jeep. I push the dolly a little faster, taking long steps. It's nice out, cool and clear, the type of afternoon where you want to be outside raking leaves or hiking a trail on a mountain somewhere. But the idea that people may be watching pushes my head down between my shoulders, and the back of my neck gets hot.

One Bullet

Instead of opening the rear hatch of the Jeep to store the dolly, I shove it across the back seat and hop up front. Drop the moneybag on the passenger seat beside me. Press the button to move the driver's seat back, and wait while it slowly motors along until my legs can stretch out. A chime rings to remind me to put on my seatbelt, but I don't want to. I plan to jump out fast when I get back to the delivery truck.

I steer the Jeep in a big loop around the lot, and see a car with two guys sitting in it. They could be Cartel, but I don't get a good look. The road takes me around to where I parked Pudge's truck at the service vehicle access.

I pull up behind the Coin & Vending truck, and transfer the dolly and the candy boxes. As I slide the boxes into the truck, I think how good a Snickers candy bar would taste right now, but I roll the door down and close the latch. I'm not sure what to do with Pudge's huge ring of keys. I toss them up and down in my hand, and then drop them on the front seat of the delivery truck.

Pudge can come get his own damn truck.

Get back in the Jeep. I worked up a sweat and the cab fogs up. Switch on the defroster and tug the bubblegum phone from my pocket. Then I remember the guns. Maybe I'm tired, maybe it's the lack of coffee, but I've got to get focused before I meet Vlad.

It's like this after every job, though. The comedown. When you finally get hold of the money, your energy drops and you just want to sleep. But I don't have time for that. Carly is waiting for me. And Calm Ruben is waiting for her.

I run back to the delivery truck and grab the two pistols from under the front seat, plus Dwayne's laptop computer. Back to the Jeep and the defroster is still struggling to clear the windows.

Dial Tommy's number, and wonder why Vlad is using Tommy's phone. It rings four times before Vlad answers with his usual command, "Speak."

"It's Joe. I got the money."

"Yes, Hax called me. He said it was 'intense.'" Vlad laughs.

"Right. Let me talk to Carly."

Vlad says, "Carly, say something touching," and I hear her voice in the background.

"Joe, hurry, I don't want to go to Calm Ruben." She says something else, but I can't hear her with Vlad talking.

Vlad says, "Leave the airport and go to the St. Joseph Peninsula State Park in Port St. Joe. See? Three Joes. That has to be good luck for you, no?" Vlad clears his throat. "You have three hours. It will be late afternoon by the time you get here, and I'll be waiting with Carly. Enter the park, go up the trail and look for a yellow post that marks the western cut through the sand dunes. You'll take that cut and come out on the beach on the Gulf of Mexico side. We'll be there."

"Why not just do the exchange in Panama City?" I ask.

Vlad says, "Think. After your shootout at the hospital, there are cops everywhere in town. No, we need a place that's quiet. In the wintertime, the

One Bullet 323

park will be empty. And standing on the beach, you can see people coming from a long distance. Safe for me, and safe for you. And Carly." He says her name softly.

It's a set up. It has to be. The moment Vlad has the money, he'll kill me and then kill Carly. There is no reason for him to keep us alive.

The phone feels very heavy. I lean my head back against the seat and say, "Okay. I'll be there."

Put the phone on the bag of money, and back the Jeep out slow. Sitting still isn't a good idea because the Cartel might have a few guys just wandering the lot. On the way out, I pass a little shuttle that takes people in from the long-term parking.

I need to make one last phone call, and I'd better do it soon. So I pull into the long-term parking but don't go through the gate.

When I get to St. Joe Peninsula, Vlad will have Simon, Lars, Jorg, Fergus, Arturo and whoever helped him murder Mr. Cypress. But there are two things Vlad doesn't know.

Five months ago, Carly and I rented a cabin in the park. It was nice. The park is beautiful, and Carly spent most of the time in shorts and a bikini top. Despite all the time we spent in the cabin, I still learned my way around the park.

So I know the ground.

The second thing Vlad doesn't know is Greater Kwan. That guy will not quit. Ever. It's his nature.

So I pick up the bubblegum phone and call Greater Kwan. I need his help, and I have something to offer.

The phone picks up and all I hear is a growl. Then he hangs up.

Ten seconds later a text message pops up on my screen. "cant talk. text only."

He must be somewhere public and can't talk out loud about all this. I'm no expert at typing and the touchscreen is awfully small for my big fingers, so my text takes a while. "its joe. need yor help. meeting vlad in 3hrs to trade $ for carly."

Sit and wait and watch the cars pass on the access road.

Kwan texts back. "u hav the $? why stay?"

"i want carly. what do u want?" I wait for Kwan's response, but I don't have to wait long.

"vlad. he killed my brother."

It takes a while to text him the details of the location, but we get it done. Finally, I type, "see u there."

Kwan sends, "no u wont see me. but i will b there."

That gives me a shiver. Lesser Kwan was the friendly one of the two, and he wasn't friendly. Greater Kwan is a big, lethal machine, like a wood chipper or a sawmill.

I know the ground, I've got Kwan, and I've got the money. This can work. The weight I've felt since Pono left falls away and I sit up in the Jeep. I feel awake. I can do this. Vlad and his goons aren't going to stop me from saving Carly. I don't even care if I kill Vlad. Let Greater Kwan do it. I just want Carly and my life back.

* * *

Chapter 55
Greater Kwan

Greater Kwan sat in the stolen Toyota outside Vlad's restaurant, watching the last of the lunch crowd leave. He had one bangstick on his lap, and the other sticking up from the floorboard like a second gearshift, plus two handguns and a shotgun he'd taken from Mr. Cypress's condominium. And the rusty, blood-sticky hatchet. He figured Vlad would come by to check the lunchtime receipts or feed money into the registers to launder, but for the past hour, he hadn't seen any members of the Syndicate.

He popped the lid off his smoothie and vacuumed up what was left at the bottom with a straw. The cold smoothie felt good on his injured throat, and the fever had stopped. Greater Kwan felt ready for war. He imagined shoving the bangstick into Vlad's forehead and feeling the jolt through his arm as the big .44 Magnum blasted the Russian's brains out.

But then what?

Vlad would be dead, and vengeance achieved. Or at least justice. But where did that leave him? His brother was dead, and would remain so. Kwan wished his brother was in the passenger seat next to him, like they'd sat so many times, talking in Korean while they waited for Mr. Cypress. Everything had been fine until Vlad got ambitious. Now nothing was right.

326 Mark Boss

Kwan's phone vibrated and he snatched it off the seat. He looked at the number but didn't recognize it. A clump of Canadians came out of the restaurant, laughing and walking slowly, patting their bellies. Kwan raised the phone and tried to answer, but only managed a growl.

He threw the phone on the floorboard. The Canadians left. A cook came outside to smoke. There was no sign of Vlad, and Kwan wondered if he should try a different Syndicate business or even Vlad's house. But who would be foolish enough to stay in their own house?

He picked up the phone, and thought. Who would call him? Who was still in play? Manila Tommy, or Fergus, not Simon, and Lars wouldn't dare. Joe? He texted the unknown number, "cant talk. text only."

Two full minutes later, a reply arrived. "its joe. need yor help. meeting vlad in 3hrs to trade $ for carly."

Kwan sat forward in the car and looked around the half empty parking lot. Joe was meeting Vlad to trade what money--the money he'd lost at the airport? And why did Vlad have Carly? Although it made sense. If Vlad wanted to get to Joe, taking Carly hostage was the smart way to do it. Always identify the enemy's weakness and exploit it. That's what his instructors in the army told him.

Still, it could be a trick. But not by Vlad's hackers. Kwan had killed most of them, and reasoned the rest would flee. He texted, "u hav the $? why stay?"

One Bullet   327

The answer came back in a minute. "i want carly. what do u want?" That also made sense. Joe loved Carly. And Joe made it clear to other men that he would protect her. To Kwan's way of thinking, Joe was simple but loyal. Loyalty mattered. Betrayal had to be punished.

Vlad's death wouldn't bring Lesser Kwan back, but it would let Greater Kwan sleep at night. He wrote, "vlad. he killed my brother"

Joe sent details of the meeting and Kwan read them carefully. He left the screen open to the text conversation and cranked the Toyota. If he hurried, he might make it to Port St. Joe before the Syndicate did.

* * *

Chapter 56
Vlad

At the marina in St. Andrew's, Vlad slid a long, plastic gun case from the back of his Porsche Cayenne. He carried the gun case in one hand and the guitar case in the other to his 35-foot ProLine and lowered them into the boat.

A sun-browned old man sat with his feet dangling over the side of an ancient sailboat, splicing a piece of rope. The old fellow looked at the gun case and the guitar case and smiled. "I hope you catch whatever you're after, mister."

Vlad smiled and waved.

The Finn stood balanced on the bow, untying a rope so they could cast off. Carly sat by the engine, arms crossed, sunglasses on tight. While Vlad locked the Porsche, he heard the ProLine's engine crank. The Finn appeared to know boats, and that made him smile. She was a valuable woman in so many ways.

He took the stern rope and dropped down into the boat. Put his hands against the bumper on the dock and pushed the boat clear so he wouldn't scratch her.

The Finn took the boat out at low speed, and Vlad was glad she didn't cause a wake. They didn't need to attract attention.

If the weather cooperated, they could make the St. Joseph Peninsula by dark. Vlad thought of the Cartel's dinner-time deadline. He shrugged. By

One Bullet

329

dinner time, Joe would be dead, and Vlad would stand alone on the beach. Victorious.

He went forward and leaned into The Finn. She stepped aside and he took the wheel. There was a light chop on the bay, but the sky was clear and the wind gentle. "It's a good day to be on the water, no?" he asked, and smiled.

The Finn nodded. "Good shooting weather. If the wind remains calm." She hauled the long gun case into the cabin and sat with the door open. She took out the rifle and rested it across her knees. Vlad looked down from his spot at the wheel to watch her.

The gun was an old Dragunov 7.62mm sniper rifle he'd stored in his garage, but there hadn't been time to buy something better.

The Finn checked the gun over and frowned. She spoke, but he could barely hear her over the motor as he increased speed. "This gun is old, and the scope mount wobbles."

"It's a Dragunov. Soviet quality. Popular in Africa and the Middle East," Vlad said.

"There won't be time to sight it in. I wouldn't trust it beyond 400 meters." She opened a cardboard box of cartridges and loaded a magazine.

"Don't worry," Vlad told her. "I sent Simon and the rest to get their weapons, and then on to the peninsula. I ordered them to wait in ambush on the trail for Joe. They'll kill him and retrieve the money. We'll probably never even see Joe."

The Finn shut the case and stood near to him. She glanced at the stern where Carly sat. "What about her?"

"Once you catch the fish, you don't keep the bait." Vlad watched the compass as he took the boat south and east.

* * *

Chapter 57
Hax

As soon as he hung up the phone with Vlad, Hax left the airport terminal and hurried to his car. He watched for the scary ranch hand or truckloads of Cartel gunmen, but no one yelled at him or tried to stop him. He pulled his Mustang into the exit lane, paid for parking, and hit the access road fast.

He took Highway 79 back to Panama City Beach, and then drove east on Highway 98 until he reached Vlad's neighborhood. When he pulled into the driveway, the garage door was down and the window blinds were closed.

Hax went to the front door and rang the bell. In the backyard, the two mastiffs barked. After a minute, he knocked hard enough to hurt his knuckles, but no one answered. The young hacker stood tapping his foot for a minute, and then tried the front door. It was locked.

The dogs liked him, but he thought going over the fence to try the glass door in back might constitute invading their territory. In which case Genghis and Amber would tear his arms off and fight over his torso.

You're a hacker, hack something, he told himself.

He pulled out his phone and called Vlad, but it went straight to voicemail. Calling The Finn wasn't an option because he didn't know her number. Hax walked down to his Mustang and slumped against the hood. Stared at the garage. Idiot, he thought. I went through the garage before to impress her, just do it again.

As soon as he pulled up the app on his phone, he punched in the code and Vlad's garage door rumbled open. Hax peeked inside to make sure no one was waiting to ambush him, but Vlad's Porsche was gone and there was no one hiding in the shadows.

He looked over his shoulder to see if the neighbors were watching, and then trotted through the garage. Inside, the house was dark and still with the blinds drawn.

Now the dogs seemed like a good idea. He went straight through to the living room and opened the glass door. Genghis bounded in, while Amber stopped long enough to sniff Hax and shrug. The dogs jogged around the house, chuffing as they searched for Vlad.

When the dogs didn't root out any Cartel killers hiding in the closets, Hax flipped on the lights and went into the kitchen. The dogs came and sat at their empty bowls and looked up at him with friendly eyes.

Hax took a bottle of Sunny D from the refrigerator. The dogs watched him. Genghis wagged his entire rear end. "Okay, okay. Hang on." He searched the cabinets and found a big bag of Iams dog chow. Poured a generous helping in each bowl and stepped back.

While he dialed Vlad again, he sipped his cold Sunny D and the dogs worked their way down until their noses hit the bottoms of the steel bowls. Then

One Bullet   333

they walked out to the living room and sat on either side of Vlad's leather recliner.

Hax left another voice message for Vlad, and then sat between the dogs with the phone on his lap. He assumed Vlad and The Finn and Carly had gone to meet Joe Barrow, and he wondered who would survive that meeting.

He gnawed on the inside of his lip, and wondered where his inhaler was. He pictured Vlad with a pump shotgun, blasting Joe in the back and the big bagman falling dead at his feet. Then it would be over and Vlad would have the money and The Finn. Hax wondered if somehow Joe could kill Vlad, but maybe The Finn could escape and return to him. He imagined taking her to Europe, and standing on the deck of a cruise ship on a hot Mediterranean day on the way to some steep Greek island.

Odds wise, he knew Joe didn't stand a chance against the entire Syndicate, but Hax wondered if Vlad and The Finn knew what Joe's last name meant. Did they know 'barrow' meant 'grave?'

* * *

Chapter 58
The Syndicate

"I have to pee," Jorg said from the back seat.

"Hold your knickers," Simon growled. He spun the wheel and parked the car. The parking lot at Eagle Harbor in the St. Joseph Peninsula State Park was empty, and a pale, orange sun fell low in the west.

Jorg bolted across the lot to the restrooms, his slung AR-15 rifle thumping against his back.

Simon looked at the sun and then at his watch. "Bloody hell. Vlad told us to get here early, not late. You wankers took forever to get your guns."

Lars knelt to lace his combat boots. "The beach Wal-Mart was out of ammo. We had to drive all the way into town to buy some."

"Wal-Mart? You smell like a pub."

"We stopped for a drink. Jorg has to work himself up. He's a nervous sort." Lars slid a magazine into his rifle. Simon noticed his hands shook.

Jorg came out of the restroom and trotted across the parking lot. "A raccoon ate all the toilet paper. I had to--"

"We don't care." Simon opened the brochure for the park. The simple map inside only showed the portion of the park from the entrance up to the cabins. The map had symbols for camping and picnic tables and showers, and Simon figured it would take five seconds to overwhelm Jorg's brain.

Simon crouched and drew in the sand with his finger. "The peninsula runs south to north, curving up toward the rest of Florida."

"Like a horse's wang?" Jorg asked.

"Yes, like an 11-kilometer-long horse's wang." Simon took a breath. "Vlad will text Joe to hike about two kilometers past the cabins, and then cut west on the trail that goes over some high sand dunes and down to the beach."

"How high are the dunes?" Lars asked.

"How the hell should I know?" Simon waved the brochure. "Does this look like a bleeding military topo map?"

"It's a fair question," Jorg said.

"Shut it, both of you." Simon drew a line up the peninsula. "There's only one north/south trail, but there are several that cut to the west. We wait between the first western cut and the second. When Joe comes whistling along, we shoot the bugger, and take the cash to Vlad. Simple."

Jorg studied the sand drawing and rubbed his cauliflower ear. "What do we do with the body?"

"Leave it for the coyotes. What do we care?" Simon asked.

Jorg stood and shouldered his rifle. "Maybe we should cut off his ears and bring them to Vlad, so he'll know we did the job."

"How would he know they were Joe's ears?" Lars asked.

Jorg's eyes widened. "That's a point. What will we do?"

"Shut up and march." Simon pointed at the narrow road. "That leads to the cabins, then we start on the real trail. Let's go!" He led them off at a brisk pace. When he looked back, each man had his rifle at the ready, and Lars knew enough to keep an interval of several paces between them so a shooter couldn't get them all with one burst.

Simon questioned his decision to act as point man, but Jorg was too nervous to handle it, and Lars looked over anxious to pull the trigger. If Lars saw a deer, he might put a bullet into Simon's back on accident.

By the time they reached the cabins, he'd told Jorg to shut up three times and taken a pack of cigarettes away from Lars. From the main trail, narrow roads led east to the cabins on the inner side of the peninsula. Simon saw a few cars parked at the cabins, but no people. The wind picked up, and he figured the cold would keep any birdwatchers indoors. That and it was near dinnertime.

They hiked another twenty minutes, and Simon looked back and saw Jorg standing in the middle of the trail, staring at something. Simon crouched and brought his rifle up. Flipped the safety off.

"I dropped my Clif Bar," Jorg called.

Simon shook his head and walked back to the other two.

A half-eaten nutrient bar lay in the loose sand of the trail. Jorg stared at the bar. "I guess birds might eat it. Or sea turtles."

Jorg's head jerked sideways. His entire face elongated, the skin stretched as lead pellets tore through, and the ex-fighter fell to his knees.

One Bullet

Only then did Simon hear the roar of the shotgun.

* * *

Chapter 59
Joe

As I drive down the narrow road of the park, branches scrape the side of the Jeep and I flinch. Sure, it's only a rental, but I hate to scratch a brand new vehicle. It's just wrong.

I told the ranger lady at the front entrance that I was just catching a quick nature walk before dark. She told me not to "walk, climb, sit or camp in the beach vegetation or dunes." I promised her I wouldn't, and she let me through.

She didn't say anything about shooting a bunch of people.

The road is tight and sandy and I have to be careful not to get the Jeep stuck. Although hopefully any Jeep product could dig its way out of some sand. I pass the marina and picnic area, and continue on to the part they call Eagle Harbor.

Sitting right there in the parking lot is a white Chrysler 300 with giant silver wheels. Simon's car. I brake and grab the Ruger off the seat. Staying still is stupid, so I pull in and look, but there's no one around.

I roll down all the windows so I won't get glass in my eyes if somebody starts shooting. The Syndicate soldiers got here ahead of me, but I figured they would. I had to drive all the way in from the airport, and they didn't. Still, I only see one car, which means four of them at the most. Maybe the rest drove in closer or took a different route, but why?

One Bullet   339

Carly is waiting, and I want to get this over, but I need to be smart for once.

I pull the bag of money onto my lap and prop it against my chest. Fifteen pounds of paper money might stop a bullet. Leave the Eagle Harbor parking lot and head north toward the cabins. I drive slow and watch the trees to either side. The park is flat and mostly small sand pines and scrub brush, but even in the winter it's plenty thick to hide in. When Carly and I stayed here, a deer walked right out of the trees like a magic trick.

Soon I see the turnoff for the first set of cabins. I pull in and see a pair of SUVs already parked. They could be campers or Syndicate or Cartel. No sense in risking it. So I take the Jeep back out to the road and down to the next group of cabins.

The second parking area is empty, and I park the Jeep nose out in case I have to leave in a hurry. I have the big Ruger with six shots in it, and the one-bullet Browning I took off the Cartel mutt. And a bag of money. Dwayne's laptop is on the floorboard--it's one of the big ones and it weighs five pounds, at least. Thick, too. I slip it in with the money and sling the bag over my shoulder.

At least if someone shoots me in the back, the money and the computer might stop it, or slow it down. Because that's what you want to feel, a bullet going through you slowly.

Shit. This is crazy.

The bubblegum phone rattles and I check the screen. It's a text from Vlad telling me to hike north a mile past the cabins and then look for a side trail that goes west. He says there's a yellow post to mark it.

The timing of his text is spooky, and I look around to see if anyone is watching me. Maybe they have a soldier hiding in one of the cabins? Or a guy could crouch down in the woods and just listen for my vehicle.

When I reach the marker, I can either go past it and circle around, or go back a little way and cut west. I know hiking in this loose sand in street shoes is going to hurt, so as soon as I see the marker I think I'll cut west. Then I'll watch Vlad and his goons from a distance and figure out how to exchange the cash for Carly.

I push the phone deep into my pocket and take the Ruger in my right hand.

Settle the bag against my back and set off parallel to the trail. It's slower moving through the woods, but the footing is better than the loose, white sand of the trail. And as long as I keep the trail in sight, I shouldn't get lost. More important, I don't want to run into an ambush.

Creeping through the woods isn't the same as playing on the beach with Carly. Every sound feels like a threat. Every time I make a noise, I flinch and wait for a gunshot. But I have to keep moving. The sun is dropping fast, the wind is up, and the woman I love is waiting.

The huge Ruger is heavy, and I stop and tuck it in my belt and shake my right hand loose.

That's when I hear a blast up ahead. A shotgun for sure, and maybe a scream.

One Bullet   341

I hope it's Greater Kwan doing the shooting, and not the screaming.

Either way, he might need my help. I shift the straps of the bag so it's hanging in front to protect my chest.

And I run north beside the trail.

* * *

Chapter 60
Greater Kwan

Firing both barrels of Mr. Cypress's Benelli 12-gauge shotgun was both better and worse than Kwan expected. His thick shoulder handled the recoil, but without ear plugs, the noise was deafening. Almost disorienting.

However, the birdshot shredded Jorg's entire face, and the kickboxer went down screaming.

Kwan dropped the shotgun, and pulled the first of two handguns he'd taken from the condo. He raised Mr. Cypress's nickel-plated .45 in the old cup and saucer grip still taught in a lot of places.

He kept his position behind the thickest pine tree he could find within pistol range of the trail, which meant about five paces.

Lars swung a tricked-out AR-15 around, but paused to look through the optic. At that close, Kwan knew he shouldn't have bothered.

Kwan pointed low and let the .45's recoil take his aim point up from Lars' groin all the way to his sternum. He fired patiently, walking the big 230-grain bullets up the target.

Lars shook, and fired his rifle into the sky.

Then the slide on Kwan's .45 locked back--the magazine was empty.

A bullet smacked the tree next to his head, scattering bark. The next one grazed his cheek. Kwan dropped low and crawled to his left. Ditched the empty .45 and drew his last distance weapon, an old snub-nosed .38 Special he'd found in Mr. Cypress's bedside table.

He searched for Simon, but the Syndicate soldier had retreated into the trees on the other side of the trail.

Simon fired three more rounds, then stopped, and Kwan realized Simon wasn't as careless as the others. Kwan crept along on his elbows and knees, with the gun forward. He had to get close. A pistol against a rifle was a losing battle.

A bullet hit a tree to his left and Kwan straightened his arm to fire, but caught himself. Simon was tempting him to fire and give away his position.

Patience. That's what his Special Forces instructors had told him. Any fool can blaze away until their gun is empty. Hunting humans takes patience.

Kwan quietly cleared his throat. He knew it should hurt, but he was so jacked up he couldn't feel the pain. He scooted forward. His elbow came down on a thorn and he eased his arm back up. Waited.

"Just give us the money, Joe," Simon called out. "You can't beat the whole Syndicate. Toss the money onto the trail and I'll let you live."

Kwan listened carefully and homed in on Simon's voice.

On the trail, Jorg rolled over onto his back and moaned. Kwan flinched, amazed the man was alive.

344 Mark Boss

Simon must have flinched, too, because the thicket of Spanish bayonets just across the trail shook.

Kwan held the stubby revolver and focused the front sight on Simon's position.

"Come on, Joe. You can't win," Simon called.

Kwan saw a sleeve, just part of a sleeve, but his eyes followed the sleeve until it disappeared into the brush. He took aim at where Simon's chest should be.

And felt the thud of footsteps through the ground beneath him.

Someone was running up the trail, fast.

Kwan looked to his right and saw Joe Barrow come through the trees alongside the trail. He had a nylon bag across his chest.

The sleeve moved, and Kwan knew Simon had seen Joe, too. The barrel of a rifle eased over a low-hanging limb as Simon took aim.

Kwan rose and threw one of his bangsticks. It missed and hit the tree behind Simon and fired. Simon turned toward the gunfire behind him.

Joe spotted Simon, raised an enormous revolver, and fired.

Kwan pointed the .38 at Simon and fired the little wheel gun--all five shots. As soon as the hammer clicked on a spent round, Kwan rushed forward with the hatchet.

But Simon tumbled face first onto the trail. He thumped into the loose sand with a half dozen holes through him. Shuddered once and lay still. Joe stood gasping for air, his gun still aimed at Simon's corpse.

Kwan stepped out of the trees and raised one hand.

* * *

Chapter 61
The Finn

The Finn looped duct tape around the plastic bag covering the Dragunov sniper rifle and sealed the weapon as well as she could. Next to her, Vlad guided the boat close to shore, running slow at trolling speed.

She touched his shoulder. "Once I'm in the water, give me a few minutes to swim ashore and get set up. With the waves and the twilight, no one will see me. Don't go more than 400 meters up the coast before you anchor. I don't trust this old thing." She tapped the side of the rifle.

Vlad nodded, his hands on the wheel to keep the boat steady as the waves hit their port side. "I can't anchor in too close. The chart says it's only five-feet deep near the shore."

"Then I suppose Carly might get her feet wet," The Finn said with a nod toward the back of the boat.

Before she could turn away, Vlad pulled her in and kissed her. His lips were wet with salt spray.

He let go, and she slipped over the side of the boat and swam to shore. The water was colder than she expected, and her clothes were instantly heavy. A wetsuit would have been preferable.

The surf carried her the last few meters to the beach. She sprinted across the open sand, lifting her boots in high steps to keep from stumbling. When she reached the sand dunes, she crawled into the sea oats and scrub brush and looked north.

One Bullet   347

Vlad piloted the boat parallel to the peninsula. He stopped and dropped anchor about six hundred meters north of her position.

The Finn clenched the rifle stock. He was too far, and she'd have to move closer. Movement was dangerous because Joe might spot her. She crawled through the dunes, moving one limb at a time, but it took several minutes to travel just 50 meters.

The Dragunov wasn't equipped with a night scope, so she hoped the starlight and partial moon would be bright enough to shoot by. The Finn crawled to the top of a dune and settled in a bed of seat oats. She rolled up her wet jacket and used it as a rest for the rifle. She'd tightened the scope mount with a multitool during the boat ride, but she didn't know what range it could handle.

Even worse, a strong westerly wind blew across her field of fire. It would carry the bullet wide of the target, so she would have to compensate. She took a quick look through the scope at the anchored boat, and saw Vlad and Carly splashing through the water to shore. Carly's clothes would be wrecked. The Finn smiled.

The Finn seated the magazine, chambered a cartridge and settled down behind the gun to wait, but her hands shook. If she had to fire to protect Vlad, the distance was too great, and the wind too strong.

* * *

Chapter 62
Joe

It's a good thing the Ruger is empty. Because I almost shot Greater Kwan when he popped out of the woods like Bigfoot.

I'm out of breath, sweat in my eyes, and the moneybag is hot against my chest. Simon is face down in the dirt, and he's not ever getting up. His blood leaks into the white sand and I don't feel a damn thing. Simon was a monster in the making. A younger version of Calm Ruben.

Hell, I'm not even sure if I hit him. Kwan is holding a smoking .38, so I know he fired, too.

Kwan looks bad. There's a bandage around his neck, and it's sweat soaked and dirty. He's lost weight and his eyes look empty. Resigned. I guess the message from Vlad was true, and Lesser Kwan really is dead.

"Thanks," I say. "I'm sorry about your brother." It's not enough, but what else can I tell him?

He nods.

"I got the money. Vlad told me to hike to the second trail that leads west, and follow the cut through the dunes and out to the beach." I look west and the sun has already sunk behind the trees, and I know it will get dark fast out here. "I'll find the side trail, and then back up and sneak through the woods. Maybe we can take them by surprise."

Kwan's mouth opens but nothing comes out. He puts his hatchet under one arm and types on his

One Bullet 349

phone. Holds it up for me to read. When I step close, he smells like blood. Or maybe the hatchet does.

The message says, "Vlad has partner. assassin. a woman. i will look 4 her."

"You can't talk?" I point to his throat and Kwan shakes his head. "Damn. Uh...okay. Yeah, if I know Vlad, he'll have her hiding nearby. I'll go to meet Vlad and maybe that will draw her out." Or draw her fire. "Then you can take her down." I can't say 'kill her,' because even if she is an assassin, she's a woman. It's wrong to kill a woman.

Kwan nods. He walks past me to where Jorg lays face up. A fly hovers over Jorg's open mouth. He doesn't have eyes or a nose. Had to be a shotgun. Lars is slumped against a little pine tree like he's taking a nap. He has six or seven red holes in a straight line down his chest--they look like buttons.

Kwan takes a rifle from Jorg's body, and checks the rifle's magazine. It's empty. He drops it and tries the gun next to Lars, but when he pulls the mag I only see a few rounds in it. He holds the gun out to me, eyebrows raised.

"No, you take it. I'll never be able to hide that and get close to Vlad. I have to get close because he has Carly."

Kwan nods and puts the rifle over his shoulder. Points at Simon. I roll Simon over but his rifle isn't underneath him. It's not on the trail and I can't see it in the underbrush. It's getting dark. "There isn't time to search for it. I'm going ahead," I say to Kwan.

350   Mark Boss

He nods and jogs into the trees. For a guy his size, he moves quietly.

While there's still just enough light to see, I pop open the cylinder on the Ruger and check the load. All empty. I'm tempted to toss the gun away, but that gives me an idea, so I keep it.

I make sure the Browning with its one shot is still secure in my belt at my back, with my shirt and jacket covering it. Then I start north on the trail. I figure Vlad kept Arturo and Fergus and his lady assassin with him, in case I survived Simon's ambush. Vlad is smart.

Slogging through the loose sand is tough, and my calves burn.

I spot an opening to my left and it has to be the first side trail. Pass by it and try to hurry. My street shoes aren't made for hiking, and the sand in them grinds my heels raw. But I can prop my bloody feet up on a chaise lounge somewhere once I get Carly back.

The thought of Vlad handing her over to Calm Ruben makes me want to scream. To roar a challenge into the twilight like a lion. But I bite my tongue and keep moving.

It's almost full dark when I reach the second cut. I go down the side trail just far enough to spot the yellow marker, then I back out slow. Go south for fifty steps and then step off the trail into the woods.

I wonder if Kwan has found Vlad's hired assassin yet. She might be skilled, but I wouldn't want Kwan and his hatchet hunting me in the woods at night.

One Bullet 351

Bushwhacking through the trees is loud, and I have to slow down. Signs back at the road warned of alligators, and it'd be just my luck to step on one. But except for a few birds, the woods are quiet. The wind cuts through my jacket. I should have dressed warmer.

The trees thin out fast and there's a few yards of scrub and then sand dunes. These magnificent, white, forty-foot tall dunes. I saw them on my camping trip with Carly, and they still amaze me. It's like Florida must have been in the way back, before the Spaniards arrived and Indians came here to fish.

The dunes are beautiful. But they're hell to climb. I take a step, slide back halfway, take another step. Up the loose sand and then I crouch and slither over the top. Down, down into a sort of tiny valley between the dunes. The wind can't reach me here, and it's quiet and still.

I creep through the valley, climb one more dune and look down on the beach.

There's a sliver of moon and a thousand stars. And a boat bobbing in the surf near the shore. Two figures, one big and broad, the other short and curvy, stand just above the tide line. Vlad and Carly. My Carly.

I lay still and look for Vlad's lady assassin. Check the top of each dune, but I can't see her. So I slide down the dune to the beach. Stand up and shake the sand off my pants.

Vlad sees the movement and steps closer to Carly.

352   Mark Boss

I walk until we're ten paces apart. Between the wind and the surf, it's loud out here. Vlad yells, "Throw your gun away."

The Ruger is empty, but it makes a great prop. I lob it into the surf like I hate the thing.

Vlad lets go of Carly.

He reaches behind her, and I know he's going to come up with a rifle. I can't outrun a bullet. But he doesn't come around with a rifle, he has a sledgehammer.

Carly screams.

I look at Vlad holding the big sledgehammer and shake my head. This is exactly the sort of dramatic, over the top shit he always pulled to impress Cypress and the other thugs. It's his pride. Shooting me would make sense, but he wants to beat me to death in front of my girlfriend to prove he's the better man.

"You planning on building a railroad?" I ask.

Vlad laughs. "Drop the money bag, Joe."

I work the strap over my shoulder and drop the bag to my left. I can feel the Browning at the base of my spine, and I want to pull it and shoot him. But one bullet won't kill a man his size unless I hit him in the head. I have to get closer.

"Carly told me a fat Hawaiian beat you senseless in the airport," Vlad says.

"He wasn't fat." I ease forward and Vlad moves toward me, and in three more steps I'll be close enough to shoot.

But Carly is standing two steps behind Vlad and if I shoot, I might hit her. I want to wave her aside, but it will give my plan away.

One Bullet 353

Then there's no more time.

Vlad charges, the hammer high in both hands.

He swings it smooth, like he's done it a thousand times. But I shuffle to my right and drive a hard hook into his ribs. I feel his rib crack beneath my knuckles and it's the best feeling in the world besides sex with Carly.

Vlad grunts, stumbles. I step in to land another, but his stumble was a fake. He drives the handle of the hammer down on my foot and it hurts like hell. His shoulder hits the side of my head.

He lets go of the sledgehammer and fires a fast, practiced combination. I block the left hook, and the stiff right, but after that it's a blur of punches. I cover up, stay low, put my head on his collarbone and throw right, left, right, aiming for his liver.

I can't find the liver, but the punches rock him back and he tries to kick me in the crotch but I've seen that move and I just scoop up his leg and dump him. As he rolls over onto his hands to push up, I stomp on the back of his leg, and then wind up to kick him in the face.

Something thumps me hard in the right thigh. My feet go out from under me. As I hit the sand, I hear the report of a rifle cut through the wind.

Vlad's assassin. Kwan didn't say she's a sniper. Shit.

Vlad is getting to his feet, and I have to hurt him before he gets moving again. But when I try to stand my leg folds under me.

He grabs the sledgehammer and raises it.

* * *

354 Mark Boss

Greater Kwan

Greater Kwan squatted in the woods, listening. It was difficult with the wind, but when he heard the loud report of the rifle, he opened his eyes and looked at a sand dune and knew she must be there. The assassin, the woman who killed his brother.

With the hatchet in his belt and his last bangstick in his hand, Kwan crept forward into the sand dunes, his eyes on a thick patch of sea oats.

* * *

Joe

With all the stars, it's bright enough to see shadows on the white sand. I see a big shadow and there's Vlad with his sledgehammer, looming over me.

He looks at my leg and shakes his head. "She fired too soon. I give you credit, Joe. You're tougher than I expected. Almost my match. And you will die as a man should."

He swings the sledgehammer and if it connects I know it will crush my skull. I launch from the sand on my one good leg. Dive in fast enough so the steel head misses, and instead the wooden handle cracks me. But I've got my left up to protect my head. My thick forearm goes numb but it saves my skull.

I tackle him and we go down in a tangle. He grabs at my wrists like those Brazilians do in jiujitsu, but there isn't time for the fancy stuff. I use my weight to shove the handle of the sledgehammer onto his throat. It's a lot easier for me to push down

One Bullet 355

than for him to push up, and all my weight sits on his chest.

A second rifle shot sounds, but I don't feel it hit. She missed! On reflex, I look for the muzzle flash.

Vlad drives a punch into my nose and I lose my grip on the sledgehammer, and we roll in the sand.

* * *

Greater Kwan

Kwan not only heard the second shot, he saw the muzzle flash. He was right. The shot came from the bed of sea oats. He wriggled forward in an army low crawl until he saw her boots poking out of the oats.

He jumped up and dashed forward, spraying sand with his steps.

The assassin rolled over onto her back, but she couldn't bring the long rifle around fast enough. She dropped the rifle and drew a small pistol. Drew and fired in one motion.

The bullet hit Kwan in the meat of the thigh, but his sheer mass carried him the last two steps.

He drove the bangstick into her forehead and blasted her brains into the dune. Blood spattered the sea oats, and then dripped onto the sand.

* * *

Joe

We work to our knees, wrestling for the sledgehammer. Vlad tries to flip me, and I let go and he's off balance. My leg is numb and my pants

356   Mark Boss

are wet with blood, but I manage to jack an uppercut into his chin.

It's a vicious punch and he falls back. I want to stomp him, kick him to death from a safe position, but my leg won't work. So I drop onto him with my good knee. It spears him in the center of his chest and I hear his sternum crack. He gasps hard, the strength going out of him, and his punches feel like nothing against my shoulders.

He claws at my face, but I bite his thumb to keep one hand trapped while I rain down shot after shot. His head thumps in the sand. He tries to turn away, but I'm on top and he can't ward off the shots and he can't breathe.

I punch until my hands won't make fists anymore.

Vlad is still. His chest doesn't move under my legs. His arms don't move. I drive one more elbow into his throat and feel it crunch, but he doesn't even twitch.

Roll off him and sit there in the sand and feel my leg leaking blood. It's still numb, and I'm not sure if that's good or bad.

I look around and Carly is five steps away. By the bag of money.

She picks the bag up.

"Carly," I say. My voice is raw. "Bring me the bag, baby. I have to give that back to the Cartel."

"What kind of idiot would give this money away?" She looks down at me and shakes her head. "You go to hell, Joe. And take your stupid code of honor with you. "

One Bullet   357

I've never heard her talk like this--full of contempt and hate. Does she hate me? "It's their money," I tell her. "Vlad stole the Syndicate's share, but that cash is the Cartel's. They only care about the money. If we hand it over, they'll leave us alone. I have to give it back. That's the deal."

"No, that was your deal. Your deal, not mine." Carly slings the bag over her shoulder.

"Carly, don't."

"Or what? Are you going to chase me down? Run me over with a car like you did Dwayne? You're a punk, Joe, you just can't admit it to yourself. That code you talk about is bullshit."

I try to get up. I really try. But my leg folds and I drop back in the sand. Carly turns toward the boat. "Carly," I yell it this time.

She walks away.

I try to get up again and I fall. Reach under my shirt and pull out the Browning pistol with its one bullet. Raise the gun, but then my arm sinks. I can't do it.

She slogs through the deep sand toward the boat. In two more steps, she'll be out of pistol range.

My arm jerks up.

The bullet hits her between the shoulder blades, dead center. Carly takes one more step and collapses. Her face goes into the water and the foam swirls her hair out like a dark halo.

I hold the Browning pistol and watch the wind yank the smoke from the barrel. Then I crawl to her, and pull her up into my lap. She is beautiful, even in death.

It takes every bit of my strength to haul her a few yards clear of the surf. Her hair is a mess and Carly would hate that.

We sit like that for a while, until I see a big figure limping down the beach toward us. Greater Kwan. I guess he found the assassin.

I take out the bubblegum phone and squint at the screen. Somehow it's just barely getting a signal. Dial from memory and wait.

Ernesto answers on the first ring. "Yes?"

"This is Joe Barrow. Tell Calm Ruben I'm bringing him his money."

THE END

Thanks for reading ONE BULLET. Please search your preferred bookseller for my other novels:

HIRED GUNS
THE CULTIST
DEAD GIRL
DEAD GIRL 2: FADER BOY

Visit my author site: http://markboss.net
My very random blog:
http://www.chimpwithpencil.com
Or sometimes on Twitter: @markbosswriter

Made in the USA
Charleston, SC
21 March 2015